W9-BNZ-564

"Life—fierce, painful, unyielding, complicated—bursts from every page of *The Tiger Flu* ... Lai inventively and provocatively centres the archetypes of the exile, the monster, and the dispossessed, fleshing out her characters with ferocity, genius, and vulnerability all at once."
—*Autostraddle* ("Best Books of the Year")

"Starting with an atmospheric opening page, in *The Tiger Flu*, Larissa Lai goes wholly maximalist in her world-building ... A surprisingly enchanting vision of post–Peak Oil dystopia."
—*Toronto Star*

"A compelling read about ostracization, disease, technology, tolerance, and survival in a society facing extinction from a horrific pandemic."
—*The Advocate* ("Best Books of the Year")

"A tantalizing novel, replete with the kind of detail that recalls the world of Margaret Atwood's *MaddAddam* trilogy yet belongs to another territory entirely, thrillingly its own. With Atwood you're in a world that's odd but recognizable, whereas with Lai, you're in a world that's completely strange— until it shocks you with a flash of the familiar."
—*Quill and Quire*

"This is an ambitious work and Lai is wonderfully successful in her effort to mash up cinematic science fiction, magical realism elements and fascinating characters with a fierce concern for gender and racial justice."
—*Vancouver Sun*

"A compelling cyberpunk thriller ... Lai draws inspiration from the feminist science fiction of Marge Piercy and Joanna Russ, exploring questions of reproduction, lesbian separatism, and biopolitics in the often absurdist and even surrealist world of Saltwater City."
—*Booklist*

THE
TIGER FLU

a novel

LARISSA LAI

ARSENAL PULP PRESS
VANCOUVER

ARSENAL PULP PRESS
Suite 202 – 211 East Georgia St.
Vancouver, BC V6A 1Z6
Canada
arsenalpulp.com

The publisher gratefully acknowledges the support of the Canada Council for the Arts and the British Columbia Arts Council for its publishing program, and the Government of Canada, and the Government of British Columbia (through the Book Publishing Tax Credit Program), for its publishing activities.

Arsenal Pulp Press acknowledges the xʷməθkʷəy̓əm (Musqueam), Sḵwx̱wú7mesh (Squamish), and səlilwətaʔɬ (Tsleil-Waututh) Nations, custodians of the traditional, ancestral, and unceded territories where our office is located. We pay respect to their histories, traditions, and continuous living cultures and commit to accountability, respectful relations, and friendship.

The author also acknowledges the people of Treaty 7 in southern Alberta, which includes the Blackfoot Confederacy (comprising the Siksika, Piikani, and Kainai First Nations), the Tsuut'ina First Nation, and the Stoney Nakoda (including Chiniki, Bearspaw, and Wesley First Nations). The city of Calgary is also home to the Métis Nation of Alberta, Region III. The author offers humble respect to the fire, earth, metal, water, and wood elements and all the living beings both human and non-human who inhabit these territories.

This is a work of fiction. Any resemblance of characters to persons either living or deceased is purely coincidental.

Cover and text design by Oliver McPartlin
Edited by Hiromi Goto
Narrative ethics read by Warren Cariou
Copy edited by Shirarose Wilensky
Proofread by Alison Strobel

Printed and bound in Canada

Library and Archives Canada Cataloguing in Publication:
Lai, Larissa, 1967–, author

    The tiger flu / Larissa Lai.

Issued in print and electronic formats.

ISBN 978-1-55152-731-4 (softcover).—ISBN 978-1-55152-732-1 (HTML)

    I. Title.

PS8573.A3775T54 2018   C813'.54   C2018-901958-1
                                      C2018-901959-X

For my birth sister, Wendy
And my chosen sisters, Rita and Hiromi

Tyger! Tyger! burning bright
In the forests of the night,
What immortal hand or eye
Dare frame thy fearful symmetry?
—William Blake, "The Tyger"

They say that at the point they have reached they must examine the principle that has guided them. They say it is not for them to exhaust their strength in symbols. They say henceforward what they are is not subject to compromise. They say they must now stop exalting the vulva. They say that they must break the last bond that binds them to a dead culture. They say that any symbol that exalts the fragmented body is transient, must disappear. Thus it was formerly. They, the women, the integrity of the body their first principle, advance marching together into another world.
—Monique Wittig, *Les Guérillères*

When Heaven sends forth its engines of destruction, the stars are moved out of their places and the constellations metamorphosed. When Earth sends forth its engines of destruction, dragons and snakes appear on the dry land. When Man puts forth his faculties of destruction, Heaven falls and Earth is overthrown. When Heaven and Man do so in concert, all the disorganised phenomena are re-established on a new basis.
—ascribed to the Yellow Emperor, *The Yin Fu Ching*,
trans. Fredric Henry Balfour

CAST OF CHARACTERS

SALTWATER CITY

Isabelle Chow, inventor, CEO of HöST Light Industries

Chan Ling, a factory worker, founder of Grist Village

FIRST QUARANTINE RING (SALTWATER FLATS)

Woodward's Building

Kora Ko, a fifteen-year-old girl

Kai Wai Ko, her uncle

Charlotte Ko, her mother

Godwin Austen "K2" Ko, her older brother

Stash Sacks, K2's friend

Delphine, Kora's pet goat

Cordova Dancing School for Girls

Madame Aurelia Dearborn, headmistress

Myra Mao, leader of the dancing girls

Tania Manuel, a different kind of leader

Velma

Modesta

Soraya } *dancing girls*

Mirabelle

Anna

Pacific Pearl Parkade

Marcus Traskin, lord and CEO of the Pacific Pearl
Parkade, leader of 100 tiger men

COAST SALISH TIMEPLACE (SOVEREIGN)

Jemini (a cloning company, in exile from Saltwater City)
Kai Tak Ko, Kora's father
Everest Ko, K2 Ko's twin brother

SECOND QUARANTINE RING (COSMOPOLITAN EARTH COUNTRY)

General Manuel, leader of the CEC
Cousin Sloane, Tania's cousin, a border guard

THIRD QUARANTINE RING

Pente-Hik-Ton
Billy Armstrong, a Syilx man
Maria Armstrong, his mother (deceased)

New Origins Archive
Elzbieta Kruk, high priestess of the New Origins Archive
Buttercup
Vera } *attendants*
Rose

FOURTH QUARANTINE RING (GRIST VILLAGE)

Kirilow Groundsel, a groom
Glorybind Groundsel, her mother double
Peristrophe Halliana, a starfish, Kirilow's lover
Radix Bupleuri, a doubler
Bombyx Mori, Radix's groom
Corydalis Ambigua
Calyx Kaki } *Grist sisters*

PART I

CASCADIA YEAR: 127 TAO (TIME AFTER OIL)

UNITED MIDDLE KINGDOM CYCLE 80, YEAR 42 (WOOD SNAKE YEAR)

GREGORIAN YEAR: 2145

FOURTH WAVE 1

NODE: SUMMER BEGINS
DAY: 15

BEHIND THE CLOUDS OF THE NEW MONSOON, THE ANCIENT MAINFRAME Chang rolls too fast across the sky. He's a big guy, but he appears much bigger than he should because his orbit is deteriorating. His period is down to two hours now, and he casts a veiled shadow over the rooftop of the old Woodward's Building, engulfing Uncle Wai's carefully cultivated garden.

Kora leans against the fence that holds old Delphine in her pen. Stares mournfully into Delphine's golden eyes.

"Uncle Wai's got it," she tells the goat.

The tendril information scales Kora's got plugged into the single-band halo that circles her head wave gently. For all Chang is so close, the people of Saltwater Flats don't have access to him anymore. Only the citizens of the glass towers in Saltwater City can tap in. As soon as she can afford it, she'll add rings to her halo, or even a full helmet, so she can get wiser quicker. She needs all the help she can get.

"Ma-aaa-aaa-aaa," says old Delphine.

"K2's also sick."

"Maaaaaa-aaaaaa-aaaaaaa!"

"Uncle Wai says that so is big brother Everest, though I've never met him. If he comes back to us, he could save us. But I don't think he's coming back."

"Maaaaaaaaaaaaaa-aaaaaaaaaaaa-aaaaaaaaa."

"And Charlotte's got it." Kora never calls Charlotte *Mom*. It seems too corny. "Women aren't immune you know, Delphine. If they're hungry enough, if they're depleted enough, women can get it. If Charlotte's got it, that means I'm the only one left in our family who doesn't have the tiger flu."

"Meh."

"Don't be like that." Kora knows Delphine cannot actually understand her grief and dread, but still, the tendril scales atop Kora's head droop.

She scratches the old goat between the eyes. Delphine's hair is pleasantly coarse, and her forehead is warm. "Soon it will be you and me against the world."

Behind Kora, the jars in which Uncle Wai grows potatoes lean against crumbling retainer walls. The jars are huge, each one big enough to hold Kora, her goat, and a couple of tigers too. Forty floors below those walls, in the streets of Saltwater Flats, women—young and old, healthy and ill, happy and sad—go about their daily business, shop for a bit of chicken for supper, a few vegetables, a bicycle, a second-hand cake mixer. A wealthy few rest in quiet cafés, sip tea, and eat steamed buns. Others stand on street corners arguing. There are no men in the streets. The men are shut up in houses, covered in lesions and coughing their lungs out, the nasty and condescending beside the gentle and well intentioned. Or else, they are already dead. Except for the tiger men, a small contingent of male survivors who have the flu in all its contagion but whose symptoms never proceed beyond a modest cough and the occasional lesion. Miraculously, they thrive in the privacy of the Pacific Pearl Parkade, doors closed to the world.

Although the tiger flu has a taste for men, it doesn't discriminate against the wealthy. In fact, the first to succumb to the fourth wave was the hated despot Aloysius Chow-McPherson. The citizens of Saltwater City rejoiced, as did the denizens of the surrounding quarantine ring known as Saltwater Flats. Then Chow-McPherson's kindly brother, Ferdinand, took ill. The people still rejoiced, because, though kind, Ferdinand was a high-ranking member of a despotic family. The family company, HöST Light Industries, ruled the city in its own best interests. Chow-McPherson's wife, Sophia, took charge. But she too got sick. Then his daughter, Isabelle, took over. As Kora is all her family's got, Isabelle is all the city has got. She better be enough.

Far behind Chang, the backup mainframe Eng rolls in her expanding orbit. If Isabelle could open diplomatic channels with the Cosmopolitan Earth Council, which controls the last remaining rockets outside the United Middle Kingdom, perhaps they could be convinced to help right the orbits of Chang and Eng. Otherwise, Eng's elliptical orbit will only deepen, and hundreds of years will pass between sightings.

Delphine lies down in her bed of straw. "See you tomorrow, sweet goat." Kora places her hands on the highest rung of the fence, hikes herself up so she can lean in and plant a kiss on the goat's rough forehead.

Something rustles behind the shed. She drops her feet back to the ground.

"Who's there?"

No answer. She goes to look, but before she's taken half a step, a young man leaps out and grabs her from behind. "Boo!"

"Mother fuck! Get off me! Who the hell are you?"

Actually, she recognizes him. He's a friend of her brother's—Stash Sacks. He looks awful. His face is covered in weeping sores. His eyes ooze pus.

"What happened to you? How did you get up here?"

"K2 gave me the keys. We lost our jobs this week because we're too sick to lift the elk at the abattoir."

"That's awful."

He grips her tighter, nibbles her ear.

"Please let go."

He doesn't.

"I mean it."

"You don't want me to hug you anymore?"

"Stash, I would rather hug a Grist sister. Let go, really."

"Dirty Kora Ko," says the boy. "There's no such thing as Grist sisters. They're just a story told by scared old men." The bear hug from behind turns aggressive.

"Let go of me!" Her scales writhe.

"When I wasn't sick you liked me just fine."

"I did not. I hardly know you."

"The last healthy member of the Ko family." He leans in, licks her face with his white tongue.

"Agh! What are you trying to do?"

He bites her cheek hard enough to break skin.

"Trying to give me your disease?!"

He's fierce, but he's thin, even thinner than Kora. She might be hungry, but she's tough as an old shoe, whereas he's pale and wasted. She kicks a foot out from under him.

"Little whore! What did you do that for?" He pulls her to the ground with him. Rubs his face into hers, tries to stick his tongue in her mouth.

"Get off me!" Rolls him over.

Gripped by jealousy and desire, he won't let go. On the battered concrete floor that once kept water out of the apartments below, they roll over one another, closer and closer to Uncle Wai's potato jars and the crumbling wall. They'll go over the edge if they aren't careful. Kora throws her weight in the opposite direction, towards Delphine's pen. She's heavier than Stash. Back they roll. Her weight on him makes his heart pump. He finds fresh strength. Towards the wall they turn again.

"You little shit! I'm going to beat the fuck out of you." Kora won't be defeated. She jams her shoulder hard against his and forces their momentum back Delphine's way.

Rage grips him, makes him superhuman for a moment. They spiral furiously into a jar. It tips over and hits the wall. Fragments of loose concrete clatter to the ground forty floors below. The wall gives. The jar crashes overboard and smashes onto the sidewalk.

"I'm not gonna die just 'cause you are!" She forces him back, and they roll all the way to Delphine's fence. The old goat bleats panic.

"It isn't fair!" He pushes on top of her again. Rolls her towards the brink as she attempts to pull her arm free to punch him. Here's the edge. There's no wall to protect them. Holy shit, holy shit, they're going to fall! Over the ledge they go. Kora grabs a coil of loose rebar. The sick boy clings to her waist. "I don't want to die!"

She could kick him in the belly and he would plummet.

She feels the temptation. Her arm begins to quiver. She can't hold their weight for much longer. She has to decide now. She hoists them both back up to the safety of the rooftop garden.

"You little fuck!" she hisses.

The monsoon clouds burst open and shower them.

Stash trembles, flat on his belly beside her. Gets ahold of himself and gives her a crooked grin, half-malevolent, half-teasing.

"Piss off," Kora says. "I don't care if you are my brother's friend. You're not welcome in my house."

THE STARFISH GROOM 2

NODE: KERNELS PLUMP
DAY: 1

EVEN IF SHE IS OUR LAST DOUBLER, I DON'T WANT AUNTIE RADIX TO have Peristrophe Halliana's eyes. Auntie Radix already took Peristrophe Halliana's liver a week ago, and one of her kidneys four weeks before that. Auntie Radix says that it is the duty and nature of a starfish to give. I tell her it is the duty and nature of a doubler to know when to stop asking. Peristrophe Halliana and I have seen the new monsoons only nineteen times each. We are barely old enough to do what we do. Auntie Radix has been drenched by the rains forty-eight times. It should be her job to sacrifice for us, not the other way round. It's a good thing that memory is not a part of the body that can be cut out, or no doubt she would ask for Peristrophe Halliana's memory too.

I bite back my resentment. Radix Bupleuri is our queen, not to mention the eldest of the eighty-three sisters who live at Grist Village and a direct descendent of Grandma Chan Ling. She is well past a healthy age for child-bearing, but she is also our last doubler. With our death rates, we Grist sisters go the way of the dodo, unless she keeps birthing puppies. Yes, from her midnight egg space and—pop!—out her hoo, once plump and fresh, now floppy as an old sock. Still juicy to her young groom, who loves her. For me, nothing about her is juicy. Everything is duty. That means grit and grin, through every whim and tantrum.

I sigh. I clean then sharpen my knives on my precious whetstone. Don't you know that diamonds are a girl's best friend? We made the whetstone ourselves, crushed so many engagement rings from skeletons of the time before, six glass towers full of nice ladies, sweet so sweet. Purty, the scavenger Aunties tell me, purty as covergirl, wonderful wonderbra, guess? by georges marciano.

Purty and thin as skin and bones. They had time to work off the weight. Time to rot, time to mummify. For every season there is a reason. Off their skinny dead fingers the scavenger Aunties took their diamonds. Crushed those doggies to a coarse salt and made me my whetstone. Now I smooth my blade, one, two, three. All that love from the time before rushes into my shiv.

That's the way the cookie crumbles, I tell my beloved Peristrophe Halliana, as I work my knives. Once they are good and sharp, I wipe them down with mother moonshine. We make it ourselves in claw foot tubs from the time before. With potatoes cropped from our own fields, you know, Mistress Mary, quite contrary, how does your garden grow? We pretty maids, we Sisters Grist, some call us tub puppets, fuck moppets, matchstick monkeys. Who cares? We will outlive them all, in beds of our own making.

As I prepare my knives, I rant the chant the grannies gave me, the one that Grandma Chan Ling heard from the dirt, so long ago. My mother double, Glorybind Groundsel, smoking medicinal marijuana in the old rosewood pipe she inherited from Grandma Chan Ling herself, chants with me to make sure I get the words right. She teaches me my genealogy. You know, like, where we came from. What we're here for. "You must hold these things, Kirilow," she tells me. "We hold all that remains of the old world's knowledge in our raw brains. That means we need to be extra smart."

She teaches me how to be a good groom to my beloved Peristrophe Halliana, the last starfish among us, the last giver. It isn't easy, you know—to have and to hold, to kiss and to cut. Slit sluts, that's what they call us in Saltwater City. I'm not ignorant, I know what they say. It's why they expelled our grannies eighty years ago. For having and holding. For slicing and stitching. What did they expect from us anyhow? That they could keep making us again and again and again and again? Bust us from their greasy bottles like so many cheap gene genies? As if.

Grandma Chan Ling invented the partho pop, you know, how we egg ourselves along—I mean, the long, lizardy love of the Grist sisters. We split, we slit, we heal, we groom, self-mutated beyond the know-how of the clone company Jemini that spawned us, and the HöST scale and microchip factories that bought our grannies to work for them. But there are flaws in our limited DNA—the DNA of just one woman. We mutate for better and worse, for sickness and health. But more for sickness and worse. Only our starfish can save us, by regrowing whatever grooms like me cut out of them. Grandma Chan Ling invented the kiss cut, the repair job—what do you say? The fix, the patch. The first starfish gave her liver, her kidneys, and, at last, her red-hot heart to the first doubler. And so it was, in the beginning.

I chant loud as I can to push down the dread that roils in my belly:

Our Mother of milk and mildew
Our Mother of dirt
Our Mother of songs and sighing

Our Mother of elk
Blessed are the sheep
And blessed are the roses
Blessed are the tigers
Wind, bones, and onion flowers
We remember you and we remember rain
We remember mushrooms holding the globe
    in their mycorrhizal net
We remember dust
We remember meat
We remember fibre in its weave and fibre
    in its weft
The shifting and wobbling of the intentional
    earth

After we escaped the sister factories of Saltwater City, Grandma Chan Ling herself doctored it all. Our great progenitress—not only the first doubler but also the first groom, inventor of the loving transplant, the sexy suture. It feels good, you know, don't doubt it. We mutated the first forget-me-do, not that Isabelle Chow, not those Saltwater killers who claim it for who knows what new wickedness. Forget-me-do makes you feel pain as pleasure. It takes away all memory and feeling of pain, leaves nothing but a craving to be cut again. We cultivated it for the sisterly insertion and the doublers return, two holy ways for one to become two.

Peristrophe Halliana sips six slugs of mother moonshine infused with forget-me-do. I wipe down the last blade with a seventh. Then the flame, hot so hot. My precious bunsen burner salvaged from the very lab where Grandma Chan Ling was made, in old Saltwater Town, the ruin that somehow keeps on being a city. All railway tracks, mouldy stucco, and tarnished glass skyscrapers. All rain, mud, bedbugs, and rodentia. Rock-a-bye baby, in the cradle of civilization. Not that I've ever been there, but my mother double teaches me all the songs and all the history she remembers.

Thinking about the filth of Saltwater City makes me will my knives super clean. Pour more vodka in to burn baby learn. I'm being followed by a moonshine shadow. Peristrophe Halliana is prone to infection. The cutting might be no big deal, but healing's a bitch. So knives must shimmer clean, a lean mean clean. I mean, sparkle, twinkle like the lemon muscle man from the time before. Clean as mister. Even though the mistresses are master here.

The first cut is the sleekest. At the corner of the eye, at the zygomatic process, where the top of the skull attaches to the side of the head. I know my bones. My mother double taught me well. Foot bone connected to the heel bone. Heel bone connected to the ankle bone. Peristrophe Halliana sighs a sleepy sigh of pleasure-pain. I move my fingers beneath her eyeball, the tiniest blade concealed between middle and index. Nudge it out and softly slice the root. She groans. I tug at the globe, and it releases with a gentle squelch and click.

"Those are pearls that were her eyes," I sing as blood gushes from her left socket. I cinch it shut, and suture with my finest lichen fibre thread. From her right eye, she gazes at me with love.

I give her another couple of slugs of mother moonshine. Then, careful so careful, I work my blade on the right. Again, the root. Another squelch, another click. How can Peristrophe have so much blood in her head? I staunch the flow with mushroom gauze, press into the wound until the hot pulse of blood subsides. I stitch her up quick.

EARTH APPLES 3

NODE: KERNELS PLUMP
DAY: 1

UP IN THE ROOFTOP GARDENS OF THE CRUMBLING WOODWARD'S
Building, where the Ko family has lived for generations, Kora
spills potatoes and earth out one of the large earthenware jars.
The jar is huge—big enough to hold three Koras and her beloved
goat. Although one is lost, there are eleven more on the rooftop.
They are old and cracked now, and so fragile that the earth Uncle
Wai filled them with last fall pushes at their walls and threatens
to split them open.

She picks up a potato. It is not very big—barely the size of her
fifteen-year-old fist. Gnarled and slimy, its rotten surface crawls
with wireworms. It smells, not of sweet earth but of putrefaction.

"Soil's depleted, uncle," Kora says. "Do you think we could
convince the wet market gardeners to sell us more?"

Uncle Wai coughs. They both know the wet market farmers will
never help them. It's 2145, and the dollar is dead. The wet market
farmers want renminbi, a currency no one in the Ko family earns.

She examines the potato in her hand, watches a fat white worm
wriggle over its rotting skin. She shudders. But if she can accept

this horror, then she can accept the unknown horrors coming. She imagines dislodging the white squirmer and putting it in her mouth.

"Stop daydreaming, Kora," shouts Uncle Wai as he quickly sweeps earth back into the jar. "Hurry up. Looks like monsoon season is early this year."

She raises her gaze skyward. Clouds the colour of bruises rumble across the face of Chang. Kora worries about his increasingly close orbit. Although HöST has vast powers over the citizenry of Saltwater City and Saltwater Flats, it has little power over objects in space, even when that space is relatively close. If HöST were friendly with the neighbouring Cosmopolitan Earth Council, it might be able to push him back out to his original orbit. But HöST is not on friendly terms with the CEC.

Chang's actual size doesn't change, but to those on Earth his lumbering form appears larger with each passing day. The clouds that drift overhead cover his logo-pocked face, grow thick, and threaten to split.

"Come on, Kora. Let's go."

She can't help it. The worse things get, the more her mind turns to visions of the future. She sees the men waste and die. She sees whole houses shut their doors against the flu-ridden city, only to be consumed from the inside. Houses packed to the rafters with the corpses of men and boys, and the girls and women who stayed too close. Houses bursting with rot and sorrow. She sees these things so intensely that they have become the world she already inhabits. She moves through the present as though through mud.

"Kora!" Uncle Wai's got a jar lowered halfway, and it's slipping from his grip. She rushes to help him.

There was a time when he could empty the jars on his own, guiding them to the garden floor with one hand, while controlling the flow of earth and potatoes with the other. But today, it takes two of them, one old man who is not actually very old and one young woman who is actually still a girl.

"Soon, niece, you'll be strong enough to do this on your own. You just need to eat more meat." He glances up at her through rheumy eyes.

She works quickly now, wills herself to focus. From the darkness of the rickety shed, Delphine bleats. The goat is already seven years old. Uncle Wai says they'll have to slaughter her soon, before the meat gets too tough, and while he still has the strength to do it without hurting her. Kora has known the goat since Kora was eight. She dreads having to play a part in the goat's death, but Uncle Wai says Kora can't be so soft if she wants to survive in the world that is coming.

"We'll do it kindly," he says.

"I love the goat, uncle."

"I know, child. I know."

She begins to tilt another jar. The clouds open suddenly, and the acid torrent drenches them. The water is slightly viscous. Her hand slips, and the jar crashes to the garden floor and splits into a hundred sharp pieces. Dirt and potatoes scatter everywhere.

There is no time for recrimination.

"You get the potatoes. I'll get the earth," says Uncle Wai. He dashes for the broom.

Kora digs out a bamboo-fibre sack from the storage bin beside the goat shed and gathers potatoes as fast as she can. Many of them are so rotten, they squelch in her hand, but there is no time to sort. She fires them into the bag while Uncle Wai sweeps the precious dirt into a corner and covers the heap with waxed bamboo cloth.

He covers the rain barrels too. This rain is too contaminated to be useful.

Soaked through, they scurry down the rooftop hatch, carrying the bag of potatoes between them.

They lurch downstairs like an old bear with two heads. Inside the apartment, they wipe their hands and faces with towels hanging at the foot of the stairs. They remove their tattered raincoats. Kora's coat hasn't protected her from much. She goes to her room to change. There, she discovers a new rain burn in the blue cotton dress sent to her by Kai Tak Ko, the father she's never met. She likes it because it has lots of pockets. She shouldn't have worn it to the roof. She rinses the burnt corner in the basin of good water reserved for washing face and hands. Where the fabric was stained by bad rain, a hole presents itself. *Damn it.* She pulls on her only other dress, the one made of mud-brown bamboo fibre that Uncle Wai gave her for her birthday two years ago. She goes to the kitchen.

At the kitchen table, Kora's mother and older brother sit, peeling and cutting potatoes. They slice out the rotten parts. They squish wireworms. Charlotte and K2 have a pot going on the stove to cook the good parts into a soup that they can freeze at least until they run out of bamboo to fuel the generator. If the potatoes were healthy and whole, they'd store them in the empty apartment next door, abandoned by their neighbours after the father and brothers succumbed to the flu last winter. But these motley chunks of potato flesh won't keep on their own.

Charlotte looks exhausted. Although she's not yet forty, her dull black hair is streaked with white, and dark pockets of loose skin sag beneath her eyes. She's the only family member who still has a job, as night nurse at a nearby hospice, and she looks after the whole family on top of that.

The tall, once handsome Godwin Austen "K2" Ko slouches at the table, thin and pale. Although his twin brother, Everest, never lived with them, the absence that has always haunted K2 seems to scream from his skin. There's a red, angry lesion on his cheek that could be a rain burn or a sign of the flu worsening. He just turned twenty, but he's so malnourished and sick with flu, he looks sixteen. He had a job working at his friend Akal Arnouse's abattoir, just over the border in the Second Quarantine Ring, but Akal was forced to fire him when K2 could no longer lift the carcasses.

"Your icky friend Stash was here yesterday."

"I gave him a key. He's lost his family and has nowhere to go. I thought maybe he could hang around here sometimes."

"He knocked a potato jar over the ledge. Me and Uncle Wai cleaned it up this morning. So that's two jars we've lost in two days."

Uncle Wai grunts his displeasure.

K2 says nothing.

Kora says, "Don't you even give a shit? Where do you think our food comes from?"

"Stash has lost more than a potato jar," says K2. "Cut him some slack already."

"He's kind of gross." Should she tell K2 what actually happened? He's so demoralized already.

"Yeah, I know, Kora. He's sick okay? And sad. Be nice to him."

Kora doesn't want to be nice to Stash. "Tell him he's not welcome. He gives me the creeps."

More intense than her loathing for Stash is Kora's fear of losing them all. It's not just a fear. It's a coming certainty. With the heat from the stove and the burden of her grief and worry, Kora can hardly stay awake. Her limbs weigh like depleted earth. The light of the bare fluorescent bulb stings her eyes and her lids droop, then fall.

She goes down into the dark. In her dream, she sees the Marine Building, engulfed in the flesh of an earth-crawling squid. She has a knife and slices flesh from its side. It makes a thin wailing sound. She puts the flesh in her mouth and chews. It tastes like raw goat.

In the dream, families line up outside the building. She recognizes neighbours from across the hall: the Drs Bloom and their sons, Avery, Adam, and Archer. The Blooms go into the building through the door that has become a toothy mouth. The sides of the squid-building pulse with a soft pink light. It reaches its tentacles into its crown and tosses the Blooms up into the sky so high they land on the moon.

Kora has seen the moon lots of times, during monsoon season, when the heavy rains wash the acid sky and reveal what lies high above. But she knows about the moon mostly because of the memory scale that Uncle Wai gave her last year for her fourteenth birthday. With the scale neatly planted in her brain through her halo, she remembers the moon in all its phases—waxing, waning, full, gibbous, new. She remembers that the moon still pulls the tides, though Chang's deteriorating orbit interferes with the original pattern more and more.

Avery, Adam, and Archer sit on the surface of the moon, smiling and waving. And then someone else is smiling and waving, so close their face is like the moon. The moon speaks: "Kora, come back to us."

A hand passes over her still-closed eyes, making the flickers of light she dreams go suddenly dark. She blinks her eyes open. Her pupils narrow, adjusting to the nasty fluorescent light of the family kitchen. It is not the moon speaking, it is her mother. She is talking to Uncle Wai now.

"I wish you wouldn't give her those things, Wai."

"She needs memory scales to understand the world that was. They don't hurt her. She's gifted is all. And her gift will help her live."

Charlotte notices that her daughter is awake. She pats Kora's arm.

"I saw the Drs Bloom," Kora tells them. "I saw Avery, Adam, and Archer. They walked into a giant squid. It tossed them to the moon."

"She's lost her senses," Charlotte says, stroking Kora's sweaty hair. Her hand catches on the memory scale and Kora's brain vibrates gently. For a second, she sees the moon again, round and full.

THEY HAVE EATEN THEIR POTATO SOUP. KORA IS IN HER ROOM NOW, trying to sleep. She can hear Wai and Charlotte fighting about the goat.

"You have to do it now, Wai. Before—before—"

"Before what?"

"Please. Don't argue, just take care of it."

"Before the muscle wasting sets in? Before the lesions? Before the dementia? Or just sometime before I give up the ghost entirely? What?"

"Please don't."

"You're like a child. Do you understand what it means when you act like a child? It means that the children have to act like adults. They need a mother, Charlotte. Kora especially. You see how she sleeps all the time? She's depressed ..."

"What do you mean, 'Kora especially'? It's because you favour her. It's because you think Godwin Austen is going to die. Who's equivocating now, Kai Wai?"

Kora wills her music scale to rifle through its song list, seeking the strongest antidote to family dysfunction. It takes her a few seconds to find the song she's looking for, during which fragments of their argument continue to seep in.

"We shouldn't have—"

"It's the only way."

"Talk to K2. Perhaps we can change our minds."

"One of us must survive, and she is the only one with a chance. This is how we give her the opportunity."

"So it's too late. You're a coward."

She wills them to shut up. They don't, but soon the voice of Molten Mabel slides over her, claustrophobic and smooth as heavy cream. She shuts out the noise of their fighting by falling into the lyrics.

> *In the world that is coming*
> *Under the reign of ancient Chang*
> *The Weather Girls are so lonely*
> *So lonely, so holy*
> *So hopeful, so different, so changed*

She doesn't remember the album finishing. This could mean she slept, though she doesn't feel rested. It's so early that the sky is still dark. Eng hangs low over the glass towers and emits a pale blue light through the smoggy clouds that cover her face. Kora imagines her family sleeping. She thinks of potatoes growing slowly in the dark. The rain that began yesterday afternoon intensifies, beating against her window. She wants to cry and she wants to sleep but can do neither. She is miserable in a way an old stone is miserable, present to everything but cold, still, and stuck.

The rain stops at dawn, and a thin yellow light comes through the sheer curtains. She sits up, drops her feet to the cold floor, and shuffles around until she finds her tattered bamboo-fibre slippers. She pushes the curtains of her window aside. That yellow light pressures the heavy layer of pollution that lies over Saltwater City all through the dry season. On the western horizon, Old Chang rises. She gazes at him and wonders about all the things he once did for the people of the time before.

A STRANGER IN THE WOODS 4

NODE: KERNELS PLUMP
DAY: 1

I LAY OUT THE PRECIOUS HARVEST ON ICE BROUGHT DOWN FROM THE mountains by our first-year initiates, all thirteen-year-old girls from Grist Village. At the door to my cave, Auntie Radix's young groom is waiting. Soon the eyes that are darkening in that old doubler's head will shine bright as halogen headlights. Not that I've ever seen halogen headlights, but I know the songs. Maybe you can wash my car, yes, I'm gonna flee a star. I know what stars are. They twinkle a little. They light up my wife. I know what cars are too. They are what the people from the time before used to get around, instead of walking. They doubled as wheelbarrows, for transporting food and herbs and found treasures.

"I'm so tired, Kiri," my beloved Peristrophe says when Auntie Radix's young groom is gone.

"I know, my love, I know." I gather Peristrophe's frail, over-harvested body into my arms. The exhilaration of the cut has left me, and I'm gripped by a sudden melancholy. Our old cave, with its battered armchairs and tattered tiger-skin rug from the time before, suddenly looks grey and grim. The herbs I hang from the rafters shudder as the room grows colder, casting sinister shadows on the crumbling earthen walls. "Take some more moonshine, dear one," I tell her, thinking about how I'll release the mushroom stitches in a week or so, when her new eyes begin to push into the empty slashes. "To ensure the memory of the pain won't linger."

"So tired," she whispers.

I rock her gently. "Sleep, my sweet." I refuse the fear that I've really done it this time, imagine tamping it under a thick layer of warm earth. Still, doubt seeps into me like the draft that has entered the room. Does she feel it too? Her body exudes a mournful kind of trust so palpable it is almost heat. I could not bear to lose her. And bad as it would be for me, it would be worse for Grist Village. She is our last starfish.

NODE: KERNELS PLUMP
DAY: 9

WHEN AUNTIE RADIX ASKS FOR PERISTROPHE HALLIANA'S HEART, I tell her no. I'm at her bedside, summoned here after her new groom cut her wrong. Her old groom died last year of the flu, and her new groom is young and green—too green for the job she does. She should still be with the other initiates, running ice down from the mountains on clear days when the air at altitude is breathable. Her small hands are dexterous but unpractised. Her eyes glow the emerald green of excess forget-me use.

"Green grow the rushes O," I sing.

The new groom doesn't sing with me. She doesn't know this song. The initiates have no one to teach them the rhymes of the time before.

I feel dirty, cutting Auntie Radix for her, slipping my digits into Auntie Radix's floppy sockets. This isn't the ritual. This isn't the way it's done. The chivalry of the shiv says each groom takes care of her own—doubler or starfish, depending on fate. You don't take care of another groom's sexy suture. It's not right. It'll make Chang fall faster than he is already falling. This is the alternate hour, when he hangs directly above Grist Village, too round and too low in his deteriorating orbit. His gross gravity tugs at my liver and makes me queasy.

I stay with Old Radix and her new groom until Eng rises on the southern horizon, blue and small but still visible through the smoky air outside the four windows built into the wall that closes off Auntie Radix's cave. The elites of Saltwater City control Eng's insides, as they control those of her brother, Chang, but we can still enjoy her glow. We worship her an avatar of Our Mother. As her period lengthens, her gravitational effects get weaker. My heart aches the special ache it only aches for her. I should get back to Peristrophe Halliana.

Auntie Radix blinks her peepers open, gazes at me through the true brown eyes of my own best beloved. Jeepers creepers.

"My heart is failing, Kirilow," she says, misty mournful as lonely Eng, though not nearly as sweet.

Oh no, I think, though I don't say it. She's our last doubler, and coming to the end of her fertility. We should have stopped calling upon her to pop out young ones a decade ago. She's a miserable whiner, but the teachings of Our Mother say,

Behold, the last
Doubler is gold

I sat that class carefully.

It means, Glorybind Groundsel told me, if the Grist is dying down to the last doubler, her word is flesh, her word is god. You can't say no.

But all my fibres scream it. No more I love yous. My own

heart howls like a child's. My mouth says, "I don't quite get your meaning, auntie."

She takes a deep breath, then narrows her eyes. "Arrhythmia, Kirilow. Don't pretend you don't understand."

I sigh. "I hear your concern."

"Well, then?"

"If Peristrophe Halliana gives her heart so soon, she might not make it." I would really rather not be having this conversation.

"Not my problem," says Old Radix. "You may not respect me much, Kirilow Groundsel, but you have a duty to the Grist sisterhood. Without me, the sisterhood won't make it."

"Who says I don't respect you?" I protest, alarmed as I say it to feel whatever respect I had for her dwindle to nothing.

"Spoiled child. Don't you dare think I don't know. But I don't care what you think. I need a new heart soon. You know your duty."

I cogitate with all my being. Too slow, I say, "The Grist sisterhood won't survive without the starfish Peristrophe Halliana. Mama Glory says a balance must be struck."

"Humph," says Old Radix, because she knows I have a point.

"I'll consult with my mother double and tell you what's possible."

I escape Auntie Radix's dark cave and rush out into the night air, fresh and bright as the day's smog recedes back to the city it came from.

NODE: KERNELS PLUMP
DAY: 12

I FEEL THE PULL OF CHANG AS HE RIDES UP THE EVENING SKY. TONIGHT, he faces us, and through the smog I can see the logo of HöST, the company who made and launched him in the long-ago days of oil. Every day he orbits closer. Old Glorybind says that he and Eng are the same size, and that once upon her time, they had periods of twelve hours each and appeared to earthbound Grist sisters just slightly larger than the moon. Now, Chang rules our sky, rises and sets every two hours, while Eng spirals away from us, high and unpredictable.

"HEO," says Mother Glorybind. "For highly elliptical orbit. Once upon a time, people could calculate. Maybe in Saltwater City they still can. We Grist sisters feel our way to other knowings."

I nod, though I have no idea what she is talking about. Gotta learn faster, before I lose her. I don't want to think about that and push it from my mind.

Tonight, Chang's gravity tugs at the spindly trees and makes their leaves rustle. A thin metallic light drifts through the pollution and illuminates the forest floor, making everything glimmer ghostly.

Below the bluff that shapes the path between my cave and Auntie Radix's, I see something shift and jerk against the wind. The bluff rides high and steep over the valley below. Invasive eucalyptus crowd in on me and hide the figure running down there. A body of smoke from the forest fires up north fills the valley. A breeze nudges trees in the valley, revealing then obscuring the forest floor. There's a red flash of hair. It's a biped, like us. One of those sneaky creeps from Saltwater City? But unlike us, tall, pale, and gangly. Our genes don't express like that. We manifest crow-black hair, autumn-leaf skin, and short legs.

I shudder, remembering last year's militia attack. We were lucky. It was a small advance guard, and we got them all. In my humble opinion, we should have moved the village afterwards, but Auntie Radix was against it.

I track the Salty along the edge of the bluff, meek and sweet as hello kitty. I catch a whiff of its shit and sweat stink on an updraft, and gag softly.

It stumbles into a clearing. Gotcha! I throw a knife at it, neatly severing its left hand. It screams and dashes into the brush.

The severed hand lies there in the clearing, reflecting Chang's metallic light. Blood pools from the cut veins. I step off the path onto the loose gravel, through more eucalyptus and spindly sage that give onto the valley floor. My first step lands solid, but the second sets a cascade of gravel flowing down the escarpment. I ride it, thankful for the sturdy elk-skin boots that Peristrophe Halliana sewed for me while recovering from her last surgery.

I walk cautiously forward, brace through the thighs to keep it slow and steady, though the slope wants me to run. When I think it can't get any steeper, the path becomes a straight drop. I turn around and climb backwards as though down a ladder. When I reach the narrow ledge at the bottom of the drop, I turn again. A pair of eyes watches me from the forest just beyond the clearing. The Salty I saw? What if there is a full Saltwater City militia in the forest, watching and waiting to ambush me?

My gaze darts between the eyes in the forest and the severed hand, that gleaming horde of genetic treasure, right there in the middle of the clearing. To nab it on my own would be risky. If I were smart, I'd leave it, bide for a better chance when I have Glorybind Groundsel or a posse of initiates with me.

I'm not smart. I scramble the rest of the way down, half running, half rolling, and dash through rough bush and brambles into the clearing. The Salty rushes out. Dives into the clearing, blood still dripping from its hastily bound wound. It snatches up the severed hand just seconds before I get there, then stumbles back into the woods. I tear after it, muttering, "Our Mother who art artful, Our

Mother of moss ..." I follow the shuddering of the trees and the intermittent blood spatter staining needles, earth, leaves, and stone. I follow fast as the winds that hail the new monsoons.

Slam! Here's Mourning Rock. The forest lies dead still. The blood trail is gone, and the Salty is nowhere to be seen.

"WHAT DO YOU SUPPOSE IT WAS LOOKING FOR?" I ASK PERISTROPHE Halliana back at our cozy cave.

She sits up. "Will you take out my stitches? My new eyes are deuce itchy."

My tunic is torn, my hair is full of burrs, I'm covered in bruises, and my hands are filthy. "Give me a minute to wash up." I open the tap and let run a precious trickle of water from our rooftop cistern, opened to the sky only on clean rain days. Dip a dry rag into the half-full sink, and in the precious mirror from the time before, check my face for dirt and blood.

"I suspect it was looking for us," she says. "You better catch it." She slumps back onto her mushroom-fibre pillow.

WET MARKET ENCOUNTER 5

NODE: KERNELS PLUMP
DAY: 2

KORA WATCHES THE SKY BRIGHTEN. SHE GAZES AT CHANG UNTIL HE is full and round. Then she puts on the brown bamboo-fibre dress Uncle Wai gave her and layers on her warm padded jacket. She slips out of the quiet apartment and up the stairs to the roof to begin the morning's chores. She can hear Charlotte and Wai shouting at one another the moment she lifts the rooftop hatch. She comes up into the light. Her eyes burn with the horror of what she sees.

Delphine swings by her hind legs from the ceiling of the shed. Thrashes fearsomely. Blood gushes from her hooved friend's throat and soaks the bamboo-fibre mat on which the goat slept last night.

Charlotte stands before the pen wielding a bloody knife, eyes blazing sorrow and desperation.

Uncle Wai clutches the kicking body, trying to calm the goat and staunch the gushing blood. At the same time, he yells at Charlotte, "No shame and no self-control! You're a child. How will Kora and Godwin Austen feel? You're selfish. You think of no one's feelings but your own."

Charlotte doesn't yell back. Instead, her voice comes deep and low and slow. "If you'd agreed to kill that bleating nanny a year ago, the kids would have had some decent food to eat instead of your lousy rotten potatoes. K2 might not have gotten sick. You're the selfish one, protecting Kora's feelings at the cost of K2's life."

"Don't be melodramatic. K2 is still alive, and he might get better."

The bleeding, bleating goat kicks and thrashes. Uncle Wai looks like he's gone for a swim in a red pool.

"You don't know anything of what I've suffered. I should never have left your brother."

"Don't say that." He grips the goat as its thrashing slows.

"We'd be living in wealth and comfort instead of shame and poverty."

"Our love was real."

"Was it, Kai Wai? Really? Aren't you a little old to believe in such garbage?"

The goat kicks, then grows still. Uncle Wai gazes into its dying eyes. "Yes," he says. "I believe in such garbage. And I believe in Kora."

"Well, good," Charlotte says. "You better treasure her and make sure she lives. Because I have only two children now."

He stares at her.

"That's right. My eldest son, Everest, is dead."

Kora realizes she's been holding her breath.

"Dead?"

"His father left a message this morning."

Though she never knew Everest, a wave of grief slams Kora. She draws in a great, gasping gulp of air.

Her uncle sees her and dives towards her. But Kora has already turned. She runs down the stairs, through the apartment, out the door, and into the main stairwell, all the way to the ground level. Down Hastings Street she flees, past the N-lite junkies stoned on history, past the scale exchange where denizens routinely swap out shimmering flakes and tendrils of information in a desperate attempt to know and so fix the broken world.

Uncle Wai lumbers along behind her like a sick bear. In her mind's eye, Kora sees the goat's throat gush red and furious. She runs faster, turns the corner, and scuttles into the wet market. She darts in and out among the stalls of cans recovered from the time before, whirls and turns through the market in a frantic, antic dance, tears past sellers of salmon jerky from the Coast Salish Timeplace, lush fruits from the UMK, salvaged coffee from Seattle Before, squashes and fresh rabbit from Houston North, elk-skin gloves and raw forget-me-do purportedly from the mythic village of Grist. Everywhere she turns there are women from all walks of Saltwater City life—vendors and engineers, dockworkers and office staff.

At last, the flap of Uncle Wai's tired feet against ancient concrete stops. She pauses to catch her breath by a stall of can sellers.

"Hey!" shouts a voice. "Thief!"

"I'm not stealing." Kora turns to face a girl her own age, a fearsome one with kohl-rimmed eyes and spiky scales jutting out in all directions.

"Well, what are you doing then?" The girl taps the counter beside her, on which are laid out a heap of precious-because-extinct tuna tins. "Empty your pockets."

"As if," scoffs Kora. She turns to find the next corner around which to disappear. But there are two more ghoulish girls behind her, their eyes rimmed dark. One of them hisses at her through a set of brown and jagged teeth.

Kora empties her pockets. There is nothing in the left but a dirty handkerchief. The right has a hole in it and produces nothing.

"Ptaw," says the girl behind the counter, glaring. "Pathetic! All that scurrying about and you don't even have a little can of clams in your pocket?"

Kora has bought cans like these from Cordova Dancing Girls before, very rarely, for her uncle when he couldn't get out of bed. But the only conversations she's had with them have been bartering ones.

She swallows phlegmy fear and shrugs her shoulders. "Should I?"

"Well, why are you darting around like a little robber if you aren't one?"

The girl with bad teeth exhales foul breath in her ear.

Kora digs deep for bravado. "None of your business, tin-can lady."

"Oooooooh, feisty, is it?" says the counter girl.

Kora takes a long silent inhale, then snatches her handkerchief back. "Well, see ya."

The fearsome girl grabs Kora's wrist. "Not so fast. What sheltered brat comes running into the wet market unless she's after something? Or running from something, is that it?"

Kora tries to pull her arm back, but the other two girls close in behind her so tight that lice leap from their dirty skins and scamper across Kora's bare neck. She draws her knee up quick and gives the table a good swift kick. Cans of salmon, tuna, crab, and char roll off in all directions. The fearsome girl lets go. Kora turns, elbows one henchwoman sharp in the guts. Gulps. Slaps the other hard across the cheek. Then runs back the way she came, suddenly eager to be home.

THE SALTY'S HAND

NODE: GRAIN IN BEARD
DAY: 1

MY MOTHER DOUBLE AND I ARE OUT HARVESTING FORGET-ME-DO—OUR most precious crop, bred alongside us three generations ago in the factories of Saltwater City, refined by us here at Grist Village, and now seeded through mallow, agave, and sage. Through its use, we cultivate what we remember and what we forget in order to make Grist history. Under my mother double's watchful eye, I developed my own strain to suit first and foremost the needs of Peristrophe Halliana.

I'm absorbed in selecting the brightest leaves and at first don't notice the trees rustling and shivering below us as a creature moves through them. It steps into an open patch of light and stops. I draw my opera glasses out of their pouch and whip them up to my eyes. It's the same Salty I saw two days ago, grey-eyed and weak now. It pauses, as though it senses my presence. Raises its gaze to the bluff and draws its right hand up to shield its eyes from the light.

By Our Mother's blues and shoes, its hand has grown back! Through the magnification of my marvellous opera glasses, I can see that although the hand is not to size, it is perfectly formed. It looks a little pink and raw but healthy. A new starfish!

I rush along the bluff.

It stumbles, vulnerable. My heart beats faster. A clearing opens down the path in front of it. I take my chances and hurry ahead to a spot just above the clearing. Watch like a young coyote, eyes intent, tail twitching. Quick as a brown fox, I drop a womb bomb over it—Glorybind Groundsel's latest invention, a translucent wrapping sack made from modified black squirrel bladder cells. With a quick, sharp tug I draw the womb bomb tight, bundling the thing neatly. It shrieks like a wounded rabbit as I rush down the bluff to where it flails. Whistle for my mother double.

Glorybind Groundsel emerges from the trees seconds after I reach the sobbing Salty. These creatures are so pathetic. I don't understand how they could ever have disdained us, much less expelled us from Saltwater City.

"Whenever I want you, all I have to do is preen," I tell it. "So shut up, Little Susie."

The thing whimpers.

My mother double says, "There's no need to be cruel, Kirilow."

I glare at her. I say nothing but lead her gaze with my own to its new hand.

It can starfish, she mouths.

I nod.

"Let me go," blubbers the thing.

I yank the womb bomb tighter. "By the foulest breath of Our Mother, would you please shut up?"

It bawls.

"I can't stand these things, Mother Glorybind," I say. I pull out my needles.

"When will you grow out of this murderous phase?" Old Glorybind Groundsel sighs.

One of the needles is a little tarnished. I pull out a cloth and begin to polish it. "I don't know why you're so squeamish," I say. "The Salty barbarians want us all dead. You should thank me."

"We need this one for its starfish wisdom."

"At least let me bleed it a little."

"Kirilow."

"All right," I say. "I wasn't going to hurt it anyway. But you can't stop me from hating. You yourself told me the stories—of how they rounded our grandmothers up by the thousands, lined them up along a barbed wire fence, and shot them. And didn't they discover, raid, and torch our far forget-me-do fields just last year? Why should you care if I hurt it or not?"

"The war is over now, Kirilow. Just stun it."

"The war is not over. It's just quieter than it was in Grandma Chan Ling's day."

"Stun. That's all."

"Pardon, master. I will be correspondent to command."

"That's enough cheek for one day," says my mother double. "The knowledge I feed you from the time before is solid jade. You have no right to abuse it."

Tenderly, as though this putrid Salty were my own best beloved Peristrophe Halliana, I tap a needle into its skull and then all down the meridian of sleep. The Salty stops weeping. Its eyes dim and its eyelids flicker down. It dozes softly.

I pick up one end of the womb bomb, and my mother double picks up the other. Swinging the Salty between us, we take it back to our lab and lay it out on the examination table.

I'M IN THE KITCHEN WARMING A BIT OF RABBIT STEW FOR PERISTROPHE Halliana when I hear rustling in the lab. I pull aside the curtain to see what's going on. The Salty is awake.

"I found you," it hacks. "You have to come to Saltwater City. The people are dying. You have to cure them."

"Why would I do that?" I ask, eyes incredulous wide. "Far as I'm concerned, the sooner you murderers go extinct, the better for me and my sisters. It's about time you brewed a flu strong enough to kill yourselves off."

I move towards the medicine pot to get it a cup of forget-me-do tea. I open a small hole in the womb bomb where its mouth is and press the cup to it, urging it to drink.

"Please, no," it begs. "Not yet." And then, "We didn't all want rid of you, you know. It was the Chow-McPherson government. It was the militias. Some of us hate them as much as you do."

I put on a mushroom membrane glove, stretch its thin elastic skin over my rough hand. I press my palm to its stomach. Even through the glove and the thick fibres of the womb bomb, I can feel the excess bile in its belly. Sickly and sickening.

"I don't believe you," I tell it. "So drink."

"Please," it wails. "When you see them, your heart will fill with pity." Tears dribble down its pimply cheeks. A river of snot runs from its nose. How can they be so repulsed by us when they themselves are so disgusting?

I press the cup harder against its lips. "Drink, Salty."

"I have a mother and a father," it says, smiling ever so slightly through the mass of snot and tears. "And two brothers. We could help you."

Vomit pools in my throat. I grip its jaw and force it open. Pour the tea into its already gurgling, foaming mouth. As soon as I let go, it coughs and sputters, then spits the whole cup of tea over its front. I want to be sick, and stumble away towards the water closet.

I hear old Glorybind's voice then and am astonished to realize she's been sitting in her rocking chair this whole time, smoking a pipe of sage and pot. "Steady, Kirilow. A good groom doesn't get excited over nothing. What will you do when you have a real emergency on your hands?"

Chang stares right in through the middle of the three windows that grace our cave's sister-built wall. I choke back my puke. If I don't learn everything my mother double has to teach me before she leaves this world, then Peristrophe Halliana doesn't have long to live, and nor do I.

"These things disgust me, Mother."

I know they have a second sex they call "men," and that men are useful in Salty doubling technology. When I was a sprout, Glorybind Groundsel showed me a pair of post-storm slugs on a log slipping and sliming over one another. She intended to demonstrate that it was natural.

"It's not so bad,' she said. "Some Grist sisters like the idea of reintroducing men to the Grist. Not you, I suspect."

I remember so clearly the great glob of mucus that dripped from the combined bodies of the two slugs, oozed over the log, shimmered wetly, and plopped to the ground.

"Not me," I told her.

My mother double laughed. "When you get older, you might not find the idea so repulsive."

"It will be repulsive no matter how old I get," I told her. I took forbidden sips of forget-me-do for a whole week afterwards to try to erase the knowledge of how Salty doubling was done.

Now, Old Glorybind draws a great puff of smoke into her lungs and exhales. "Sometimes it is all right to feel pity."

"Am I obliged to feel it? They made us to use us. When they ran out of uses, they murdered as many of us as they could and exiled the rest. Why should I feel anything at all for them?"

"They aren't all the same," says my mother double.

"They lack sisterly feeling."

"I'm just as human as you are," the Salty whines through the walrus goo that oozes from its facial orifices. "Will you please unbind me?"

"We aren't human," my mother double informs it. But then she puts down her pipe, goes over to it. She pulls the womb bomb back farther, until its head is free from the tidy wrapping. Strangely wistful, she strokes its head, still covered in sticky, threads from the bomb. A loose hair pokes up from the Salty's temple, seemingly with a will of its own. It looks like a cockroach antenna. Two more spring up. They quiver with curiosity. Disgusted, I shudder.

"You shouldn't honey it," I say. "What would happen if it told the other Salties where we are? We'd be finished then, wouldn't we? Done and dusted like so many rusted-out car shells." I hold its face steady and take a swab from its nose. "Let's see what kind of disease it has. With any luck, it's a plague that'll kill them all good and dead, and then the Grist will be free at last. High day!"

"Kirilow, be careful what you wish for. The Grist may have evolved beyond its former masters, but we are not immune to their illnesses."

I reach into the casing at the creature's shoulder and pull its right arm out, grab its wrist, and feel its slippery pulse. An unbidden image rushes into my head—Peristrophe Halliana's mother double laid out on a white table under bright lights as Salty doctors poke and prod. I don't want to see. I let go of the thing's hand. Shuffle over to the plant bench and begin to prepare substrate for mushrooms.

"You'll help me then?" whispers the Salty.

"What are you?" I hiss.

"I dream about time," says the Salty. "Time past and time to come. I can show you your history."

"My mother double teaches me my history," I say.

"I can show you how the Grist sisters might survive. I can show you how they might die. I can help you make a path." Its eyes plead. Its weird independent hairs wave. I don't trust it.

"All your kind ever did was use us and lie to us. Your word is dross!"

"I know you saw your sister," says the Salty. "I can show you things. In Saltwater City, they hate the ones who dream about time. But we have our place. The city is changing. If you help me now, you'll pave the way for the Grist sisters to return as full and beloved citizens."

"What kind of mark do you take me for?" I snarl. I throw a fresh womb bomb over it and yank. Inside, the thing whimpers. That's better.

I DON'T WANT THE SALTY TO KNOW THAT IT HAS UNSETTLED ME. I GET to work preparing substrate for ganoderma as though the Salty isn't there. The music of the spores will soothe. Perhaps the path to Our Mother's salvation lies not with animals but with plants. If I could make the perfect substrate, I could capture the perfect spores. If I were a perfect groom, I could modify the longevity bestowed by the ganoderma to become immortality, and then there would be no need for doublers or starfish. Auntie Radix could cut the greedy grasping. Peristrophe Halliana and Glorybind Groundsel would stay with me forever.

These are the things I think as I water my substrate, massage and knead the sweet, earthy-smelling stew of rotted fibre and bone, fruit and flesh.

I'm so absorbed, I don't hear the snipping and cutting sounds until it is too late. Old Glorybind has cut the sick Salty from its sack. They whisper together.

"Mother Glory, what are you doing? I bagged that thing up for a reason!"

The Salty passes something dry and purple to Mother Glorybind. She tucks the strange gift into the folds of her robe, then passes a hand over the Salty's forehead.

"Stop that! You of all people should know how dangerous those things are. Bomb it now before it's too late."

I move towards the Salty to wrap it up again, but there's a thump at our old wooden door. My mother double opens it. Standing there in the piss-pouring rain is Auntie Radix's new young groom.

"Kirilow, you have to come quick," she says. "There is something wrong with Radix Bupleuri's heart."

"Did you take her pulse?" I ask. "Did you take her temperature?"

"There is no time," says the groom. She sweats and jitters. "Bring your mother double too."

"Naw," I tell her. "Auntie Radix's every sneeze is an emergency."

"This time there's really truly a problem," the young groom says. Her eyes brim with shameful tears.

"I better come with you," says Glorybind Groundsel.

"Someone has to stay with that. We can't let it run amok through the lab."

Old Glorybind casts it a glance. "Just bundle it, Kirilow. This might be serious."

I sigh like a put-upon old lady. If she hadn't freed the Salty from its second womb bomb, I wouldn't have to waste a precious third. I draw it from the deep pocket of my tunic and, with a flick of the wrist, cast it over the Salty.

This time, the Salty doesn't struggle. It curls up and seems to sleep.

My mother double and I take our elk-wool overcoats from their hooks and hustle into the ashy air. The forest fires that have been burning through the dry season rage on to the north. I wish the rains would come, as Glorybind says they have on the coast, but here it's much too early.

ISABELLE SHRINE

NODE: KERNELS PLUMP
DAY: 3

WHEN SHE APPROACHES THE GATE TO THE APARTMENT BLOCK, THERE is a whole crew of ragged girls waiting for her, scales wriggling in all directions, eyes all raccoony. Mostly they wear tattered fatigues from Arm-a-Gideon, the police force that used to patrol Saltwater City before Isabelle Chow brought in a new one under HöST. Some wear clothes from the time before: jeans and T-shirts, miniskirts with fishnet stockings, hoodies, and baggy pants. One wears a curly blue wig and a gold lamé dress that sparkles under the solar street light.

Kora goes around the building, thinking that those nasty girls won't know about the back gate, but she sees a crew of them loitering there also. They haven't spotted her yet, though.

There's a fort Kora found with K2 when he was well, hidden in the blackberry bushes down by the water. When she last visited, its floor was littered with N-lite tubes, pigeon shit, and scale shells. Her nostrils wrinkle in anticipation of the stale urine and rotten fish smell. But the fort is hidden from the beach and the road. She prays that the tin-can girls don't know about it.

Before she gets inside, the sweet scent of sandalwood incense rushes out to greet her. Someone has hung a piece of red satin over the door. It's stained and frayed at the edges, but it has been hung with care. *Please don't let there be anyone inside.* She pushes the curtain back. Enough light comes through the cracks in the walls for Kora to see that the fort has been converted into a shrine in honour of the great inventor and CEO of HöST Industries, Isabelle Chow. Embedded in the altar is a smiling photograph of her from when she was awarded Woman Leader of the Year, taken those few short years ago when it wasn't a given that all HöST's leaders were women. Beneath the photo on a wide shelf are neatly arranged statuettes and figurines of female deities as though they were all her avatars: the Virgin Mary, Kuan Yin, a nine-tailed fox lady, Green Tara, the Venus of Willendorf, Athena, Heng'e, and many more besides. Below that sits a small box of sand into which incense, cigarettes, and candles have been stuck and lit.

The sandalwood fragrance is strong. Whoever lit it was here recently. This is not the great hiding place she'd hoped, but the alternative is surrendering to the Cordova girls. *You'll never catch me, witches,* she thinks. Because the shrine seems to want her to, she kneels on the cushion left for precisely this purpose and says a little awkward prayer to Isabelle.

Hail Isabelle, full of place
Richer than the moon
Give us this day our daily cans
And lead us not into the flu
But allow the denizens of Saltwater Flats
To live long and well
Especially Uncle Wai and K2
And even Charlotte, though she killed

The best friend I ever had
My beloved goat, Delphine
And may Delphine's spirit rest in peace
And may I never eat her
For thine is the kingdom the power and the glory
Forever and ever

She takes a match from the box beside the altar and lights one of the half-burnt candles. In the sand beside it, someone has stuck a long fine filigree of gold. It takes her a moment to recognize it as a scale—not the cheap kind she buys in the wet market when Uncle Wai gives her pocket money but a state-of-the-art, posh, and highfalutin one, the kind used by the people in the glass towers at HöST.

She pulls it out of the sand. Cleans it off with a gob of spit and the corner of her bamboo-fibre dress. Removes one of her own precious scales—the one about the phases of the moon—and plugs in the filigree.

The minute she inserts it, Isabelle appears before her, ever so slightly larger than life. Her long dark hair flows around her and moves in a gentle breeze that Kora cannot feel. Her eyes look tired, but her flesh looks so tender soft that Kora reaches out to touch it. But there's nothing to touch in the space she occupies. Kora pulls her hand back as though she's touched a corpse. The figure retains its appearance of solidity. Begins to speak.

"Always they want a piece of you. I'm so tired, my love, so tired. I've been going day and night. If we don't perfect this bloody LiFT soon, the UMK will beat us to it, or the Cosmopolitan Earth Council will. Don't you know it's a contest for the world now? Someone's got to win, and if it's not me, then I'm as good as dead. HöST is as good as dead. That's the way it works these days, you know? Oh sweetie, please send me a message soon and say that you'll never leave me. Please? I don't think you understand how alone I am, and how terrifying it is.

"When do you think you can deliver those men of yours? They're going to die anyway, aren't they? So we're doing them a favour? You know this project is meant to be a humanitarian one. I couldn't bear the thought that my work might hurt somebody. You said they'd welcome the LiFT, even if it isn't perfect. It's not perfect. I'd call it life-giving, yes, I believe it is. But life on Quay Sera, it's not the same, not yet. It's better than dying, if you're going to die anyway. I'd recommend it for those who don't have a choice. But for those who imagine a one-to-one trade-off between life on Earth and life on Chang? I can't honestly say I have that to offer.

"And since Jemini moved to the Coast Salish Timeplace last year, their price for a single clone has quadrupled. We need those clones to improve verisimilitude. So I need at least a thousand test subjects. How will I ever afford a thousand? Eventually, we'll reel those Grist sisters in, but if you're willing to provide a hundred flu-sick men in the meantime, sweetheart, you have no idea how grateful I'd be. I love you. I love you so much my liver hurts. Please message me back soon. Are you sure you don't want a direct connection to Chang? I could set that up. So many kisses!"

As quickly as she appeared, Isabelle Chow vanishes.

Kora stays in the shrine until the sky grows dark and the air cools. The night fills with its own noises. Through the slats of the fort, she sees a fire light up on the nearest street corner. Around it, dark figures gather. She hears their laughter, full of threat. It's no time to be out in the city. She will have to stay the night.

It starts to rain. She pulls her hood over her head and hunkers down in the driest corner. Her stomach would grumble with hunger if she weren't so thirsty. She sticks her head out the back corner of the fort, puts out a finger to test the water. It sizzles slightly on her skin.

She closes her eyes. Sees her beloved goat Delphine, writhing in a wet, whirling cloud of death blood. Kora can't bear it. She opens her eyes again and stares at nothing. She sleeps.

It's still dark when she wakes. The sky is clear now that the rain has washed it clean. Through the leaves, brambles, and unripe blackberries, she watches peaceful Eng rise in the south and journey across the blue-black sky, smooth and lazy. Eng appears large some years and small others, depending on her proximity to Earth in her wide elliptical orbit. She is larger this year than she was last year. Closer satellites cross her path like bright insects. Great Chang rises suddenly and obscures Eng's face. For a brief moment, he is so close Kora can feel his gravitational pull. If Eng is self-effacing, Chang is bloated, angry, and sick. He leans towards Earth way too intimately.

Kora tries to imagine how people from the time before got them up there. Uncle Wai told her once about a thing called "rocket," and black, sticky stuff that used to make the world go round.

"Get me a scale?" she'd asked.

"Expensive," he'd said. "Maybe for your next birthday."

Fast as he came up, Chang goes down.

Was that projection of Isabelle that Kora saw real? Perhaps, in her rage and sadness, she dreamt what she saw?

Kora shivers. Lit only by the pale light of Eng and a smattering of starlight, the shrine has become dead creepy. Isabelle's photographed eyes and the eyes of all the little statuette-avatars scattered beneath her stare at Kora. She is cold, hungry, and very thirsty.

She doesn't feel sleep when it descends upon her. She only knows she's slept when she wakes, just in time to see Eng set quietly in the north, as the sky begins to grow light. Chilled to the core and still full of sorrow, she darts back onto the quiet streets to the rear entrance of the Woodward's Building.

Two scale-covered girls doze side by side against the chain-link fence. She approaches quietly. Asleep, they are all bone. Their pale, pocked skin lies over their meagre flesh like scum on a dirty puddle. She doesn't get too close, but still they don't smell good.

Softly, softly, she unlocks the gate and pushes it silently shut behind her. She dashes into the building and takes the elevator up to the fortieth floor.

THE LAST DOUBLER 8

NODE: GRAIN IN BEARD
DAY: 1

AUNTIE RADIX CHOKES FOR BREATH. HER FACE BURNS BRIGHT AS A RED apricot in the season when kernels plump. Peristrophe Halliana's beautiful brown eyes bulge from her fleshy face.

My mother double rushes to her side. "Calm now, Radix," she soothes. "Breathe, slow and easy. Kirilow is here. She will save you, but you must calm down."

> *Behold the last*
> *Doubler is gold*

In the interests of the Grist, I swallow my rage, direct its energy towards the work.

"Willow bark!" I shout.

The young groom should already know this. She rushes off to get it while Old Glorybind and I help Auntie Radix lie down.

Auntie Radix huffs desperately. I lay both palms firmly over her chest and begin to pump, one two one two, just as Glorybind taught me when I was a child and she was the village's best healer.

The groom returns with willow bark, which we give Auntie Radix to chew. Pump thump. Pump thump. She chomps and I knead, but the old engine number nine beats fainter and fainter. I pump faster, but the beat skips, then slips. I push deeper into her chest. Pump thump. Pump thump. Pump thump.

There is strength there again!

Pump thump pump thump pump thump.

All on its own! Praise be to Our Mother who loves us all, young and old.

The young groom comes to Auntie Radix's bedside, tenderly takes her hand. "Much gratitude, Groom Kirilow."

I smile and nod.

We wait for a few minutes to make sure she is stable. Then Mother Glory and I head back to our cave, chanting the happy rhyme of Grandma Chan Ling, who led the Grist sisters to this holy place eighty years ago:

> *Jemini factory returnee*
> *Saltwater City not so free*
> *First Plague Ring and Saltwater Flats*
> *Where you're at is where you're at*
> *Second Plague Ring, Cosmo Earth*
> *Places of hope, no more dearth*
> *Third Plague Ring and NOA*
> *Nearly there, not far away*
> *Princeton, Syilx, Hedley, Pente*
> *Rest for many, places of plenty*
> *Fourth Plague Ring and through the wood*
> *Home is food is brood is good!*

We're barely at our door when Auntie Radix's young groom runs up behind us, out of breath. "Groom Kirilow, Auntie Glorybind, you've got to come back. Her heartbeat has slipped again."

Our Mother have mercy. I run behind the groom fast as my young legs will carry me. Mother Glory limps behind, shouting "Go ahead! Don't wait for me!"

When I get there, Auntie Radix is gasping desperately. I return to the ministrations I only just left off. Pump thump pump thump. She takes a great inward breath. Pump thump pump thump pump thump. Her fourth partho breast, one of the extra pair that all doublers grow, flops over the side of the bed. I push it back to join its sisters.

Pump thump pump thump pump thump.

Crack. I feel the sharp snap of a rib.

Pump thump pump thump pump thump pump thump.

She chokes.

Pump thump.

Auntie Radix can barely get words out, but somehow she manages. "I told you, Groom Kirilow—"

"Concentrate on the beat, auntie."

Pump thump.

"Too late—"

"There's time."

Pump thump pump thump.

"You should have given—"

"I'm going to save you! You must try too."

Thump pump.

"Selfish—"

Her heart gives what I think is its last feeble push. Thump thump. After a long delay, a surprise follow-up. Pump bump.

Then nothing.

I push into her chest one last time.

But that was it. Before Mother Glory even makes it to the door, Auntie Radix is gone.

My mother double enters. We are all standing at the bedside, numb with shock.

Glorybind Groundsel catches her breath. Takes a moment to be sure of what she sees. She whispers, "Our Mother be praised. Though we may not understand her actions, her will is done." She bows her head reverently.

The young groom sits, twitching. Her whole being vibrates with a restlessness that is not exactly grief. We sit with her as she twitches like this, for an hour, then longer. We sit with Auntie Radix's body as it cools, palpably releasing its heat. I wonder if it is too late to retrieve Peristrophe Halliana's eyes, but I know the question is not appropriate. I push it down. At least Peristrophe's heart is safe, for the time being.

"I could use a drink," I say to the young groom, hoping she'll offer something from Auntie Radix's stash—and have something herself to stop the twitching. But she sits silent.

At last, she says, "I hope you are pleased with yourself, Kirilow Groundsel."

My jaw drops.

"This is not the time, Bombyx," says Old Glorybind. "We must mourn Auntie Radix now. She was our queen, and the Grist has lost its last doubler. Kirilow is our best and most gifted groom. You should revere her as a teacher. She did everything she could for Auntie Radix."

"That she didn't," the young groom says. "Auntie Radix needed a heart transplant. Kirilow Groundsel knew this, and it was within the power of the starfish Peristrophe Halliana to give."

"It was not," I hiss-whisper. "It was not."

"I know you've already got plans to replace my lady. I know you have a Salty in your cave. You've robbed me. You've robbed the Grist itself, Kirilow Groundsel. You're a yellow, a Salty sympathizer, a traitor. When will you be happy? When the whole Grist sisterhood is dead and gone?"

"That Salty is a starfish," I say, getting out of my chair. "I have no replacement for Auntie Radix." If she's not going to offer the least little sip of mother moonshine, I'll help myself. I step towards Auntie Radix's medicine cabinet. She comes for me then, but Old Glorybind is faster than I thought she could be.

She takes the young groom by the shoulders. "You still have duties to Auntie Radix, my friend," she says. "Auntie Radix's daughter doubles will want to know, even if they weren't getting along. And the high priestess and groom elder should be here to administer last rites."

The young groom knows Glorybind Groundsel is right. She casts me a last resentful glance but does what she's told.

I take a good swig of Auntie Radix's moonshine and allow myself to feel relief. Mother Glory and I sit with the cooling body. Evening descends outside Auntie Radix's four wide windows and, with it, a heavy coat of ash. The sorrow of loss seeps into me. Although I didn't like Auntie Radix much, the Grist sisterhood has lost its last doubler. Stricken also with the deaths of three young folk to non-productive mutation this past year, the village is not long for this world, unless we get more doublers, and more starfish.

The young groom returns with a contingent of Grist villagers. "The high priestess has been signalled. She can't come but will send a proxy. Proxy arrives tomorrow," she tells us. Glares at me. "I get *my* duty done."

I scowl at her. But as custom and solidarity demand, I stay with the young groom and Old Radix's body until dawn.

GOAT STEW

NODE: KERNELS PLUMP
DAY: 3

CHARLOTTE IS MAKING A MODEST BREAKFAST OF HASH BROWNS AND mushrooms. Once, they would have had eggs to go with this meal, but the rooftop chickens have long since been eaten.

"There you are," she says, as Kora slinks in. "Well, I hope you're pleased with yourself."

Kora smiles wanly. She grabs a glass from beside the barrel of drinking water, fills it, and guzzles it down. Refills and repeats. Water has never tasted so good. She sits at the counter, hoping to be fed.

"We should send you to live with those girls who were at our gate all night. How would you like that?"

"I wouldn't." Her head is still full of the strange projection she saw. Maybe she should have kept the filigree scale. But someone could have come after her for it. It's better that she left it at Isabelle's shrine.

"You know they trade with the Coast Salish Timeplace."

"I don't know anything about that." Which is a lie, because they all know that the Coast Salish Timeplace across the river, and the Cosmopolitan Earth Council of which it is a member, offer a route to a better life. HöST Security forbids any communication across the Stó:lō. But it's a public secret that some of the wet market girls have a way of bypassing the police, though they do so only for the purposes of trade.

Charlotte plops a plate in front of Kora. The diced chunks amount to almost a full potato. The mushrooms have been quartered. Kora counts nineteen pieces, which is nearly five whole ones. Charlotte doesn't know how long their supply is going to last, so she has to ration. "I'm sorry, kiddo. I know it's not a lot. There will be stew later."

Kora shoots Charlotte the evil eye.

Charlotte says, "When you're done, can you please take some to your uncle?"

Kora is too hungry not to eat. She scarfs the meagre breakfast down in two seconds flat. "Is he really sick?"

"Your uncle is in bed. Thanks to you."

Uncle Wai is asleep in the old oak bed salvaged by his father in the aftermath of the first wave of Caspian tiger flu. His breath stutters. He's thrown off all the covers in his sleep. When she gets closer, she can see why. He's sweating copiously. The sheets are drenched. She puts the tray down and rushes to get a damp cloth and thermometer.

The thermometer is made of low-quality plastic and is cracked in several places. Charlotte thinks the Drs Bloom bought it in the last days of the time before, from a place called "Dollar Store."

"What's a dollar?" Kora asked the first time Charlotte showed her the thermometer.

"Dollars were units of exchange," she explained. "Kind of like renminbi, only from here, not the United Middle Kingdom."

She places the fragile instrument in Uncle Wai's ear, gently so she neither breaks the thermometer nor wakes her uncle. Miraculously, he sleeps on as the red stuff inside the thermometer rises. Ethanol, that's what it's called—the same stinky liquid they use to power the world's last remaining hummers, the ones that HöST Security use to police their streets.

It was Uncle Wai himself who taught her how the thermometer works. She watches the ethanol climb to 37 on the C side and 98 on the F side. Normal. It seems to rest there for a moment before climbing farther. 99, 100, 101, 102, 103 ... It vacillates between 103 and 104, then settles at 103 and a bit. His temperature is very high but still below 105°F, the temperature at which brain damage occurs. Uncle Wai is by far the smartest member of the Ko family. They need his brain.

She mops his forehead with a cool, damp cloth. He moans softly. "Daughter, is that you?"

"Niece," she says. It's not the first time he's made this mistake.

He doesn't speak again but soon drifts back to sleep. She leaves the breakfast tray in case he wants to eat something when he wakes up.

She goes back to get some food for K2. Her mother stands in the kitchen, the right half of the goat's split carcass slung over her shoulder. It reeks of death and urine.

Kora runs to her room.

She can hear Charlotte yelling for her to come back. She puts her hands over her ears and closes her eyes. She doesn't want to see, hear, or feel anything. But she can't close her nose. Soon, the savoury smell of goat stew wafts through the cracks around her door. She tries to shut it out, but her stomach has other ideas. It rumbles insistently. In her mind's eye, she can see the pot, simmering gently on the old stovetop. She hears Charlotte periodically shovel fuel in. Lately, they have been supplementing their diminishing stock of bamboo with broken-up furniture from the abandoned apartments around them.

Charlotte knocks on her door. "Are you going to eat, Kora?"

"No way!" she shouts, without opening the door. "Butcher."

She hears Charlotte place a tray on the floor in the hall. She ignores the sound. She puts on her headphones and turns on Molten Mabel. Stares up at the row of toy owls she's collected from plague house garbage bins on her periodic forays out of the apartment. They stare back. Her stomach growls indignantly, but she won't be betrayed by her flesh.

She spends the day in her room, hungry and furious, listening to album after album. When hunger overwhelms her, she wills herself to sleep.

In the middle of the night, she jolts awake. Eng is at her window, high and distant. Kora has the impression of a face staring in. Although it must be cold now, she can smell the bowl of goat stew sitting on the other side of the door. Maybe Charlotte has made potato bread to go with it and she can eat that. She opens the door. There is no potato bread, just the bowl of pure meat stew, with a spoon and a napkin beside it. It is cold and congealed. A thin skin has formed on the surface.

Kora is ravenous. She snatches the bowl up and gobbles the whole thing down. For a brief moment, she feels satisfied. Then her stomach begins to churn. She runs to the bathroom and barely makes it to the composting toilet before the poor dead goat gushes out of her mouth.

When her stomach is empty and the convulsing stops, she gets up off the cold tile floor. Rinses her mouth with good water from clean rain days. Drinks a little. Goes back down the hall, not to her own room but to Uncle Wai's.

He lies there, bathed in Eng's blue light, snoring softly. She has a terrible feeling she is never going to see him again. She sits at the foot of his bed and soon is fast asleep.

DANCING FOOL 10

NODE: GRAIN IN BEARD
DAY: 2

I'M GLAD TO GET OUT OF AUNTIE RADIX'S CAVE AND AWAY FROM HER angry young groom. Old Chang rises behind us, backlit by the pale yellow glow of the distant sun. Glorybind Groundsel and I follow the bluff back to our own cave. We are only halfway there when we hear the music.

> *Moon mother moon mother*
> *Moon sister moon brother*
> *No time like the present*
> *No rain like the torrent*
> *No flood like the recent*
> *No wind that ain't decent*
> *You and me*
> *Forever free*
> *From the stranglehold of Jemini*

I laugh out loud. "There's a choir at our house, singing the old songs! Such voices!" It's not that I've forgotten Auntie Radix. It's that I don't want to think about her.

Glorybind Groundsel scowls, then smiles. She begins to run. I run after her, cackling gleefully.

Peristrophe Halliana has risen from bed and the Salty has burst from its bomb. They've got some of the old junk from the time before out of the storeroom. Like a couple of glad rabbits, they bounce around the room, shake and shimmy as though their hearts could burst. Burst like poor old Radix's heart or a fairground balloon. Burst and laugh and burst again, like fireworks from the time before. Peristrophe howls and hoots as though the time of all time, past and present, future and distant future wants to rush from her lungs. I open my mouth to chastise her and find that I'm howling too. What is this music? What is this machine? To my shock and horror, Old Glorybind begins to dance, tentatively at first, but soon her body falls into a rhythm. I gape like an idiot. I grit my teeth and clench my arms at my sides. I won't be touched by this dirty Salty's forest-of-the-night magic. But then my feet begin to move too. I shuffle reluctantly. My feet are not my own. An electric vitality rushes into them and I'm a dancing fool.

The Salty leans to the time-before machine and turns a dial. Blue and green lights flicker hideously. The music grows louder and stranger.

My body surrenders to the nightmare dance.

I dance the dance of the grannies' expulsion. I dance the dance of Chang and Eng at their mythic launch. A rocket blasts skyward in my mind's eye.

"Stop," I croak. "I don't want to see."

I dance the dance of nuclear fission, of oil, of coal, of wood and straw. I dance for wheels and automobiles, when they were like living creatures drunk on the rotted bodies of species long dead. I dance for the tiger flu, for Ebola, for AIDS, smallpox, measles, tuberculosis, Black Plague, and death. I dance for stem cells, devilled eggs, cloning, and mutation. All the long path of chance and science, money and murder that Old Glorybind taught me was my messy legacy. Although I can't say I understand it, I know its songs, its oranges and lemons, its ring around the rosy. My body knows something that my mind can't refuse.

Shimmy, shake, hop, and leap, I fall into a movement I never knew, feel the feel of all the old ones living and dying and living again, back way back in the gist of mist, the time of rhymes, the how of now. I can't control my laughter. It ripples from my throat like the hoot and holler of a moony coyote. Sweat runs from my pores, my brow, my armpits, my stinky lady crotch, and still I can't stop the dance, young and sweet only seventeen. All the songs Old Glorybind taught me from her raw memory burst from the drumbeat, the trumpets, the saxophones, the violins, lutes, harps, zithers, and guitars of the time past, the time present, all pumping humping volume, itchi gitchi ya ya hee-yah, voulez-vous coucher avec moi?

Then, as suddenly as it erupted from the ponderosas and sagebrush, it grinds to a halt, mwah waaaaaaaaaaaaaa.

"There goes my battery," says the Salty. "But come back to Saltwater City. You can listen to music every day. You don't know what this machine is, do you? Not your fault. It's really old. We haven't used a CD player for a hundred years. But you can have the music. All you need is a scale. It goes right into your head, a little pinprick, just like the ones you gave me, and then you can have it anytime you want. You don't know what a scale is either, do you? Never mind, ha ha ha ..." And then its laugh becomes a cough, and it coughs and coughs and coughs and coughs, and it can't stop until Mother Glory gets it a glass of water.

We all come to our senses then.

"It bewitched us, Mother Glory."

My mother double slowly becomes her old self. "Astonishing, strange. And not right, not right at all."

"You better go," I say to the thing. "But you need your tea first."

"No," says Mother Glory. "We need a cell scraping and a blood sample."

Peristrophe Halliana begins to cough. She coughs and coughs and cannot stop. I knew it. That Salty came to infect us.

"Out! Get out!" I yell, awake now to the truth of our situation. "We don't want your devil music and we don't want you!"

Glorybind Groundsel wraps Peristrophe Halliana in a blanket.

I'm still yelling. "Out, out, out, out, out! We don't want your dirty blood, your dirty biomatter."

"It needs its forgetting tea or they'll be upon us before the day is out," says Mother Glory.

"It would be easier just to kill it," I observe. "And better."

The Salty dives for the door. I lunge, grab it by its strange red hair. It screams bloody murder, but I won't let go. I yank it towards me and pull it into a headlock.

"Gentle, Kiri," says my compassionate mother double. "You must learn. I don't have so many days left to teach you."

I wrestle the Salty to the floor, try to do so gently, though it's not really possible. My mother double goes to get the teapot.

I hold the Salty down and pry its jaw open. Mother Glory pours the forgetting tea in, and I pinch its nose shut until it swallows. Twice more. Mother Glorybind administers the needles of sleep. We put the Salty in our rusty old wheelbarrow and wheel it into the valley where we first caught sight of it and dump it unceremoniously in the dirt.

When we get back, Peristrophe has clear symptoms of the flu—a runny nose, weepy eyes, and a temperature of 102. I'll give that Salty a painful death if it ever comes back.

I make a strong ganoderma broth from my best mushrooms and feed it to her spoonful by agonizing spoonful.

"How is she?" Old Glorybind asks when Peristrophe is asleep and I'm out in the living room by the fire, drinking what remains of the broth.

"I don't know, Mother," I say.

"If we lose her—" she begins.

"Don't say it, Mother Glory. I just can't."

"All right, Kirilow, all right." She reaches into the folds of her robe and pulls out something moist and purple. It's the hand that I severed from the Salty's wrist. She lays it on the table and we stare at it in wonder.

"I hope I never see that Salty again," I say.

Mother Glorybind is circumspect. "It was a starfish."

"I don't care. It was a killer."

"I hope your tea took," she says. "Otherwise, it could tell its friends about us."

"The tea took. My teas are excellent teas."

"They are that, my child. Whatever your flaws, you have your gifts."

PLEASE DON'T LEAVE ME

11

KORA KO // SALTWATER FLATS

NODE: KERNELS PLUMP
DAY: 4

SHE WAKES UP THIRSTY AND LIGHT-HEADED. ARE THERE ANY MOLECULES of Delphine still in her? She wants to be sick again, but her stomach is empty and dry. It heaves, reminding her of her betrayal. She drinks a little water from the cloudy glass on the nightstand.

She's still furious with Charlotte, and with Wai for not stopping Charlotte from slaughtering Delphine. And she's famished. She lingers in bed for as long as she can bear it, then goes to the kitchen hoping for a bowl of potato soup.

K2, Charlotte, and Uncle Wai are there at the beautiful teak table they salvaged from an abandoned apartment on Level 22. Uncle Wai is so pale, as though he's already got a foot in the next world. If he's upset with her for making him chase her, he doesn't express it. But he's got a proposition. He wants to send Kora to the Cordova Dancing School for Girls.

"I don't want to go," Kora says. "I want Delphine back. Murderers."

"I want her back too," Uncle Wai says, eyeing Charlotte with simmering rage. "But that has nothing to do with the Cordova School."

"Those girls are all so stuck-up. Besides, who will help you take care of the rooftop gardens?"

"Don't go," Charlotte whispers, so soft they can barely hear her. "Don't leave me alone. I cannot weather the grief by myself."

"You killed Delphine. If I go, it'll be to get away from you," Kora says. If she could be meaner, she would.

Uncle Wai says, "Don't be so selfish, Charlotte. And Kora, it's your duty to go. One of us must make it in the world that is coming."

K2 says, "Uncle Wai is right, sis. Young women don't get the flu as much, it's true. But what will you do when we're all gone? Old Madame Dearborn is willing to take you. It's the best chance you've got."

The ancient Woodward's Building shifts on its foundations. Its concrete rumbles fearsomely.

"Those girls are not nice girls," Kora says, picking at her moon phase scale. It is slightly infected, and the infection threatens to spread along the path of the halo. Did that come from sticking spit, sand, and who knows what germs from the altar in her head last night? She has no renminbi for the alcohol solution you're supposed to rub on it. "Last night you were trying to protect me from them. Now you want me to live with them? They despise us."

"That isn't true," Uncle Wai says. "Some of them are very kind. Don't they bring us cans from the time before sometimes? And firewood when we can't collect enough of our own?"

"They sell us the cans for renminbi we can't afford. They give us nothing. And the food in those cans is spoiled half the time," says Charlotte.

"They have to charge," says K2. "Cans are getting scarcer."

"I don't want to go," Kora says.

Uncle Wai says, "In times like these we put aside our individual desires, Kora. In favour of the larger collective. In favour of survival. You are fifteen now. Old enough to accept duty when it calls to you. You've had a formal invitation."

He lays the open scale on the table and turns it on. The invitation flashes up in pink and silver. It bears the three-dimensional chop of the Cordova Dancing School for Girls' venerable matron, Madame Aurelia Dearborn.

"I don't want to ..." Kora whines.

"It's a prestigious invitation," says Uncle Wai. "And it is time." He begins to cough, and then spits a clot of bloody phlegm into his handkerchief.

Kora bows her head, ashamed.

"Please don't go. Don't leave me," Charlotte whispers in a thin sad voice. She puts her hands over her face then, so they all know she's crying.

THE LAST STARFISH
12

NODE: GRAIN IN BEARD
DAY: 3

PERISTROPHE HALLIANA'S COUGH HAS MOVED INTO HER LUNGS. WHEN I place my hand on her chest, I can feel the mucous trapped in the spaces where only air should go. Little gooey globules of rot move deep within the flesh, worm their way into the crevices where my needles can't do any good. She coughs now, she hacks. Thin spittle runs from her lips. Our Mother curse that slimy Salty and its black hand. May all Salties go to the hottest and most agonizing reaches of the hell they dream for us.

Peristrophe Halliana says, "If anything happens to me—"

"Best beloved, nothing is going to happen. Drink your ganoderma tea and sleep some more. Rest is what will help you now."

"I've rested enough, dear one. There is only so much you can do. You have to accept it."

"I refuse to let you go."

"You're a good groom, Kiri." Her new eyes have grown in ever so slightly, and she gazes at me now with a sad maturity that no one our age should have gained yet. "But you know that in the end, only Our Mother has power over life and death." Her gaze moves skyward to where Eng rises once again.

"I have power," I tell her.

"Great power, dearest. But not the ultimate power. I know you understand me."

I drop my head into my hands.

"If I don't make it, you must go to Saltwater City. Many of our sisters still live there—in captivity, to be sure, serving the scale factories of HöST. Find a new starfish and a new doubler and bring them back."

"A new doubler, yes. Half a dozen of them. But we don't need a new starfish. We have you."

"You must see the truth, my love," rasps Peristrophe Halliana, squinting at me now through her barely developed eyebuds.

"You have a good eighty years ahead of you," I tell her. I try to look at her, but the tears rush up and I have to turn away.

When she is asleep again, I go outside to rail at Eng.

Our Mother of bread and roses
Our Mother of dirt
Our Mother of loaves and fishes
Our Mother of love
Please keep Peristrophe Halliana in stable health
Until the salt flu passes
Bless and water
All the sisters of the Grist
In their meagre variety
In the guise of the good guys
Now more than weather
A slice of forever

I make my prayers up as I go. Will Eng, with all the knowledge she holds, hear me? The old world is long gone, and in this brave new one we must make everything all over again.

NODE: GRAIN IN BEARD
DAY: 4

I GET UP EARLY TO CHECK ON PERISTROPHE HALLIANA. SHE SLEEPS so silent heavy. My gut muscles quiver with worry, but I leave her to rest.

When Chang is halfway up the western sky on his second ascent of the day, I go to wake her. She lies very still. She doesn't budge when I call her name.

"Peristrophe Halliana. Dearest beloved." I take her arm. It is warm, but not as warm as it should be. My gut turns over. I move my hand down to her wrist, search it for a reassuring sign of life. Her wrist is thin, and cooler than the rest of her.

"Peristrophe."

Her pulse kicks so, so faintly. "Kiri, my love."

"Please, my only star."

"You were a good groom to me." Her pulse is fading.

"No, please—"

"In Saltwater City, you'll find—" She speaks so softly I can barely hear her.

"No, Peri—"

"Listen, you must do as I ask."

Her pulse is so faint, I can no longer feel it. "Peri, please. Please no."

"Find—another—"

"No. You have to try harder. There will never be another."

"St-sta-star—"

"No. Don't leave."

"—love—"

I press my thumb in deeper. Nothing. I place my hand over her heart. Stopped as an unwound watch.

My brain understands that she is gone, but no other part of me accepts it. My hand remains over her heart for a long time.

My mother double comes to pull me away. "Kirilow."

I take my beloved's dead hand, though she won't squeeze mine back.

"Kirilow, don't cling or you will fall into the other world with her."

"So be it. I don't care."

I can feel her concerned eyes bore into my back. "Daughter, it is not your time."

I refuse to move. I stare at her with the eyes of the dead.

"If you won't think of yourself, think of your gifts and your duty to the Grist." She strokes my hair.

"I can't."

"You must. You are needed." Tugs my arm insistently.

I pretend I don't hear.

"I need you."

I allow my mother double to pull me away.

"Bonfire night is coming," she says, as if she imagines I might find this comforting. She leads me to the fireplace. "We can send Peristrophe Halliana and Radix Bupleuri to Our Mother together."

"The beauty and the despot," I say. "Blasphemy. I won't go."

"It would do you good to cry," my mother double says, pulling me into a fierce hug.

The emotion that takes me is not sorrow but rage. I push her away, run out into the forest to that place along the bluff above the clearing where we first saw that dirty Salty. Just two days ago, though it seems a hundred years. There I sit for the rest of the day, stewing in a vengeful hatred of all the Salties in the world.

CORDOVA DANCING SCHOOL FOR GIRLS

13

NODE: GRAIN IN BEARD
DAY: 2

THE NIGHT KORA ARRIVES, THE CORDOVA GIRLS ARE HAVING A STEW called "bourguignon," made from an animal called "beef." It smells so good, Kora almost can't bear it. She stands in the foyer, fairly swooning.

A girl of seven or eight comes to bring her up to the hall. She introduces herself as Velma. "We've just started. You're lucky it's a heist day. Myra and Tania broke into a HöST supermarket and got us real beef. You know that fancy one, what's it called ... Gupta-Anderson ... And bananas too, from the time before. For banana cream pie. Have you ever had bananas before? They're extinct, you know. And only Jemini can make them again, if and when they decide to. Heist day, feast day, heist day, feast day!" she chants merrily. "Myra and Tania were wearing Madame Dearborn's catcoats."

"What's a catcoat?"

"Catcoat, thinskin, catcoat, thinkskin, catcoat, slink in!" chants young Velma. "You'll see, Kora. By Our Mother, you're on easy street now. Was your uncle very sick? Tania says you didn't want to come, but your family will be dead soon and so you have no choice. Myra says you should be grateful to be here. So, are you grateful?"

She leads Kora up the creaking stairs of the old Cordova Dancing School for Girls. It was a theatre once, and before that, a firehall. Even more than the Woodward's Building, the ground on which it has been standing for the last 200 years has shifted. Everything slants east now. Kora really notices it in the stairwell.

At the top of the building, in a wide hall, the girls are seated at long narrow tables. The air is thick with the delicious smell of beef bourguignon.

"Come on," says Velma. "You can sit with me." She points to an empty space between two other small girls. All the little ones sit together. If Kora sits, she'll be an awkward potato jar among a cluster of germination pots.

"Maybe I should sit over there," she says, moving towards a table of girls her own age.

The girl at the head of that table lifts her head from her stew, and Kora recognizes her from the market stall two weeks ago. Her hair is black and matted, and her eyes are rimmed with so much kohl that she looks like she's stepped straight from the steaming guts of hell. "DON'T ... YOU ... DARE!" the girl hisses.

"You better not, Kora," says Velma. "That's Myra, and this is her heist feast. You better just do what she says."

Kora backs away and sits at the table of younger, smaller girls. One of them scoops her a bowl of stew. It tastes a bit like Delphine. Knobs of slippery mushroom and onion swim among the chunks of meat. Unfamiliar spices tickle her taste buds, too spicy and oddly floral. She huddles with the seven-year-olds and tries her best to enjoy what is, in spite of its unfamiliarity, a really good meal.

From the head table comes much raucous laughter and shouting.

Kora doesn't understand a word of it, until she's hit in the head with a buttermilk biscuit. She hasn't seen anything made of wheat since she was six or seven, and there are no biscuits at the children's table. She snatches it up and crams it into her mouth. The hilarity at the head table increases as she chews.

"How's the biscuit?" calls a girl with memory scales sticking out of her ears.

"Good," Kora says, not knowing how else to respond.

"She likes her biscuit, Our Lady of the Flu," says the frightful girl. "You've fallen a long way, Flu Lady!"

"We're all flu ladies," Kora says, as blandly as possible. "Because we live in a time of flu. What makes me so special?" She continues to chew her biscuit.

"What makes you so special?" the girl repeats. She's missing a front tooth. "What makes Lady Kora so special, my friends?"

Scowling, Myra raises her head from her steaming bowl. "Don't you even know, Kora Ko?"

"She doesn't know ..." whisper the girls at the head table, giggling.

"She doesn't know," says the frightful girl. "Better tell her, Sister Myra."

Sister Myra smiles broadly. All her teeth have been replaced with hard memory scales, and her grin glints with their metallic light. "If not for *you,*" she intones, "all of the men—our brothers, fathers, uncles, and sons—would be alive today. Saltwater City would be a city of prosperity and wellness. If not for *you,* there would be no Cordova School."

Kora swallows her fear and holds her head up. "I am most deserving of a space here then," she snarls, with all her mightily mustered courage.

"She doesn't even know," says the frightful girl.

"She doesn't know ..." whisper all the others, shocked.

"Tell her, tell her now," the frightful girl says.

"How can you be so ignorant of your own past? How can you not know what you are?" Myra calls.

Kora shakes. She can no longer control it. She glances at Velma, but Velma only looks at Kora in horror and wonder. Kora is truly on her own. "You invited me into your midst," she says. "Why would you do such a thing if you don't want me here?"

"She doesn't know, she doesn't know ..." the girls at the head table whisper.

Kora's ignorance and mortification will kill her if she lets them. She grits her teeth. "What's the big deal?!" she shouts. "If you can't say it to my face, then it can't be true."

"Ha," says Myra. "Of course it's true, Lady Kora of the House of Ko, re-animators of the Caspian tiger and purveyors of Caspian tiger-bone wine. How could you not know that you and your family are the source of the tiger flu? How could you not know the misdeeds of Lennox Ko, your very own grandfather? Madame Dearborn wants you here because of it."

Kora is stumped. She searches her memory for any hint of tigers in her family's past. Uncle Wai never said anything to her about them. Nor did her mother, nor K2. She's never met her father, Kai Tak, or the brother, Everest, whom Kai Tak took to ease Charlotte's burden and his own loneliness. She'll never meet Everest now.

There are, of course, those jars, big enough to hold a tiger and cover it with water, oil, or wine. She pushes away the thought.

"I don't know what you're talking about," she says. "It can't be true."

"Of course it's true," says the frightful girl.

"As true as the life and being of this school," says Myra. She begins to laugh. "Gotcha, Lady Kora. Don't you know the place you come from? We want you here because of it. How can anyone be so ignorant of the place from which she comes?"

"Yes, how?" whisper the girls.

"In order to survive in the world that is coming, we need to know our history," says Myra. "Knowledge, my sisters, is the most important tool we have. We must learn everything Madame Dearborn has to teach us. We must learn from our families—those of us who still have them. And what we don't have, we will get from the marvellous memory scales that the great inventor Isabelle Chow has deigned to send us. Make use of all the technologies you've been given, sisters. Technologies come and technologies go. So we must make use of everything we've got."

Madame Dearborn enters the room then. She's tall and stately, with high cheekbones, a flat nose, deep brown eyes, and bright red hair streaked with white. "I apologize for my lateness, girls. I had a lead on a new litter of kittens. Kora, go sit at the table with the girls your own age. I hope they are treating you well."

Kora gives a little smile. She can't say why, even to herself, but something about Madame warms her.

BOMBYX MORI'S SURPRISE 14

NODE: GRAIN IN BEARD
DAY: 5

MY SISTERS BUILD AN INFERNO AT MOURNING ROCK, TALL AS AN OFFICE building from the time before. It's bad for the sky, but the rites must be observed. A green-robed delegate from the New Origins Archive oversees the proceedings as proxy for the high priestess. Her name is Vera. She is young but seems self-assured. My sisters take direction from her without complaint.

Now the oldest of the Grist sisters, Glorybind Groundsel watches disapprovingly as my sisters add more and more logs and branches. "The Salties will see us and come for us."

"It's the Night of the Firefly," Calyx Kaki tells Glorybind Groundsel, as though she doesn't already know. "Bonfires will burn all through Old Cascadia. So don't worry, Auntie Glory. Salties be celebrating their own Midsummer Festival, the end of oil, the ascent of Our Mother, and the ancient launch of Chang and Eng. They won't notice us in any particularity."

Old Glorybind still has her doubts, but the young sisters shout her down. She does not have the gift of governance that Auntie Radix had. Some say she had it, but she lost it when she lost the power to double, right after the birth of yours truly, born live, and the rest of my sister litter, all stillborn. The sisterhood needs a new queen, and a queen should be a doubler or a starfish. It should have been Peristrophe Halliana, I think bitterly. It is a starfish's turn.

Every kind of wood that migrated north to us as the climate changed feeds the fire that burns in the wide clearing: blue gum eucalyptus, canyon oak, scrub oak, incense cedar, ponderosa, Torrey pine, Tecate cypress, pinyon pine, and the bark-peeling arbutus that some sisters call madrona. All the varieties of trees that grow around Grist Village must be used so that Our Mother doesn't feel we've neglected any of her children, long established or newly arrived.

There is food for the feast too, from our forest gardens, cultivated with seeds from the New Origins Archive, where Mother Glory took me for the first time just last year—zucchini, kabocha, butternut, carrots, potatoes, and beans. Also shared are some of the newer fruits that began to take at Grist Village with help from the New Origins Archive around the same time the Caspian tiger was brought back. All these returned within the span of my own life: bananas, pineapples, coconuts, mangoes, starfruit, lychees, dragon fruit, and durian. They require a lot of water and a lot of care, but they grow. And there are meats to stew or roast: elk, deer, rabbit, bear, and pheasant. There are renewed meats too: Queen Charlotte caribou, passenger pigeon, great auk, and Pyrenean ibex, in addition to Caspian tiger. Some of the sisters are against eating tiger. They say that tiger is the source of the flu the Salty brought to us, the flu that killed Peristrophe Halliana. But others say the Caspian tiger is no different from us—a creature that would not live now except by human intervention. We should embrace it in love and sacrifice.

I sit at the darkest part of the circle and watch my fifty-two sisters celebrate through a haze of grief. In the sandy soil that surrounds the firepit, I draw a long row of eyes with a stick. I should have said no to Auntie Radix a surgery ago. I don't care what we eat or drink. I don't care how high the fire goes. If the New Origins Archive could return Peristrophe Halliana to me, that would be a gift worth having. Otherwise, I don't care about much.

"She's with you all the time," says my mother double. "Look around you, Kirilow."

All around the fire my sisters gather, their beautiful faces lit by orange light. Each is the slightest variation of the next. Give or take a scar here, a wrinkle there, the length of hair, the choice of dress, any of them could be Peristrophe Halliana. If Auntie Radix were still with us, her partho breasts would mark her variation from the rest of us. As would the wrinkles in her face.

"They look like Peristrophe, but they are not Peristrophe," I tell Glorybind Groundsel. "She is gone and Auntie Radix is gone, and soon it will be as if Grandma Chan Ling never escaped Saltwater City and Grist Village never existed at all. We'll be remembered as captive mutants without honour, who all died in the first wave of tiger flu in the crowded scale factories of Saltwater City."

"Not all city sisters died. That Salty's new hand is proof," says Mother Glory. "Grandma Chan Ling used to talk about a Grist commune in Saltwater City. Maybe it still exists. Maybe it's time for a journey."

"Don't look at me," I say. "Whatever I had is burning on that pyre. Ask someone else to go."

But Old Glorybind does look at me. "You've also got duty, Kirilow. Don't forget duty."

"Please, Mother Glory," I beg. "Don't talk to me about duty today." If I had courage, I'd jump into the fire. Instead, I move away from my sisters to the edge of the forest and lurk there like the creepy creep I'm bound to become.

I'm leaning against a tree, smoking a pipe of pot and sage with a pinch of forget-me-do, when someone tugs at my arm. The smoke has sent me elsewhere. It takes me a long moment to realize who it is. Auntie Radix's young groom.

"My name is Bombyx Mori," the groom says. "In case you ever wondered."

"I know," I lie.

"I'm sorry I was such a jerk the day my Radix died," she says. "It was more than I could bear."

"It was more than I could bear too."

"I'm sorry about Cousin Peristrophe," she says.

"I'm sorry about Auntie Radix."

She gazes at me to see if I'm sincere. "I've got something I think you should see," Bombyx Mori says.

Chang hangs close tonight, in sinister sympathy with the Grist sisterhood and our double loss. "Maybe another time," I say. "I have to get back to the fire. It's my Peristrophe Halliana they are burning." A small family of bats zigzags out from their nest, a hole high in the body of a tall Tecate cypress.

"It's my Radix Bupleuri," she says. "Peristrophe Halliana would want you to see what I've got to show you." Her eyes shine clear and brown as earth.

A shadow moves across the open face of Chang, large and oblong. The pipe I've smoked helps me see it as a floating whale, turning the sky to water as it moves.

"By Our Mother's stinky hole," Bombyx Mori curses. "It's a batterkite."

"Batter ... who?"

"The latest invention of Isabelle Chow. Don't you know?" Smugness. I trust it more than her seeming honesty, though I have no idea where the young ones get their knowledge. "It's a ship that works as its own battery. Isabelle engineered it from seal bladder and oyster material. It's a hydrogen cell and a transport vehicle both."

It pulses across the sky, horrible, gorgeous, and shimmering. I shiver. I've got to find Old Glorybind.

But we are both mesmerized by the sheer size of the bio-ship. It glides above us, smooth and slow, covers two-thirds of Chang's face. Figures begin to drop from its underbelly. My stoned eyes see the sky bloom with airborne jellyfish, militia men dangling from their spindly tentacles. My senses turn inside, feel for cell-knowledge of my relation to the awful life forms coming at us.

"Come on, come on, Kirilow, they saw our fire. We're under siege. You have to come with me! No choice now, hurry!"

"I've got to find Mother Glory—"

But the young groom has got my arm and drags me through pinyon and succulent so fast my feet don't touch the ground.

"Kirilow, come on, snap out of it. There's no time."

I am stoned and writhing inside. The outside world turns on a giant wheel so slow. She pulls me jarringly fast. How can anyone move so quick against this slow horror?

"My duty—I can't leave Mother Glorybind—I'm the only daughter double she has—" I groan.

Oily jellyfish swarm through drifting ash above us. Each grows larger, like the pupil of a giant eye trying to see in the dark. I tug away from Bombyx. There's screaming now from the bonfire.

"Mother Glory!" I try to cry with them, but my cry creaks from my throat as an unearthly groan.

I don't see the jellyfish directly above us until it crashes through the treetops. I surrender to Bombyx Mori's pull, and we fly through the trees in a furious, woozy stupor, zigzagging wild as the little bats I saw. Could it have been just seconds earlier? A cold wind rushes at us and the wails of the sisters at the fire reverberate in my drug-addled ears as though the sisters themselves flail in my auditory canals. Their pain knifes my eardrums and I wail-howl with them, "No, no, no, get away from me, you monster, you Mother-cursèd Saltwater beast, you animal, you human, you scum of the sky, not Our Mother, you heaven and hell demons who destroy everything dear and warm and earthy and good."

"Shut up, shut up, shut up, Kirilow!" Bombyx Mori yell-whispers. "It's following us."

"Our Mother of milk and mildew, Our Mother of dirt," I chant, soft now, both here in the murderous present and there in the genocidal past. The wind sears my skin cold and sharp, and the branches of trees whip my face. We run through the terrified forest all curls and whorls, run until there is no breath left in our lungs, run until our legs threaten to collapse beneath our furiously pumping hearts. Run so fast and long we don't notice we're no longer being followed. Praise be to our generous Mother, surely she is kind. We slow to a walk, search for our bearings. The wind keeps coming. It reeks of bonfire smoke, but there's also a cold dampness in it.

I recognize a secret wild olive patch, the one that hides the abandoned magic bus. I mean, the tour bus that Grandma Chan Ling pirated to take the first Grist sisters from Saltwater City eighty years ago. It lies on its side now, rusted and rotting. We have to climb up its underside to go in the broken door, once at its side, now open at its top. We climb into the dark. It reeks of shit and decay. And something else, animal and sweet. I hear a soft keening.

Bombyx Mori pulls a small jar of fireflies from her vest.

At the back of the crumbling bus, hunkered down in a bed of ancient seat cushions, leaves, and dry grass, lies a young girl I recognize as one of this year's initiates.

How did I not notice until now the partho marks, three pale yellow moles in the cup of the clavicle? Her belly is swollen so huge it seems twice the size of the rest of her. She moans and heaves with a squirming strength no one so young should have.

"Please," says Bombyx. "I'm sorry I was such an asshole before. Please help Corydalis Ambigua pop her puppies."

"I'm trained to groom starfish, not parthos," I tell her, my drugged eyes bugging wide.

Corydalis wails. Her womb contracts visibly.

"Did your mother double not teach you?"

"Theory, yes. Practice, no."

Bombyx bursts into panicked tears.

"Okay, by Our Mother's teats, don't cry!"

Through the waves of my own terror, I find a soldier's calm. I go to Corydalis. Her legs are open and drawn up by the wisdom of instinct. I squat between them. Bombyx holds her hand, mops her sweating forehead with a cleanish rag from inside the folds of her tunic.

"You need to breathe," I tell Corydalis. "Inhale deep."

She does, eyes wide.

"Okay. Now exhale and push. Scream if you want, no one's listening." For all I know that batterkite has the ears of a bobcat, but it can't be helped.

She bawls like a demon from the other side.

"Inhale."

Again, she does.

"Exhale and push."

"I can't," she howls, gripping Bombyx's hand so hard that Bombyx howls too.

"You have to."

She screams. She pushes.

"One more. Inhale."

She whimpers.

"Inhale."

She draws the air in, thinner than I'd like.

"And exhale."

She breathes out, and gives a steady, controlled heave.

"One more time."

They both bawl and scream like the animals they are. I guess we are all animals.

"Again."

By the grace of Our Mother's loving heart, the downy head of a sister puppy appears between Corydalis's damp legs.

"One more. Inhale." I nod encouragingly. "Exhale. Push."

"Mama!"

"Come on."

She groans and pushes. The little sister slips out of her holy hole covered in blood and womb snot. One section of umbilical cord attaches to the belly button, but another section branches back into Corydalis. I know what that branch means. Mother Glory taught me that a young partho can birth as many as ten.

"First is worst," I tell Corydalis, as her womb contracts again. "Breathe in."

The howling hours pass in a bath of blood and mucus. Finally, all the sister puppies are out.

There's more new grooming to do. May Our Mother guide

me. I snip the umbilical cord at each of seven branches and tie the knots for their little belly buttons. We wipe them off with rags that Bombyx had the foresight to gather and put two of them on Corydalis to suckle. I swab up blood. I suture the dark place below where she's torn. She's so young, her extra breasts are barely developed, though when I place two more puppies at them, the youngsters seem to latch and find milk.

"Were you given the nursing surge?" I ask Bombyx.

She lifts her tunic. "Your own mother double did it for me at my groom initiate ceremony when I was thirteen." She lifts her right breast to show me the small scar.

"Good," I say. I pass her two more puppies.

The seventh, I pull to my own right breast. Glorybind Groundsel gave me the nursing surgery when I declared my intention to become a groom at age ten. But I've never done this before either. Our Mother of bread and roses, the surge works. I'm squirting sister juice like a regular heifer. For a minute I'm disgusted, but soon I relax into the sensation. I'm washed in family love as the three of us nurse together.

"Why didn't you tell anyone?" I ask Bombyx Mori.

"My Radix would not have liked it."

I nod, understanding her messy emotions at Auntie Radix's deathbed differently now.

The screams of the sisters by the fire tear at our ears afresh.

Bombyx and Corydalis's eyes bulge wide and terrified.

A jolt of fear runs through me, wants to come full throttle. I push it down so as not to feed it to the suckling sister puppy.

"Remember your prayers," I say to Bombyx and Corydalis, hoping my own need for comfort doesn't show.

While we nurse, we sing for our sisters young and old, "Our Mother of songs and sighing, Our Mother of stone."

The screams from the clearing are broken by a bout of machine gun fire. Disembodied fear rides ungodly shrieks, tears through the forest and in through the door of the magic bus. We shudder collectively. We chant.

> *Our Mother of light and darkness*
> *Our Mother of soup*
> *Our Mother of wood and city*
> *Our Mother of owls*
> *Now is the hour*
> *Of our holiest howl*
> *Birthing and bleeding*
> *For the ones to come*
> *Remember night for us*
> *As safety under cover*
> *Rest and gestation*
> *Deliver us from humans*
> *For thine is the garden, the pathway, the story*
> *Forever in cycles*
> *Now until the hour of our rebirth*

THE WORST THING DONE FOR FOOD

KORA KO // SALTWATER FLATS

NODE: GRAIN IN BEARD
DAY: 6

"WHAT'S THE WORST THING YOU'VE EVER DONE FOR FOOD?" IT'S Myra, the scary one with charcoal-rimmed eyes who leads them all.

"Raid a garbage can?" Kora's pretty sure the one with curly black hair and neatly darned camouflage pants is called Soraya.

"Steal from us at the wet market?" The wiry thin one with large brown eyes, torn yellow T-shirt, and white-blonde hair is Modesta.

"Catch and roast a rat?" Cropped brown hair, green eyes, and the kind of mushroom-fibre tunic more commonly worn in the quarantine rings. The frightful one from the night of Kora's arrival. Tania.

"Ha ha, we saw you doing that, you and your brother. We saw you chase it down that alley," taunts Myra. "We saw you bludgeon it with a shovel. We saw you build a fire, roast it up, peel the skin off, and gobble it down. You're a rat eater. Don't lie. Your mom and dad were too poor to feed you properly."

"Not true! Don't bring them into it. And Wai is my uncle."

The memory makes Kora's stomach lurch. She turns away. She doesn't want them to see her retch. She retches.

"Ha ha. You gonna puke?" Soraya says. "If you puke it means you ate it. If you puke we'll make you eat your puke."

She pukes. The four girls grab her and shove her face in her own vomit.

Others surround the fray. "Eat it! Eat it! Eat it!"

They begin to kick her head. "This is what you did to that rat. Because you're a rat. A dead rat."

"Stop! Stop hitting me!" she screams.

They mush her face around in her own vomit.

"We won't stop until you lick that all up."

"I won't," she wails.

"You will." They kick her until her ribs scream.

She opens her mouth and licks. The acrid, rotten taste of her own puke brings up more. For the second time in a two-week solar node, she barfs and barfs and barfs.

Finally, they stop kicking her and leave her on the street outside the school in a pool of tears and blood and vomit.

NODE: GRAIN IN BEARD
DAY: 7

"What's the worst thing you've ever done for love? Your family can't love you much if they've sent you here." Myra is on Kora again.

"They sent me here because they love me more than anything," Kora says.

"If they loved you, they would keep you at home," says blonde Modesta. "They would give you the tools you need to survive."

"They couldn't."

"Because they were too poor. What's the worst thing you've ever done for food?" Soraya asks, menacing.

"Nothing. Please."

"Do you have a boyfriend?" Tania asks, and not in a friendly way.

"No. I don't know any boys except my brother."

"Maybe your brother's your boyfriend," says Myra.

"You're sick. Of course he's not."

"Maybe your father's your boyfriend."

"I've never met my father."

"We saw you with an older man. You look like him."

"He's my uncle."

"Maybe your uncle's your boyfriend."

"Shut up. I'll kill you with my bare hands."

"Ha ha, pussy. You can't kill anything bigger than a rat. You want to go kill a rat?"

"No."

"You do. Go kill a rat."

"Maybe she likes girls."

"I do not."

"Do you like me? Huh? I'll do you if you want."

"If I liked a girl, it wouldn't be you."

NODE: GRAIN IN BEARD
DAY: 8

In addition to teaching a dance class every morning, sourcing kittens, and pressing catcoats, Madame Dearborn runs the Cordova School clinic. She's tired all the time, grumpy, and worried. What will become of these girls when she is no longer able to care for them?

When Velma brings Kora down to the clinic, Madame Dearborn is furious.

"When did this happen?"

"Two days ago," says Velma.

"Why didn't you bring her right away?" To Kora, Madame Dearborn says, "You look awful. What happened to you? Myra and Tania?"

Kora says nothing.

Velma says, "Yes. Soraya and Modesta too."

"I don't understand the girls these days."

Velma helps Kora up onto Madame's examination table. Madame pulls out a precious flashlight imported from the United Middle Kingdom and shines it into Kora's eyes to check for concussion. Sure enough, the telltale pupil dilation.

"Those little shits. For all the good they do the school, they do twice as much harm."

"Maybe not twice as much," says Velma. "But they aren't very nice."

Madame gives Kora a cold pack from the barely running freezer and some precious-if-stale ibuprofen from the time before, foraged by Myra and Tania a few seasons ago. "They are the best leadership we've got to replace me when I'm gone. Which is to say the school is in deep trouble. I'll beat them myself."

Velma says, "Maybe you shouldn't. Last time ..."

"Yes, I know. I was more hurt than they were. I'm too old for this."

Kora groans. "I want to go home."

"They just went off into the quarantine rings to forage. You're safe for a few days," Madame Dearborn says.

"Well, darn." Kora smirks to hide her feelings. Modesta and Soraya are still here.

"I've fixed you up the best I can. Stay down here overnight," says Madame Dearborn. To herself she mutters, "This school needs a real doctor."

STORM TRAVELLERS 16

NODE: GRAIN IN BEARD
DAY: 6

> *Our Mother of carts and horses*
> *Our Mother of shoes*
> *Our Mother of fish and roses*
> *Our Mother of flames*
> *Now is the hour of great decisions*
> *The hour of time and place*
> *The house of beginning and ending*
> *The howl of the long O*
> *Circling and diamonds*
> *Wise as wolves*
> *Edging a clearing*

WHEN OLD CHANG PEERS THROUGH THE DOOR OF THE MAGIC BUS ON his early-morning route across the sky, I leave Bombyx Mori, Corydalis Ambigua, and their new litter curled together in a sleep of exhaustion and dread. It's still dark out, but I can't stay in here anymore. I go look for my old mother double, muttering the old songs under my breath.

I'll sing you one, O
Green grow the rushes, O!

Along last night's trail of terror, I retrace my steps. How could I not have seen that Salty for what it was, the advance guard of HöST Security, or one of the for-hire militias deployed from the towers of HöST sent to protect and purify Saltwater City and its surrounds? Why did I not fight my sisters over their ridiculous bonfire? Ha, there's vanity. I wanted honour for my beloved Peristrophe Halliana too desperately and closed my eyes to the extent of the danger. Against the edicts of Our Mother, I made too much of my own grief. And now, it's payday. Payday and May Day. If I ever see that Salty again, I'll burn it alive on a pyre twice the size of last night's, I swear I will, just you wait and see. I should never have let it go. If these are the proceeds of my generosity, then my generosity is over and done. I'll hunt that Salty like an animal. I'll stick a knife in it, slice it open like the walking carcass it is. If this is war and all is fair, I'll get my share.

Under the forest's cool cover, at the edges of Mourning Rock clearing, I lurk, scan the area to make sense of last night's atrocities. The clearing is quiet, strangely so. There are no bodies, no hawks, eagles, ravens, crows, or carrion birds of any kind. Just a heap of charred logs, still smouldering. How can this be?

I pull my knives out, one for each taut fist. Step one foot into the clearing. There's a rustling.

I duck back under cover, then stumble over something warm. I let out a sharp gasp, which is echoed by the warm thing's own quick intake of breath. I pounce like a coyote on a rabbit.

It yelps, then kicks and thrashes.

By Our Mother's milk. It's a sister. I turn her over. Calyx Kaki.

Her eyes stare a wide, terrified green. She has drunk way too may cups of forget-me-do.

"What happened?" I demand. "Did you see?"

Her too-green eyes water, and a thin stream of drool runs from the corner of her mouth.

"Sister Calyx, come on. What's wrong with you? This is no time for a party. Snap out of it!" I shake her.

She jumps at me so sharp I jump too.

"Batterkites," she whispers.

"What did you see, Calyx? What happened?"

"A whole fleet of them just passed over."

She closes her eyes and falls back into her forget-me stupor.

"Sister Calyx!"

She's gone all floppy, completely inert.

"That was last night. They're all gone now," I say. "Let's get you out of here."

But as I speak, I hear a scuffling sound. And from the same direction, on the other side of the clearing, a groan.

"Mama ..." moans Calyx, echoing the voice on the other side of the clearing.

"Who's over there?"

"Don't go look ..." she rasps.

"Grist sisters or Salties?"

"Don't go there. You don't want to see ..."

"Are there sisters there, Calyx? Have you seen Glorybind Groundsel?"

"Womb bomb ..."

"I've got one here. Let's go."

"No go. No, no, no …"

"Don't be a baby. Come on."

"No!" she cries.

"The sisterhood is truly not long for this world if all that's left are the likes of you," I say. It's mean, but I don't care.

She lets out a sob, then draws in a great croaking gasp of air.

As my mother double taught me, I skirt the clearing on the lightest feet. There is pine and dry brush to push through, but it's better than exposing myself to sight. Dark shapes move over my head, above the trees. A second batterkite attack? I glance up. No. Only storm clouds promising the first floods of the rainy season. They are dense and dark. A flash lights up the whole forest. In the distance, thunder rolls. I pick up my pace, less heedful of the sounds my feet make as they snap bracken.

The next lightning bolt strikes bright and close. Fearsome thunder roars on its heels. I think I hear screaming beneath the roar. I run towards the sound.

A third flash lights up the beast. A hundred arms and legs writhe, tangled in a strong mesh net. A hundred bright eyes stare out. The whole mass groans. How could I not have seen it before?

I step back in horror. There's another crack of lightning. Our Mother who art artful, it's not a beast. It's my own Grist sisters, bound up tight in a mesh net, not unlike the womb bombs that my mother double and I make to catch wayward Salties who stumble too close to our woods. But this womb bomb is huge—vast enough to swallow a whole village of sisters shivering and howling in terror.

I reach for my knife as I hurry forward. The rain descends in sheets now, and the sky grows so dark it feels like night. My trapped sisters shout and cry as I attempt to cut the net.

"Keep still, by Our Mother's nasty nails! I don't want to cut you."

The fibres are finer and stronger than I've ever been able to achieve. I hack and hack, but my blade just slides off. Each strand takes slow, agonizing minutes to cut. The sisters shout and clamour the whole time. I don't realize they are speaking sense until I recognize Old Glorybind's voice, pleading with me through the fray.

"Up, up, up! Look!"

"Mother Glory?"

"Look up, Kirilow! You have to run!"

The deepening dark I registered a moment ago was not cloud darkness after all. A giant batterkite fills the sky, bulbous, fleshy, and pulsing.

"Mother Glory!"

"Run, Kiri!"

"I won't! You are almost free!" I hack at the strong, slippery fibre with the strength of the desperate.

"You need to be smart now. Not so stubborn. You're not a child anymore. Go to the city and find a new starfish. My friend Elzbieta Kruk at the New Origins Archive will help you. Remember everything I've taught you. Find your feet. Play fewer games."

I hack and hack and hack.

The batterkite crashes through the treetops. Splinters fly in a thousand directions as pine and eucalyptus come crashing down.

I keep hacking.

"Go, Kiri!"

One last hack and the strand I've been working on breaks.

"Go! Now!"

"Mama ..."

"*Run!*"

I do as she says. I turn and flee, scramble just ahead of the trees as they fall behind me. I cry like the little child I cannot be anymore, tear away from the depression in the forest floor, the writhing mass of my very own sisters, and the massive, hungry ship that descends on them.

I glance up. I see the chain of sisters, clinging hand to hand as they fall through the hole in the mesh. Miraculously, none fall to the ground as the batterkite rises high above me and sucks the whole tangled, howling mess of net and sisters up into its undermouth.

As I run, my heart bursts with days and intergenerational years of hatred for that wicked Salty. I should have knifed it in the back. What an idiot I was to let it live. *Rock and a hard place,* says the voice of my mother double within me. That Salty with the starfish hand remains a chance to save the sisterhood—if I can find it.

There is a flash of orange hair in the trees. It can't be. I turn towards it. It runs, tall and gangly. I don't care if it's my tricky mind or the real thing. I take off after it, never human but now superhuman in my rage and grief. For all its awkwardness the Salty is fast.

The sky grows dark overhead. The batterkite follows me just above the treetops. Its massive oily belly bulges into the branches and leaves a slick of mucus wherever it brushes. Something thick and fleshy pushes out of its distended belly, a suction tube made of quivering, greasy meat. The Salty is so close I can hear its ragged breath. The tube's puckering orifice makes a grab for me. I dodge, zigzag through tight-knit woods. It makes a hideous suctioning noise, whacks the trees out of the way. I throw my knife at the Salty—a last desperate attempt to bring that hateful creature down. The batterkite's grasping arm swipes at me. I roll quick as a cub into the lucky hollow of an ancient arbutus. The tube gropes around the forest floor for me, sucking up leaves and branches, pulling up smaller trees. The kite hovers so low that I can hear my sisters wailing inside its belly. The arbutus is an old one from the time before, a tree that has survived all the changes. Its roots go down into the spacious earth. I follow the path of a thick, twisted root with enough space underneath for a Grist sister to slide down. I follow its spiralling length as low as it will go. In the womb of the earth, I curl myself into a ball. Above me, the ripping and sucking continues. I can still hear my sisters sob and howl, though faintly now. Inside the hollow cavity of my chest, my heart thunders, threatening to burst open like the sky at the start of the new monsoons.

At last, the batterkite gives up. I hear the trees spring upright as it lifts away. I stay furled in my hiding place for a long time.

A torrent of rain hits the ground above. Water rushes into my hiding place. I attempt to scramble back up the way I came, but it's slippery and I fall back in. Water gushes over my face and I gasp for air, scramble-wriggle furiously to get out. I dig my claws into mud. I've survived a full HöST invasion; I will not drown in the roots of a tree, not even a very old one. I squirm. I claw. I'm tossed up onto the slippery forest floor, covered in mud like blood but otherwise intact. One lucky sister, praise be to our Holy Mother, truly she is great.

I scour the forest floor for my knife, kick at dead pine needles, sand, succulent, and sage. No luck. That cursed Salty has taken everything. I will hunt it and murder it to little pieces. At least I've got my second, smaller knife.

IT SEEMS LIKE HOURS LATER WHEN I REACH BOMBYX MORI WAITING for me still inside the bus.

"Did you see the batterkite? Did you hear it? Just after the storm? By Our Mother's feet, I wonder what they came back for, we're so lucky it wasn't us ..."

The grumbling, snoring carcass of Calyx Kaki lies in a heap of leaves beside Corydalis Ambigua. "Did any others, besides this fine specimen, come to you?" I ask.

"None."

"Then I'm going to Saltwater City to find them. And I'm going to catch that dirty Salty on my way. If they've harmed Glorybind Groundsel in the least little bit, I will kill them all." I whip out my remaining knife so she knows I'm serious.

"Put that away, you silly fool. You're scaring Corydalis Ambigua." Bombyx Mori casts a glance to the rear of the bus. "I checked the sister puppies this morning for partho marks. And starfish ones too. There's nothing."

I sheath my knife. "I guess this means you're not coming to the city with me."

Bombyx Mori shakes her head. "We might be the last Grist sisters in the world," she says. "But Corydalis Ambigua could fruit again. My duty and yours are not the same. Remember that place in the mountains where you took down that old bull elk last summer?"

I remember. He gave me such a chase, and when I finally caught him, the look of sorrow in his eyes was almost unbearable. I nod.

"You didn't know I was following you."

"You couldn't have been."

"That was a well-hidden valley. If the Kainai will give permission, I'll take the sisters there. I'll begin a new Grist Village."

"I'll take Calyx Kaki with me. She's sipped a lot of forget-me-do. You've got more important things to take care of."

Bombyx casts her eyes over our sleeping sister. "Calyx Kaki, of all the sisters who could have made it."

"Our Mother says gratitude above all else. We'll be okay."

"Come find us when you've got your mother double and our other sisters back."

She picks up a stick and scratches a map in the dirt to show me where the hidden fertile valleys are.

"There were many expulsions to those places," I tell her. "Expulsions older than the expulsion of Grandma Chan Ling. Who knows what ... or who ... you'll find."

"I have no choice, Kirilow."

"Neither of us do."

We hug for a long time. Bombyx, Corydalis, and the new Grist litter head immediately east. I return to the sad cave I shared with my dearest beloved and my mother double to pull supplies together before heading to the city.

PART II

CASCADIA YEAR: 127 TAO (TIME AFTER OIL)

UNITED MIDDLE KINGDOM CYCLE 80, YEAR 42 (WOOD SNAKE YEAR)

GREGORIAN YEAR: 2145

HOMESICK

NODE: GRAIN IN BEARD
DAY: 9

"HOW ARE YOU FEELING?"

"Better."

"Want to learn the tango?"

"Tango?"

"It's the dance that fights back."

Madame leads Kora around the floor. Slow, slow, quick quick slow.

"How is this going to help anything?"

"It's the first lesson, and you must learn it well. The other dances are harder, because they are secret. So come on now, move like you mean it."

NODE: GRAIN IN BEARD
DAY: 11

IN SPITE OF MADAME'S KINDNESS, KORA FEELS HOMESICK LIKE CRAZY.
She's forgotten the hunger. She's forgotten the strife. She wants to see Charlotte, Kai Wai, and K2 so badly she thinks she might burst.

On a moonless night, after Chang has set, she leaves her narrow cot in the sleeping hall. Pads softly down the stairs all the way to the basement, past Madame's private quarters, to the back door. Unlocks it and lets herself out into the night.

The city is blissfully quiet. Kora walks quietly to the street corner and looks off in the direction of home. The giant *W* atop the building still turns on its axis, though the light it gives off is dim and flickering. Still, it's bright enough to make her heart leap. She hurries towards it on the lightest feet she can manage.

Here's the path to the Isabelle shrine. She feels a sudden urge to have a look.

Instinctively, she looks left and right in case there are any kohl-eyed girls lurking nearby. Smirks inwardly, remembering she's one of them now. Scurries down the broken sidewalk, past haunted alleys full of trash, two plague houses, and a crumbling church towards the water.

The Isabelle shrine is more lavishly decorated than before. Someone has painted an image of Isabelle in profile on either side of the door, looking right on the left, and left on the right. The torn satin curtain has been replaced with red velvet. Kora approaches softly and pulls the curtain aside just slightly at first, in case there's an attendant or priestess inside. A recently lit candle burns on the altar. It casts a warm glow. Beside it, smoke wafts up from three sticks of incense. But no one is there.

Kora steps inside. Kneels on the cushion and mutters an awkward prayer for Charlotte, Wai, and K2. Hesitates. Grumbles one out for Madame Dearborn, Velma, and the other Cordova girls, including Myra, Tania, Soraya, and Modesta.

When she's finished, she notices a red filigree scale stuck in the sand beside the candle. Was it there before? Once she pulls it out of the sand, she can see the plug is standard. She wipes it off as before, with spit and the corner of her dress. Pulls out one of her own scales and inserts the filigree.

The Isabelle projection kneels this time, her face uncomfortably close to Kora's, her cheeks streaked with tears. "I guess you chose her after all. I can't believe it, after all we've been through together. What was I thinking? I guess I'm a girl and stupid. Nix that. I'm not stupid. You're an asshole. To think how much I loved you. Well, I hope you're happy and I hope you're screwing yourselves silly, because it's not going to last, do you hear me? I know you don't. You don't take my messages anymore, I know. I'm not even talking to you, I'm talking to the ghost of you I keep in my moronic little heart, like an idiot, like a chump. Oh God, I can't believe I feel this. I can't believe I let you do this to me." Her eyes are fountains, gushing water. Kora twitches, but she can't stop watching the emotional slaughterhouse.

"Well, don't imagine for a minute that you have the last word. LiFT is still only at eighty-five percent verisimilitude, you know. And neither you nor that little bitch—how could I have ever called that charity case my best friend?!—have the smarts to generate the other fifteen percent. So you're going to sell a defective product to the desperate. I'll make it again, and I'll make it perfect. There will be no contest. And then just you wait, because I'm amassing an army, do you hear me? You don't get to treat me like this and live!"

The transmission ends there. Kora is in shock at the intensity of Isabelle's emotions. Isabelle—the brilliant inventor, the cool and canny CEO of HöST and heroine to millions of girls surviving the tiger flu, girls who will far outlive their boyfriends, brothers, fathers, and uncles in the streets of Saltwater Flats and beyond. How can she be such a mess? How could anyone hurt their golden princess this much?

This time, Kora leaves the Isabelle scale in her head. Sticks the old moon phase scale in the sand beside the candle as a kind of offering. She no longer needs it in her halo because her brain remembers most of its content anyway. She pushes the red velvet curtain aside and departs the shrine. Takes the path by the ocean towards the Woodward's Building.

She doesn't see them waiting for her until they step out of the shadows.

"Think you can get away from us so easily, spoiled girl?" It's Modesta, in charge in Myra's absence. Shit.

"After all we've invested in you?" And Soraya. Crap.

Modesta grabs her by the ear as though she's a delinquent child. Soraya takes her firmly by the arm. They drag her back to the Cordova School.

STATE YOUR INTENTIONS

18

NODE: GRAIN IN BEARD
DAY: 7

THE NEW MONSOONS HAVE ARRIVED DECISIVELY. THIS MORNING'S rain falls in torrents. I haven't slept, but I spent the night coiled in the fragrance of Peristrophe Halliana's hair. I didn't cry, and I won't. I wash the dishes from our last meal together, fold and put away her clothes, then move to Old Glorybind's room to make sure it is in order. Peristrophe was never tidy, but my mother double always was. Her room is just the way she left it every morning—a quilt of tiny squares laid perfectly over the bed, her four tunics hanging neatly in the closet, not a speck of dust on the old pine dresser built by Grandma Chan Ling herself. Atop the dresser lies my mother double's pipe. I put it in my pocket. I pack the tent that Peristrophe made for me, half a dozen womb bombs, a few basic herbs, a handful of needles, plus dried foodstuffs—elk, chicken, mushrooms. Also knives, scalpels, and of course, my precious whetstone. The pack will be heavy, but it can't be helped.

I rest for a moment and watch the rain subside at the little window where my mother double used to sit. Chang follows the dark clouds as they roll away.

Calyx returns from her own cave with an old knapsack of

Glorybind's I gave her, packed with her own things. I help her load it onto her back, then hoist my own.

If I had nuclear rockets like the Cosmopolitan Earth Council, I would launch them all and blow Saltwater City to high heaven. I would, I swear it. I would kill every one of those last little mothers and not bat a single pretty eyelash. If I could be there to watch blood run from their eyes, as I was forced to make blood run from the eyes of my best beloved, nothing would make me happier. I'd knife them through their slitty peepers myself, revel as red fountains spurted skyward. I'd make their children drink them dry from their bleeding eyes. If I could kill them twice and twice again. If I could vaporize them and gore them too, I would. I'd burn them in the hottest and deepest reaches of hell. There is no pain they don't deserve. But I don't have a rocket launcher. I don't have swords, guns, napalm, sarin gas, or any of the weapons my mother double taught me they had in the time before.

We march towards the New Origins Archive, where my mother double took me for my rite of spring just this past monsoon.

"A penny," says Calyx Kaki, trudging beside me as we descend a bluff into the thickening forest. We've walked through the horror of the morning without a word. It's mid-afternoon. Chang rises, as he does every other hour, on the western horizon. He's noticeably closer today than yesterday. The tug of his gravity irritates me.

"I won't share," I tell her. "I've got nothing nice. Nothing I should inflict on you."

She gazes at me, mournful and lost.

"Look, baby, I am not your mama. I'm not anyone's mama and never will be. Radix Bupleuri was a greedy mother who died of greedy greed. I'm done taking care of people. So don't you think I will take care of you. You can come with me, and that is all."

She sniffles, then chokes.

I don't have anything to give her.

The choke becomes a sob.

"By Our Mother's hairy crotch, *do not cry.*"

She bursts into tears.

"You stop that now, or I will leave you in the burnt village. Do you want to stay at Grist and pick the rags off dead sisters? Hmmmmmm? And eat their rotting meat, 'til you die of maggot poisoning? Do you?" We reach the bottom of the bluff. I'm appalled at my meanness, but I can't stop. "I will take you back there and tie you to Mourning Rock, I swear I will, if you don't stop testing me!"

A scream erupts from her scrawny throat.

"*Stop that.*"

She wails like one possessed, rolls to the ground. Her body shakes and quivers.

"They will find us, you stupid ninny. You better get control of yourself *right now.*"

She vibrates uncontrollably. What is wrong with her? The vibrating intensifies. Is she still breathing? Get ahold of yourself, Kirilow Groundsel. You cannot afford all this rage. You've got to get Calyx Kaki to Saltwater City. You've got to catch that Salty and find your sisters. Do it for Peristrophe Halliana.

I roll down beside her, grab her tight. "I'm sorry, Calyx Kaki, I'm sorry ..."

Her body vibrates fearsomely as she sobs. I grip her tighter. The shaking stops and she's just crying. "Don't abandon me, Groom Kirilow, you are all I've got."

"Shhh, Calyx, you are all I've got," I say, though I feel numb. "We will get them back, do you hear me? We will catch and kill that invading Salty, and we will make the others pay in fountains of blood."

"Don't talk like that, Groom Kiri. Your mother double would not want that."

"She is gone, and I'm in charge."

"We are children. We know nothing."

"I know things. High Priestess Elzbieta Kruk took me through my adulthood rites last spring. We will go to the New Origins Archive now for help."

I must pull it together. If I want my revenge, I must find patience. I have a long march ahead during which to find it, and I hope I can remember the way.

THE PATH IS NARROW AND OVERGROWN WITH SAGE. ALTHOUGH MY mother double took me to the New Origins Archive only last year, it was just the one time. I'm not at all sure of the way. I could take the longer route, which follows old railway tracks, but I've never been that way, and it goes through the city of Kim-Ach-Touch, also known as Grizzly Bear Town. The last time one of our runners came back from there, she said it was infested with flu. Better to go through Pente-Hik-Ton farther south, where the Syilx are still in control and, thanks to their medicinally cultivated immunity, have kept the flu out, at least for now. The old matriarch of that town, Maria Armstrong, was the one who helped Grandma Chan Ling back in the days of the Grist sister exodus from Saltwater City. I think her great-grandson Billy Johnson will remember me, even without my mother double.

So we pick through sage and pinyon in the growing heat, and I chant and chant to Our Mother to make my memory right. By day's end, we hit a road made of crumbling asphalt. Sage and dry grass push through the pavement at every weakness, but the road is still recognizable. I breathe a sigh of relief. We'll make it as far as Pente.

It's growing dark, and the evening rain will hit any minute. Calyx Kaki and I duck into the trees and set up the mushroom-fibre tent that Peristrophe Halliana wove, sewed, and waxed for my mother double and me last year, before our trip along this same route. Calyx and I get the tent up and shove a few scraps of still-dry wood inside just before the first drops of rain begin to fall. We dive beneath the shelter of its thin yet sturdy fabric. It still smells of beeswax and, ever so faintly, Peristrophe's thyme and orange water perfume.

The fragrance surrounds me, and my heart goes soggy with grief and longing. How will I pass a whole night inside here? When I close my eyes, her presence is so intense I almost believe I'll see her when I open them. Her impossible closeness is unbearable.

As soon as the rains let up, I exit quickly and build the lowest of fires under the flaps of the tent, where it's still dry but open to the air. Over it, we simmer a broth of dried elk and herbs. We eat in silence.

Back inside the tent, still overwhelmed by the scent of Peristrophe's ghostly presence, I tumble into an exhausted slumber.

NODE: GRAIN IN BEARD
DAY: 8

THUMP. I WAKE WITH A START. SOMETHING HAS HIT THE FINELY WOVEN roof of the tent and is now gnawing at its fibre. Squirrel? You'll make a good breakfast if I catch you. I lift the flap and climb out.

"Good morning, Groom Kirilow."

I gasp. "Who are you? How do you know my name? What do you want?"

"You're in my territory now. I could well ask you the same."

The sky is barely light. I pull my little firefly jar from the pocket of my tunic. In the pale light, a face I recognize. "Billy Johnson?"

"State your intentions, please." The Pente Syilx have guns from the time before. He's pointing one right at my face. Gone is the friendly young man I met with his grandmother last year. His demeanor is dead cold.

"I mean no harm. Grist Village was burnt out by HöST the night before last. I'm going to Saltwater City to rescue my mother double, Glorybind Groundsel." No reason to tell more than I need to. Last year, his grandmother let us pass without issue through Pente-Hik-Ton, but something has clearly changed.

Billy sits quiet, thinking. "Have you brought anything to help us?"

I offer him a small pouch of forget-me-do. "You know this plant, I think?"

"What is your relationship to the extraction companies?"

"Billy, you know that my people are products of the Jemini Group, and that we escaped them three generations ago."

He nods, still very formal. "The protocols are all the more important in these uncertain times," he says. "Any more Grist sisters in these woods?"

I hesitate. If I tell the truth that there's only me and Calyx, and he's not feeling charitable, he could take us prisoner. But if I lie and say there are more Grist sisters, he might feel threatened and still detain us. "Any more Syilx?"

"I asked you first. Why answer so slowly?"

I take a deep breath. "It's just my cousin and me."

He nods and drops the gun. "HöST attacked us two nights ago. You may pass through these woods, but don't try anything funny. We've got you surrounded." He nods in several directions through the forest. "Go before I change my mind."

I nod back politely. "Is it safe to pass through Pente?"

"Safer than through Kim. Kim is occupied. They burnt Pente down."

"Billy, I'm sorry," I say. "Your grandma was my mother double's friend."

He gives just the slightest smile then. "To trust you is all the hospitality I can afford, Kirilow Groundsel."

"What will you do?"

"Join the Cosmopolitan Earth Council, in all likelihood. I don't want to. The UMK element there is strong, and ugly. And Grandma would not approve, not in any way. But we have cousins there who can protect us and might assist us in retaliation. Alternately, we could try to build an alliance with the Coast Salish Timeplace, who are less politically compromised, but they are not well armed. Otherwise, we flee farther inland, but HöST is raiding all the villages regardless of who lives there. What will you do?"

"I have to go to Saltwater City. To fulfill a promise to Peristrophe."

"How is your beloved starfish?"

I don't answer, but he looks in my eyes and knows.

"We've both lost too much, Groom Kirilow. Go in peace, but go now. I don't have any more to offer you than that."

The squirrel is still gnawing at the tent. I swat it away. It better not have made a hole. I go inside and wake Calyx Kaki. We pack up quickly. As we head up the crumbling asphalt road, everywhere among the dark branches of the forest I see the little firefly lights of the exiled people of Pente. I hear them whispering, voices full of worry.

My brain races with the possibilities. Is HöST attempting to take the Fourth Plague Ring? And the third? Our Mother who art artful, I wish I'd paid better attention to Mother Glorybind's history and geography lessons. I thought biology was all there was. But I do know that the Cosmopolitan Earth Council controls the Second Plague Ring, and that they are a nuclear power. They captured nuclear warheads from the time before in the first wave of the tiger flu, when autochthones were the only ones immune. They took in many people from the surrounding plague rings too. Maybe even some Grist sisters. Billy's grandmother Maria did not approve of their nuclear stewardship. "But," she said, "it keeps them safe from the predations of HöST, and they protect us too, so I don't judge absolutely. I just guide my children in other directions."

The United Middle Kingdom destabilized their currency, forced renminbi on them, and via sympathizers within overtook their government. "Last I heard," said Mother Glory, "there were progressive elements inside, mostly grandchildren of the founding Secwepemc, trying to squeeze UMK influence out, but without much luck."

Still, from their base in the second ring, the Cosmopolitan Earth Council deters batterkites from crossing into the third and fourth rings. Or, at least, they did until now. They have the power to stop the occupation of the First Plague Ring if they wanted, but trade is lucrative, and active hostilities are low. Or—were low. Has HöST defeated them? Or made a deal? I ache for my mother double, who would know the answers to all these questions.

THE SLEEPING SPARROW

19

NODE: GRAIN IN BEARD
DAY: 10

IT'S MIDNIGHT. THE SMOG IS THICK AND THE GIRLS SEEM TO SLEEP particularly soundly. Kora slips out of bed and into her blue dress. She takes her battered raincoat from its hook in the hall and goes quietly as she can out the creaking front doors. Surely now, she can get through the gates of the old building and see Charlotte, Kai Wai, and K2 again. The dark is so thick, she can hardly see the broken sidewalk in front of her, but she knows it so well that it doesn't matter. She isn't two blocks from the school when someone takes her arm.

"Kora, is that you?"

She recognizes the voice, the aggressive grip. "Stash?"

"I knew you'd remember me!" He puts his arm around her.

She squirms away. "What are you doing out on the street so late?"

"I could well ask you the same question, missy."

"Don't call me missy. Who do you think you are?"

"Why are you always so mean to me, Kora? All I ever did was like you." He reaches for her again.

She steps back. "That's not true."

"Of course it is."

"Well, I don't like the way you like me."

"Kora, come on. It's my last night on earth." He takes her hand.

She tries to pull away but his grip is strong. "What the heck are you talking about?"

"Your brother. He's found a way for us to live after all. He's found a cure for the flu."

"There's no cure for the flu, Stash. That's why everybody is dying."

"Your brother has met a man who's figured it out. It's still in the test stages, so it's risky. But it's also free." He opens his eyes puppy-dog wide. "Come have a glass of tiger wine with me."

"I don't drink that stuff." She yanks hard and gets free.

"Come on, Kora, don't be such a bitch. It's my last night."

She sighs. "I owe you nothing."

"As a dear friend of your dear brother," he says, "I ask you this as a last favour."

Against her better judgment, she follows him.

He takes her to a tiny bar called the Sleeping Sparrow in a side street she doesn't usually dare cross through.

"Just one drink," she says. "Because, first of all, I'm underage. And secondly, I need to get home to see Charlotte and Kai Wai."

She orders a drink called Psyche's Labour, because she's had it before and likes its bitter kick combined with the taste of sour cherries. She's never seen so many men in one place before—young and old, tall and short, all with the gaunt faces and skin lesions that are the trademarks of the tiger flu.

Stash orders a shot of tiger whisky with a beer chaser. "Come on," he says, "I want to show you something."

Kora says, "If you try anything funny, I'll crush your balls to a bloody pulp. They teach us all kinds of handy stuff at the Cordova School."

"Jesus Christ," Stash says. "Do you have to be so hostile? I just want to show you something without showing it to the whole world."

At the back of the bar are booths with high walls. "Can we just sit up front?"

"I'm not going to do anything," he says. "Look, you sit on that side." He points to a seat from which she can still see the door. Sits down opposite her and pulls a small flat disk out of his pocket.

"What's that?"

"Two-way open scale," he says. "Look!" He flicks it on and a column of light springs up in the middle of the table. "To talk to guys who have already gone over."

"Are you insane?"

"It's a real thing. My friend Oscar did it last week." He fiddles with the disk and the light changes colour. "Hey Oscar, are you there?"

A faint figure appears in the light, gaunt and blue. "Hey man, how's it going?" says the other boy. "You're going to love it up here. We're strong the way we were before. There are cars like in the old days. And steak and beer, and girls, man, thousands of hot chiquititas like you would not believe. When do you get here?"

"You have to be polite, brother," Stash says. "'Cause I'm with a girl right now."

"A Saltwater Flats girl? Who cares, man, seriously. Twenty-four hours from now, you are not gonna give a flying fuck, do you hear me?"

"Don't say that," says Stash.

"I'm totally serious, brother. You'll forget about her, and you'll forget about that shithole of a city before the week is out." Oscar stands up, drops his pants and shakes his floppy wang at Stash, hangs his tongue out at the same time.

"Gross, Stash," Kora says. "Shut it off."

"Oscar, put that away!" says Stash to the ghostly blue boy.

Oscar keeps shaking his dick and wagging his drooling tongue. Kora gets up to go.

Stash turns it off. "I'm sorry Oscar is such a pig. We aren't all, you know."

"Oh no?"

"Life is possible there in a way it's not here. I thought I'd ask you—I mean—"

"Ask me what?"

"Girls can go too."

"You're right off your holy rocker."

"I thought maybe you weren't having such a great time at the Cordova School. Those girls are ballbusters, man. I mean really, and they don't smell so good."

"Is that so?" says a voice from the next booth. Modesta.

"I showered yesterday," says another. Soraya.

Modesta comes around the booth to where Kora is sitting. "What are you doing with this dirtbag?"

"Truly, Kora," Soraya says, "by Our Mother's blessed breath. You could at least have decent taste."

To Stash, Modesta says, "Put your little toy away now. Don't you know that they killed your friend and gave you some cheap algorithm. Talk about a big slice of gullible cake!"

"The Conductor is real!" Stash protests. "Tons of guys are doing it."

Modesta and Soraya drag Kora out of the booth, and two blocks back to the Cordova Dancing School for Girls.

THE FAMOUS DOCTOR 20

KIRILOW GROUNDSEL // PENTE-HIK-TON

NODE: GRAIN IN BEARD
DAY: 8

WE WALK IN SILENCE, PAUSING ONLY TO TAKE SHELTER FROM THE morning rainstorm under a broad-leaved maple. Towards noon, when Chang lords directly over us, the path to Pente presents itself. We take it and begin our ascent to the village on high.

An older village lies buried beneath Pente, reduced progressively to rubble in the Six Great Quakes of the time before. The village that stands there now is a renewal of the old one, built atop a high terp, surrounded on all sides by a flood plain. When Mother Glory and I passed through last year, it was a small but wealthy community of friendly, hospitable people. Today, I fear we are rushing to meet our doom.

We crush succulents and desert flowers already drowning in mud as we climb. Because of its gentle grade, the hill does not look so high, but this muddy march feels like it will never end. The mid-afternoon sun shines bright in the rain-washed sky when we get to the top. Chang meanders lazily past the sun, oblivious to our grief.

I see the birds first, waddling heavy over the burnt-out village. Their bodies are large and brown, their heads blood red and naked. They feast voraciously, plunge those red bloody heads into carrion—the bodies of the villagers who neither escaped nor got carried off. In the high post-rain heat, the flesh rots and reeks.

"Close your eyes, Calyx. Don't look," I say, ridiculously. She has to look, to pick a path through the carnage.

I survey the vast field of bodies and burnt homes. Something hits me in the head. It knocks me over and my mouth fills with fur. Nails gore my chest. "Get off me, ghost mother!" I struggle. It rolls me over and pulls off my pack. Although the sun is bright, I still cannot see my attacker, only my pack, running along the ground as though of its own volition.

Behind me, Calyx Kaki is fighting another one. "Damn catcoat!"

I rush to help her, though it means losing Peristrophe's beautiful and necessary tent. I can't see the thing; I can only see where it tears. I reach out to grab. It's sleek and soft. Swipe. Sharp across my face. Blood gushes hot down my chin, but I don't care. I pull a needle from my tunic and make a best guess about where to poke it. I hit my mark. The beast shrieks and falls off Calyx Kaki's back. On the ground, a large cat writhes, the size of a small human. I pop a needle between its eyes, and the head folds back like a hood. Inside the skin lies a slender, dark-haired girl, eyes wide and staring. She's missing a tooth and wearing way too many long dangly earrings. She's young, maybe seventeen or eighteen. But her eyes are old. I feel pity, and I refuse it. I grab the girl by the throat. "Who are you and why do you attack us? Where's my backpack?"

"Please," she rasps, just as that vile Salty did when I had it by the throat.

I sit on her stomach. "Stop wriggling. If I let go your throat, will you keep still and state your purpose?"

Her face is turning blue, but she mouths a dry *Yes*.

I let go of her throat.

"Myra, ruuuuunnnn!!" she shrieks. "I'm caught!"

Furious, I grab her throat and squeeze with all my might. Her brown eyes bulge out of her head. *Please please please.* Words formed but not spoken.

"You're a liar and a thief. You die."

Calyx is beside me. "Groom Kirilow, she could help us. Your mother double would not want you to kill."

"Don't you dare invoke my mother double!" I squeeze tighter. The girl faints, and I realize what I'm doing. I let go.

Thanks be to our bounteous Mother that I have a bit of mushroom-fibre rope in my tunic pocket. I bind her arms and legs. I pick her up and sling her over my back, weird furry skin and all. Although the girl is still out, the skin shudders. Creepy. "Let's get off the hill."

Calyx follows. "What are you going to do with that Cordova girl?"

"You know what this is?"

"Me and the other initiates ran into a pack of them around Ching Ming Festival. Getting ice at Mólkwcen Mountain, just like us. They're scavengers from Saltwater City. Really stinky, but clever. She could help us if she decides to be nice."

"We'll make her help. And get my tent back. We're going to need it to survive out here."

I start to carry the fur-covered girl down the far side of the terp back under cover of eucalyptus and madrona. The warm, furry skin continues to vibrate unpleasantly. Calyx follows close, and the late-afternoon rains begin to fall. The rain wakes the girl.

"Put me down, you animal!"

She's heavy. I'm only too happy to oblige. I drop her in mud.

"Horrible Gristie," she spits.

Calyx and I help her up. I adjust her bindings so she can walk in small steps, hands still firmly tied behind her back. I make a leash so she can't get away. "Where's your friend? And my tent?"

She says nothing. Stares at me insolently. I raise my hand to smack, but Calyx pulls my arm back. "Please don't, Groom Kirilow. Myra will catch up with us, and you will get your tent back."

How does she know the thief?

We march through the deepening mud. A quarter of the way down the terp, a soft wind comes up, like the voices of young girls whispering secrets.

"Don't worry, Kiri only seems mean. She's a doctor. She will help you. But only if you're nice."

"She'll hear us." Barest of breath from the Cordova girl.

Young girls do whisper secrets. The nerve!

"She's old, and old people are deaf. Don't worry," says Calyx. There are only a few years between us. She's a dim-witted thing.

More worrisome: Is she in cahoots with our attackers? I'll kill them both. I don't care. I've already lost everything that matters to me.

"Why did you attack us?" Calyx whispers.

"We didn't know who you were. There's unrest in the city and a demand for the things people put in backpacks. Madame will feast the ones who bring back the most and expel the ones who bring back the least. It's the only home I have. I can't lose my place there."

"You have to get Myra to give us our tent back. We need it to be safe at night, and also Groom Kiri's dead lover made it for her. She will kill you."

"I'm tougher than I look ..."

"So is she. And she's wounded, which means extra fierce."

The rain begins its full onslaught then. I stop and turn around.

"Tell her," I say, enunciating clearly as though to an idiot, "that we want our tent back right now."

Calyx's face burns red as a turkey vulture's.

"I don't have to take you with me," I say. I push the Salty to the muddy ground, squat over her, and place my hands on her throat. "I can leave you and little Calyx right here for the birds. Would you like that?"

"No," she squeaks. "I'm sorry, Groom Kirilow."

For the third time, I close my hands slowly around the girl's throat. She doesn't try to scream. She purses her lips. A shrill whistle pierces the soggy air.

"Stop that!"

I choke her tight.

"Groom Kirilow, please," Calyx begs, so pathetic. "Her sister is coming back with the tent. They'll help us."

I don't let up. How can I trust them? The girl's throat is hot in my hands. If I can't make the Salty who invaded our village pay for the death of my beloved, this dirty Salty will do.

The girl's face turns blue. Better finish her before the other one gets here.

"Kirilow—" Calyx tugs uselessly at my arm.

Bop!

For the second time today, my mouth fills with fur. The world goes black.

I'M AWAKE AND PERISTROPHE IS WITH ME. I CAN SMELL HER ORANGE water and thyme perfume. Beeswax, wet earth, woodsmoke.

"Dearest one, are your eyes healing?" I open my own. I'm inside the tent she sewed for me. There's no Peristrophe, only the dim-wit Calyx Kaki, watching me with wide, terrified eyes. My arms and legs are bound.

"I didn't want to do it, but you can't attack Tania again."

Rage floods my heart. "You ungrateful ninny."

"You—you don't understand. They are friends of the initiates. We meet them at the Mólkwcen icefields four times a year."

"So now you're gonna kill me? After I saved you from HöST?"

"Of course not, Groom Kirilow. They are your friends too," Calyx croaks. She can't be afraid of me, bound like this.

An unholy rage surges through me. "You brought that sick Salty to us. Through these weird fur-covered ones. I know it was you. And now you betray the Grist by selling your own flesh and blood to them. Our Mother curse you to the end of your days!"

"I had nothing to do with that Salty. It found us, all by itself."

A tall, muscly one enters the tent then. Thick black hair, eyes rimmed with black stuff. She thinks it makes her look scary.

"You bop me in the brain? Go ahead, kill me. I'm not afraid of you."

"Will you calm down, Groom Kirilow Groundsel? I'm Myra Mao." She squats beside me and brushes my hair out of my eyes.

"Don't you touch me," I spit. "I don't know you."

She keeps stroking my hair. "Calm down. We are not going to hurt you. We're your friends."

"Don't have friends. Definitely no Salty friends."

"Saltwater City is a big place, Groom Groundsel," says she of the excessive black stuff. "You're gonna have to let go of your bigotry."

"She needs tea," whispers Calyx, still so full of fear.

"No tea," I say. "Don't you dare groom me with my own teas. I'll slaughter you all. Don't you doubt it for one split second!"

"Are you sure this is the famous doctor Kirilow Groundsel?" Myra asks Calyx. Finally, she stops touching me.

The idiot Calyx nods. "We lost our whole village. She is not herself."

"The Salt Grist sisters been seeking her a long time." Myra says. "I didn't believe she was real, they been searching so long. Sure is a nasty thing."

"You're a nasty thing," I hiss.

"Of course she's real. I told you where I was from," says Calyx. "If you were looking for her, why didn't you just ask me?"

"Thought you were fooling when you said you were a Grist sister," Myra says. She looks at me, then Calyx, then back at me.

I squirm beneath her discomfiting gaze.

"The doctor's older, yes? But otherwise you look exactly the same. Freaky deaky."

I shoot her my most resentful stare.

The other one comes in then, with a cup of my own forget-me-tea.

"You don't groom me with my own teas! Our Mother damn you for all eternity!"

The one called Myra holds my nose. The one called Tania pours it into my gasping, spitting gob. Filthy Salties!

I wake up for a split second. I'm in a sling tied to a long straight pole. There's a Salty on either end, schlumping me down the far side of the terp. So undignified! So sleepy. Out.

FORAGE DANCE 21

NODE: GRAIN IN BEARD
DAY: 11

MODESTA STOPS KORA IN THE HALLWAY AFTER LUNCH. THE MORNING rains have just stopped and the sky looks bright. Old Chang looks benevolently down on them. "You can't just eat and not work."

"I'm willing to work."

Soraya is right behind her. "Good. We will teach you the forage dance."

"I'd just as soon go with Velma."

"Madame asked us to teach you while Myra and Tania are away. Something could happen to them at any minute and we've got to share skills. Besides, it's time. You know our main trade is in cans from the time before. We found a buried supermarket at the border to the second ring. You're going to come help us clear it out."

"Velma says there are no more supermarkets in Saltwater Flats."

"Well, she's just a kid. What does she know?"

"I don't have a catcoat yet."

"You don't need a catcoat, spoiled brat. You have to learn to do this without. That's how you earn one. By the time the day's done, you'll be a better forager than Myra herself."

They take the school's only truck and put two furry, mewling catcoats in the back. It's a long ride across the city, through the East Side where all the scale manufacturers have their factories, through the commercial zone where they sell their wares, farther east and through the massive Eastern Night Market. At its edges there are hawkers selling tea eggs and radish cakes from small carts with charcoal braziers, disposable shoes and clothing from the UMK, zeptocameras, DIY heart bypass kits, foldable motorcycles, while-you-wait genetically tailored pets. Farther in there are vendors of things from the time before: old radios, rusting bike parts, motherboards and hard drives from ancient computers, battered nylon jackets, inventive toys made from bits of old blenders, plastic bottles, incandescent lightbulbs. There are vendors who sell clothes too: warm coats made from processed seaweed, beautiful shoes with pointed toes, long skirts made of heavy zeptohemp across the surface of which old movies play. Farther still, different dancing girls flog found or stolen cans. Modesta points her index and third fingers at them and gives them the toy gun salute.

On they drive, into the uncertain suburbs that line the Stó:lō. Most houses are boarded up, sad and forlorn. But that does not necessarily mean empty.

"Watch the houses for any sign of activity, and tell me right away if you see anything, Lady Kora. Girls have lost their lives out here." Modesta speaks kindly, to Kora's great surprise.

Soraya drives them to the very edge of the first ring. They stop beside an old landslide. There's earth heaped on one side of the road, and on the other, a row of empty, dilapidated houses stands.

"Is the supermarket under there?"

"There is no supermarket. We're going to take a plague house." Soraya points to one of the boarded-up mansions, one with a gnarled old apple tree on the front lawn, just coming into bud. The lawn is overgrown and wild. The grass comes up to Kora's waist.

"A plague house?"

"We scoped it out a couple of weeks ago. There's lots of cans in there that no one needs."

"Is everyone dead?"

"We don't know for sure. If they're alive, they're not very alive. We can take them."

Kora is horrified. "I don't think Madame would want that."

"Well, Madame doesn't need to know, does she? There are no supermarkets left in the first ring. Madame wants to believe there are, and it's our duty to uphold that belief. We used to cross into the other quarantine rings, but Cosmopolitan Earth has just closed the One-Two border, even to us. The city needs more cans, and it's our job to get them. So. In you go."

"I'm not going in there."

"Of course you are."

The house is a large single-family dwelling, shaped like a horseshoe, with a long courtyard before the front door. If there's anyone alive inside, they will see the Cordova girls way before the girls see them.

"Better to go round back," says Modesta.

She makes them tromp through the wet, overgrown side and backyards, three princesses storming Sleeping Beauty's castle. There are cleaver vines growing over the already overgrown bushes. By the time they get to the back, all of them are covered in little itchy, spiky burrs. Modesta and Soraya pull off as many as they can, then put on their catcoats and vanish from sight. Kora feels exposed and alone, so far from home, with no catcoat to cover her and make her invisible.

"Come here, I'll teach you the door-opening dance," says Modesta, very close by. She presses something into Kora's hand. "This is a bump key."

"I don't want to. You do it."

"We didn't take you here for entertainment purposes. We took you here so you'd get good at the heist. Take this." She pushes a screwdriver into Kora's other hand. "Come on, try it."

Reluctantly, Kora sticks the key in the lock. By touch, Modesta shows her how to pull it out a notch, turn it slightly to the right, and tap it with the handle of the screwdriver. The first time, it doesn't work. Nor the second. But the third time, the key turns in the lock, and Kora pushes the door inward.

There is something blocking the door. It takes the three of them, shoving hard, to get it open. The back foyer is full of corpses, rotting in the advancing summer heat. The stench is incredible.

"Our Mother," says Kora.

"Can't afford to be squeamish, Princess Kora," says a voice from her other side. Soraya. "If nature's done the killing for you, then you don't need to do it yourself."

How did my life come to this? Kora thinks. She steps over the putrefying bodies, trying not to look. Her heart fills with pity for the dead. Her brain races, hoping desperately that her immunity is as good as it has seemed to be so far.

"Come on," says Modesta. "Soraya, you check the kitchen. I'll go upstairs, and Kora will go to the basement."

"I don't want to go to the basement."

"Don't be a baby. You gotta learn this somehow." Modesta pushes her towards the stairs. She presses a small pistol into Kora's hand.

"You shouldn't have," says Kora.

"In case nature needs a little help." Modesta shows her how to hold the pistol high on the grip and lay her support hand thumb over thumb. How to release the safety, line up the sights, and pull back the trigger smoothly with the pad of her index finger.

"At least come with me."

"How you gonna learn if I go with you? It's simple. Go down there and see if there are any cans. If there are, fill your bag and get out. You're the closest to the door. We have to go through the whole house."

"What if there are more bodies? What if there's someone alive down there?"

"That's what you have a gun for." Modesta fits a headlamp over Kora's head. "Don't turn this on until you're sure you don't have company."

"I can't believe we're doing this," says Kora. She has nowhere to hide her terror.

"Madame can't know, or we're all expelled. Go now."

"Dog damn it," moans Kora. "Doggy doggy doggy damn it. I want a catcoat."

"Well, you don't have one," Modesta says. "Now go."

Kora steps into the dark and pads down the stairs on the softest, lightest feet she can muster. There is enough light coming from the main landing that, as her eyes adjust, she can make out a hallway and the doors to several rooms.

She opens the first and the reek of rotting flesh rushes at her and makes her gag. She turns on the headlamp. Three half-rotted bodies curl together on a mattress on the floor. She retches softly. Pulls the door shut.

In the second room lie an adult man and woman and three

children, all dead and decaying. She tries not to let the sight into her head. She pulls that door shut too.

The third is a storage room. Full of cans, bottles, and jars of everything Cordova girls dream of. Peanut butter, tuna, tomatoes, soup, juice, beer. She rapidly stuffs her knapsack. She hears scuffling above. A scream. A door slam. Are Modesta and Soraya outside laughing? She grabs cans and jars at random and fires them into her bag. When it's full, she pulls the drawstring at the top shut and turns to leave.

"Got everything you need?" says a deep voice behind her. She looks to where the voice is coming from. There's an old man, sitting on the floor in the storage room, his face covered in lesions. He is very thin. He sucks in a great wad of snot.

"I do," she says. "Yes."

She turns and runs.

He gets up, barrels after her.

She runs down the hall and up the stairs. At the top, the door is closed. What the hell? She turns the handle. It's locked. Crawling below her on the stairs, the old man grabs at her legs. She draws the pistol, levels it at him as best her shaking hands can manage. Kora really does not want to kill anyone. Especially not a sick old man.

"You steal from the dying. Is that the kind of honour you live by?" He grabs her ankle, and she slips. The gun goes off.

"Oh Mother. Modesta! Soraya!"

He lets go of her ankle, slips helplessly back down the stairs. Did she hit him?

"Are you okay?" she yells, stupidly, into the stairwell.

There is no answer.

She could go check on him, but she doesn't. She fires at the handle and the door pops open. She runs out, over the heap of decaying bodies, and into the sunlight. Modesta and Soraya are there on the back lawn, laughing their heads off.

"I think I might have killed an old man."

"If you did, you gave nature a hand," says Soraya, eyes bright with amusement.

"Don't laugh!"

"Come on, come on, let's go," says Modesta. They run through the burrs and brambles back the way they came.

"Why did you lock me down there with him?"

"We couldn't make your work too easy."

They jump in the truck with their loot, tear back across the city. Modesta and Soraya laugh and hoot. "Wooooooooooooooooo-hooooooooooooooo! Cordova School revolution!"

Kora's head is full of the repulsive, desperate old man. Is he still alive? He could have been her uncle Wai. And she did exactly what he accused her of. She stole from the dead and dying. And then she shot him. She thinks of her goat Delphine, bleeding to death in her rickety shed. She would give anything to have Delphine back, and to go back to the arms of her family before there was sweet goat blood on Charlotte's hands.

On the other side of the Eastern Night Market, a HöST Security hummer faces them at the solar stoplight. A jolt of fear runs through her, and her breath catches. *That's it,* she thinks. *We're done for.* But the light changes, and the hummer goes right on by. Kora breathes again. She wants to cry, unsure whether it's because of loss or guilt or fear or simple relief. She stares fiercely out the window of the truck.

GROOMED FOR TRAVEL

22

NODE: GRAIN IN BEARD
DAY: 9

I WHIZ THROUGH SPACE. MAMA GLORYBIND! I'M IN A TIME-BEFORE
wheelbarrow tearing along the ruined highway at such speed. I
never knew that working wheelbarrows still existed. The desert
rips by. Where are these horrible children taking me?

My mother double and I bred this strain of forget-me-do for
intense dreams. I tumble into one. I'm in a cavern deep below the
earth. The walls shimmer the beautiful pale green of rusted copper.
I recognize my sisters all around me. Caulis Entadae, Concha Arcae,
Flos Carthami, Gelsemii Elegantis, Lapis Chloriti, Stigma Croci,
Thallus Laminariae … My heart spills over with joy and relief. I
must free them! But their eyes are wide as river rocks, their pupils
so black and round I fear falling into each sister as I pass her. The
cavern is convoluted. We follow its curves. As we go deeper, I
hear the sisters fuss and mutter. What are they doing down there?
Where the line ends, there's a woman with a knife and a wooden
block. The knife falls and Sister Lapis Chloriti screams. My sisters
have lined up to have their right hands chopped off. Then I'm not
looking at them anymore. I'm next in line.

I'M AWAKE IN THE SOFTEST, CLEANEST BED IN A WHITEWASHED ROOM hung with colourful rugs. The rugs blossom knotted flowers beautiful as Our Mother could make them and then some. I remember these flowers. I'm at the New Origins Archive. This is the same room Elzbieta Kruk put me in when I came here last year with my mother double for my rite of spring. Pale sunlight pours in through the high windows, and outside birds sing brightly. Although I'm not sure why I do it, I check my hands to see if I still have both. Flex and stretch the fingers of each, marvelling at their wholeness.

Last thing I remember, I was in Peristrophe's waterproof tent with Calyx and those two nasty Salties. Someone was holding my nose, and someone—that traitor Calyx!—was pouring my own good tea down my very unwilling gullet. Mama Glory, I'm a prisoner! What will become of me now? *Courage, daughter,* I say to myself in her voice. *You've got to be strong.*

"Finally, you're awake!" Calyx beams brightly from a chair in the corner. How did she get in here? "They are preparing a gurney to take you across Cosmopolitan Earth country before the borders close. Thought you would sleep for days! The fourth wave of tiger flu is official in Saltwater City, and the CEC is closing borders to prevent infection in the plague rings. The world is upside down as a dead deer. We gotta go now if we want to get there at all. Isn't it exciting?"

"Not really," I say. Of all the sisters who could have survived, how did I get stuck with the annoying Calyx Kaki?

"The CEC is granting a last diplomatic passage because of me. Because we initiates used to cross their territory all the time, on our way to Mólkwcen Mountain for ice." She glows with foolish pride. "Can you walk?"

"Of course I can damn well walk!"

Save me, I say to myself in my mother double's voice.

"You should have a little respect," says Calyx Kaki, as she comes to the bedside to help me up. "The CEC is a nuclear power. They could blow us all to kingdom come anytime they want."

What's that, kingdom come? Where does Calyx get this language? I let her help me out of bed. My tunic has been washed and hangs over a rail at the foot. How long have I been here?

"Daydream later, Groom Kirilow," Calyx says. "Look, I repacked your sack for you. Nice and neat, and every item accounted for. See?" She holds the top open as though I could actually see what's at the bottom. "Cordova girls may be thieves, but they didn't rob you this time. They're gonna help us find our sisters. And that Salty too."

My body aches from lying down so long. I stretch and twist. Then I yank the bag away from her and dump it out, undoing all her careful work. Needles, womb bombs, knives, and food tumble to the bed. A spare tunic and summer shoes. The precious tent. Maybe these Salties are trustworthy after all.

"Come on, Groom Kirilow. Cosmopolitan Earth is closing its borders. We gotta go *now!*"

The door opens, and the high priestess of the New Origins Archive, Elzbieta Kruk stands there, pale and lovely as a spirit of the air. "I took the liberty of paying passage for you from the Third Quarantine Ring to the second. Because your mother double was my friend," she says.

"My mother double dead?"

"You don't know that, my young friend. Go and find her now. You can pay me back when we meet again."

"Do you know what happened to my sisters?"

"All I can tell you is that four days ago, many batterkites passed over the archive. I assume there was a major offensive through the quarantine rings by HöST, since they are the only ones this side of the Pacific Pond who have batterkites. But I don't know anything for sure. You should go now, while Cosmopolitan Earth is still feeling hospitable."

"Their only condition is that we wear these blindfolds," Calyx Kaki says, holding up two soft scarves, one dark green, the other dark blue. "Pretty, aren't they?"

"I won't be blindfolded."

"You gonna stay at the New Origins Archive then, and never see your sisters again? And never catch that Salty?"

I sigh.

"Come on, engine running and eth ain't cheap. We gotta go!"

"What about them, the Salties? How are they gonna drive blindfolded?"

"Tania is from the CEC. Prodigal daughter who ran away when the UMK took over. She goes back every year, though. She's got a good relationship with her aunt, who's still a general there. So got permission to drive eyes wide," says Calyx. "Isn't that right, High Priestess?"

Elzbieta nods sagely. "You are lucky to get passage. It is because of Calyx Kaki's ongoing relationship with the CEC, and because Tania is General Manuel's niece. The CEC is jealous of its secrets, especially since the UMK came in, but if you don't challenge its requirements, it won't hurt you. Just do as they ask, and you will be in Saltwater City by day's end. Go now, Groom Kirilow. Find Old Glorybind and avenge the attack on Grist Village, as both your mother double and your dead beloved would wish."

I glare at Calyx Kaki for having disclosed to Elzbieta way more than was necessary. I cram all my stuff haphazardly back into my knapsack and pull my hood over my head.

INSIDE THE WHEELBARROW, I CONTEMPLATE THE GREEN BLINDFOLD in my hands. Calyx has the blue one.

"You want more forget-me-do so you don't feel the temptation to look?" Myra asks.

"Don't you dare try to dose me again."

"Penalty for peeping is summary execution. Penalty for allowing you to peep is summary execution. They've got UMK soldiers on the border, and they don't mess around. Might be safer to take away the temptation."

"You will *not* groom me with my own teas."

"Then you will not peep, Groom Kirilow Groundsel," Myra retorts. "Anyway, we already did."

I don't like her. I put the blindfold on.

It is nearly impossible to sit still in the backseat of the wheelbarrow. I'd rather walk—at least then I'd be moving. I shake my leg, and shake it and shake it and shake it.

"Groom Kirilow, you have to keep still," Calyx whispers.

I try, but I can't. My head races with all the things I've seen and heard since the season when kernels plump: the Salty's hand falling to the ground after I severed it, Peristrophe's last look at me from the tiny buds of her new eyes, the great bonfire, the dark shapes of batterkites, sisters pulled up in a fraying womb bomb, Corydalis Ambigua with her litter of sister puppies, Billy's anxious eyes, the dark hole of his gun's mouth gaping at me, the feast of the turkey vultures at Pente. Grief and wonder and murder course through my veins. I half remember something else, but I don't know what it means: a long curving hallway, rock walls tinged with green, and sisters lined up for some awful fate. All the while, on the shadow-haunted cave wall of my mind, it rains and rains and rains. As it rains, I shake my leg.

"Maybe the tea?" says Calyx.

"No tea," I say.

The wheelbarrow hurtles through the blindfolded dark.

I'VE NEVER HEARD GUNSHOTS BEFORE. BUT WHEN I DO, I KNOW WHAT they are.

"Oh, Creator. No, no, no!" Tania. "Please no. Don't let it have started."

"What in Our Mother's holy name is going on?" I say.

They ignore me. I can hear the sweat flowing from their pores. More gunshots.

"Tania, what is it?" Myra asks.

"You know that in the first wave of tiger flu we were bequeathed a nuclear arsenal to steward," says Tania. "By stewards in the south who were dying in droves. We keep its operations top secret. For a long time, we held an important balance of power. And then the UMK moved in on us. Many of our people find this state of affairs unbearable—including me. But it keeps HöST out. It keeps Cosmopolitan Earth country safe from the denizens of the other quarantine rings. Madame never teach you?"

"There's a scale I'll get next year," says Myra, "if I bring in enough cans."

"I'm afraid something has happened, and we're being called on to use it."

Myra is quick. "HöST or the UMK could retaliate. And scorch the whole of Old Cascadia."

"Then it won't matter if we get through or not," Tania says.

"Or they could just waste the CEC."

"We've got to get through."

The wheelbarrow slows, and I hear its wheels grind in the dust.

The slowing must not be voluntary because I hear Tania and Myra chant softly: "Let us go, let us go."

"He's letting us go," Tania says. A pause. "No. He wants us to stop."

More gunshots. The wheelbarrow stops.

There is barking and wailing and a lot of confused and frightened chatter. I've had it with not knowing. I shove the blindfold up from my eyes to my forehead.

"Pull that down! Pull it down now!" Tania shouts.

I pull it down again. But I saw. A highway dense with wheelbarrows, hand carts, tractors, bicycles, tricycle-rickshaws. Animals too—dogs, horses, chickens, large cats, and creatures unknown. Many ragged walkers with nothing but the clothes on their backs. Some huddle in messy clusters. Some stand in anxious lineups leading nowhere. Some kneel by the side of the road, surrounded by armed soldiers in identical dark clothes. To their side lies a long row of corpses, knees bent, feet and hands tied, headfirst in the mud. One of them is still alive and upright. I know that person. That person is not my friend. I peek again.

Peristrophe's killer.

I hear the wheelbarrow's window roll down by some Salty magic.

"It's the dirty Salty!" I yell. "They have to let it go!"

"Shut up, shut up, shut up, you stupid, stupid Gristie!" screams Myra.

"What have we here?" says an unfamiliar voice, very deep. A soldier's voice, with a UMK accent.

"You have to let it go! Let it go, let it go!"

"Shut her up. Now!" Myra.

"Groom Kirilow, you have to be quiet," Tania says.

"It's that dirty Salty," I hiss. "The one that brought us the flu."

Tania says to the soldier, "I'm Tania Manuel, General Manuel's niece. We have dispensation to cross through the Second Quarantine Ring today. It was arranged through the New Origins Archive."

"I know the story of the prodigal niece," says the soldier. "And your passengers?"

"That's Calyx Kaki and her cousin. They come through here four times a year on their way to Mólkwcen for ice."

"I see. Did that one have her blindfold up?"

"No, ma'am."

"I thought I saw her raise it."

"She wouldn't do that, ma'am."

"I know I saw her hand there."

"Maybe she had an itch."

"The Salty. Let it go!" I wail.

"What's she talking about then?"

"Nothing. Nothing at all. She's had a hard week is all, and she's a little off her head."

"Stay here."

The morning rains come as we wait, battering down on the roof of the wheelbarrow from the time before. They make us wait a long time.

Tania says, "When they come back, Groom Kirilow, you have to be quiet, do you understand me? Quiet as the dead. Or we will all be joining them in the underworld. I have family here, so they are being generous, but there is nothing safe about this."

"The Salty," I whimper.

"What Salty are you talking about?" says Myra.

"The one who invaded our village. The one who brought the batterkites."

"Then why do you want them to let her go?"

"So I can kill it myself, you Mother-cursèd fool! After that, I don't care what you do with me. Shoot me yourself and leave me here on this mud-and-blood-drowned road for the turkey vultures to eat with all the other victims of HöST. I don't care."

"These aren't victims of HöST," Tania says. "They are victims of the UMK, as are all my people."

"I could give her the tea," says Calyx Kaki helpfully.

"Don't you dare, you traitorous little shit!" I growl.

The windows go down and there is more than one voice on the other side, urgent and volatile.

"Cousin Sloane," says Tania.

"Normally you'd be in the dirt. Do you not have a clue what times these are?!" says the soldier. "For all your betrayals, General Manuel doesn't want you harmed. The general must love you, or something like that. Who are these passengers?"

"A sister from Grist Village in the Fourth Quarantine Ring," Tania answers. "And her kin."

"Let the Salty—" I begin. Calyx slaps a hand over my mouth.

"Giving you trouble?"

"We can handle it."

"What did she see?"

"Please, cousin, she's the doctor my school desperately needs."

"Looks like a witch doctor to me," says Cousin Sloane. "Will she talk about what she saw?"

"She saw nothing."

"I know she looked."

"We have a tea to make her forget."

"A forgetting tea?"

"Yes, they cultivate it themselves. It's one of their main medicines."

"Huh," says Cousin Sloane. "Does it work?"

"It works, I promise."

"If it works, we could use some. What I wouldn't give to put a stop to these executions of innocent travellers. We're taking in as many refugees as we can, I want you to know that. But truly, what these UMK bastards call economic partnership I call occupation, and with this tiger flu crisis, they just want to shoot everyone. If we could promise them the people could pass through without remembering anything, we could save some lives."

"I'll have her send you a shipment, if you let us go."

"I want to see it administered."

I hear them come around to the back. When the doors open, the gush of rain gets louder. Before I know it, their wet, dirty hands are all over me. "Don't you dare, don't touch me, filthy Salties, dirty city creatures! Get off me!"

There are more gunshots.

Calyx says, "Our Mother's hooves. Your Salty, Groom Kiri."

"Someone killed it? Get your hands off me! Our Mother damn you to the darkest reaches—"

My nose is pinched shut. I'm gulping my own medicine. Curse them, curse them, Our Mother curse them all!

The last thing I hear before I'm out is Cousin Sloane. "Leave the flask with me."

CATCOAT

NODE: MINOR HEAT
DAY: 1

KORA CUTS HER HAIR SHORT, CHOOSES THE SPIKIEST SCALES FOR what they help her remember, sure, but also for how they look. She checks her appearance in the scarred ballroom mirrors. A series of short, sharp scales rings her cranium like a crown of horns. The long ones spiral down like snakes. Pale, wriggling lice move through the whole ensemble and make her scalp itch, but she tries not to think about them. She examines her gaunt face instead and the eyes that arc over cheekbones high like her mother's. The blue cotton dress she wears over torn Arm-a-Gideon fatigues is worn and dirty. She wears it because her father gave it to her. She's too thin, but everyone is these days. She looks terrifying enough to frighten any Saltwater denizen.

Kora's had enough. She's breaking out on her own. If there is more to learn, she'll get it outside.

In the closet of special items, which no one is to touch without Madame's express permission, hang four catcoats. Kora claims the newest one—the one with tortoiseshell fur. She steps into the feet: left, right. She pulls on the torso. She sticks her hands into the mitts that Madame has painstakingly pulled and pressed to fit human hands. She pulls the hood over her head. The thing yowls and protests the whole time. She strokes it to calm it—and to shut it up. Stupid thing. Doesn't it know they were made for each other? When she's got it zipped up, it stops its protest. It likes her body heat. It begins to purr.

Out into night she goes. She makes a beeline for the Woodward's Building.

En route sits the Pacific Pearl Parkade, home of the tiger men, infected flu survivors who compete with the Cordova girls for caches of buried cans from the time before. It looks abandoned, but Kora remembers the Interiors and Exteriors course that Madame Dearborn taught last week. She knows the parkade holds at least a hundred tiger men. One day, she will go inside, just to see what it's like.

She can hardly believe she's left the school. Her heart pounds, all hot blood and the thrill of defiance. Emotion must not make her clumsy. She slows her breathing to regain control. Pads softly down Powell Street, past the hungry homeless girl with her cart, past the N-lite junkies looking for other worlds in their minds. She passes a plague house where people have locked themselves in, hoping to keep the flu out. She shudders, thinking of the old man in that plague house beyond the Eastern Night Market three weeks ago. There is someone at the window. Does he see her? She rushes past and turns a corner.

She passes three women in expensive dresses. They have the relaxed faces of people who live in the glass towers of HöST, walled in by the great Isabelle Chow to keep dancing girls and their ilk out. Kora sees people like this from time to time, people who come to Saltwater Flats to do things they wouldn't be allowed to do in the glass towers. At first, Kora thinks these ones aren't like that, and then she looks at their eyes. Their irises are so weirdly green and their pupils so dilated it's like their eyes are eating the streets.

She passes a girl walking solo, in frayed Arm-a-Gideon pants. Kora can't see the girl's face because her head and torso are covered by a black cowlie. But she moves with an alert sense of purpose. Her head turns and her pale face shows. She looks right at the space where Kora is walking, but she doesn't see her.

Madame Dearborn's catcoat is working.

She hears the commotion before she sees it. She's coming over the rise just past the tiger men's parkade. There's a raucous cacophony of snarling and barking, the excited yips and the low, aggressive growls of a pack of wild dogs descending on their prey. A human being thrashes on the ground at the centre of their attention, hands over head, legs splayed and kicking. If she listens carefully, she can hear its high-pitched squeal riding over the growling and barking of the dogs.

She begins her anti-canine tango. Slips out of her catcoat, picks up a large stick from the organic and industrial debris that litters the ground, and lunges, hollering, into the fray. Although packs of dogs run wild through the city and wreak havoc among the cowardly, they are brazen only with the fearful. They aren't so unlike feral dancing girls. Kora swings her mighty stick—Left! Right! Crack! She whacks rumps, heads, backs, and legs as the wild dogs fly at her.

She doesn't see the sharp-toothed young one until it's already close to her right side. The dog catches the flesh of her hand, just below the baby finger. She hisses. Pain arcs through her hand and up her arm like a lightning bolt. She pulls away, but blood gushes from the puncture wounds deep in the flesh of both the top and palm of her hand. Kora howls with rage. Shoves the hurt hand firmly into her pocket to slow the bleeding, and kicks the offending canine square in the belly, sending it sailing skyward.

Now there are only two left, nipping at her legs. Stick in her one good furious hand, she pops the larger dog hard on the skull, and it collapses, whining. She raises her stick above the smaller dog. It yelps and tears off before the crack even lands.

The man on the ground is a gory mess, like something left over from a slaughterhouse. He reeks of blood, sweat, and urine, but nothing is broken. She helps him up. With her sleeve, she wipes the blood from his face. Imagine her shock. Her flea-bitten brother.

He looks her in the eye, and then runs in the direction of the Pacific Pearl Parkade. Although her bleeding hand screams in her pocket, she chases him. Picks up a rock with her good hand and hurls it. Hits him squarely in the back. He stumbles and falls.

It's easy to catch up with him now.

"You hit me!" He pulls himself upright. He's got a cut above his left eye and he favours his right leg, but he doesn't look seriously hurt.

"I didn't hit you hard. You were running."

"Not fast. Anyway, I don't owe you anything." He begins to walk away.

Kora follows. "I just saved your ass."

"You left us." Still heading, slowly, in the direction of the parkade.

"You all made me leave!" She hides her wistfulness beneath indignation, wishing she didn't care.

He stops and turns to look at her. "You could have fought for us harder. You knew we wouldn't survive without you."

"You look like you're doing all right."

He touches the cut above his eye. "Do I?"

"If it weren't for me, you'd be doing a lot worse."

"And if you hadn't happened to be walking by? Why am I even arguing? I don't need you." He turns and resumes his limping amble. "The tiger men count me as one of their own now. They've given me a home. I look after them, and they look after me."

"Tiger men? Bullshit!"

"Don't put them down, Kora. They are my home now."

She pauses. Looks him in the eye. "You're not living with Charlotte and Wai anymore?"

"No. I'm not."

"How could you leave? Who will take care of them?"

"What's it to you?"

"Let's go back to the apartment now and check on them. I'm quitting the Cordova School. I'll move back in."

He gives her a look, half-baleful, half-disdainful. "Don't go back, sis. There's no point."

She pulls him to sit beside her on an old crate beside a warehouse. Her injured hand is awkward and bleeding. She uses it as a weight to press her dress against her thigh, ignores the searing pain. With her good hand, she rips the corner of her blue dress and begins to clean then bind the bleeding bite on his arm. Rips off another piece and cleans his other bites and bruises as best she can.

He sighs. Tears off a piece of his own T-shirt and winds it around her injured hand.

"When did you see them last?"

"Two weeks ago."

"And?"

"They were fine. Go back to the Cordova School, Kora. It's what we all wanted for you. It's the best thing."

"I miss you, K2." Her hand throbs in its snug new wrapping.

"Our paths are separate now, Kora. Go home."

"That's what I want ..."

"To the Cordova School. Go."

"Let's go see them, one last time. Come on. Please."

His eyes dart to the side. He opens his mouth to say something more, then closes it.

"Just once, and then I'll leave you to your future."

He doesn't answer.

"Please, Godwin Austen."

He sighs deeply. "Okay, sis. All right. One last time."

They head back the way they came. The catcoat lies on the ground right where Kora left it, but she is so preoccupied with the thought of seeing her mother and uncle again, she forgets all about it.

NODE: GRAIN IN BEARD
DAY: 15

I WAKE UP IN A DANK AND FOUL-SMELLING BASEMENT. WHAT IS THIS, some twisted Salty prison?

"Welcome to the Cordova Dancing School for Girls, Doctor Groundsel." A tall woman about Glorybind's age stands at my bedside. Her face is wide and flat.

"Who by Our Mother's farts are you?"

"I'm Aurelia Dearborn. I've been running this clinic and wishing for the arrival of someone like you."

"I haven't arrived anywhere. I'm gonna catch that dead mother Salty, whip its hide, then take it home to serve New Grist Village."

"I hope the Cordova School will help you change your mind. You'll have your own beautiful quarters and this nice clean clinic. We're one of the last places in Saltwater City where the denizens eat well every day. The girls are admittedly a little unruly, especially Myra and Tania. But they are generous, in their way. You won't want for anything."

"No thank you. Need to catch that Salty and need to go home." I turn away from her and close my eyes. Everything is tidy in this dark room, but I wouldn't call it clean. It smells too much of damp earth and human habitation.

I hear the door open.

"Is she awake, Madame Dearborn?" I recognize that voice. "Good morning, Doctor Groundsel. You've been asleep for a few days. That is an excellent tea you and your sisters have cultivated."

I turn my head.

"I hear you're looking for a certain Salty." It's one of the Salties I saw in my forget-me dream. No, I saw this one when I was awake, with Elzbieta at the New Origins Archive.

"Yes. I want the one with the new right hand."

"I'm afraid we lost her, Doctor."

I remember this one. Her Salt Inglish is funny. I can barely understand her. "What's a doctor? Call me Groom Kirilow."

"You're in Saltwater City now, Doctor Groundsel. You probably don't remember, but I'm Myra. This is my teacher, Madame Dearborn. The Cordova Dancing School for Girls would like to invite you to live with us as our resident physician. You'll be paid. And you'll get a new family too, to replace the one you've lost."

"I don't want a new family. I want the Salty with the new right hand."

"I believe your Salty died en route, Doctor Groundsel," says Madame Dearborn. There's sadness in this woman.

"No. That Salty is alive. I saw it at the checkpoint." The one thing I do remember.

Myra says, "That 'Salty' was shot. I saw her shot with my own eyes. I'm sorry. And please watch your language. You can call us Cordova girls."

Our Mother curse the excellence of my own forgetting tea.

These damn Salties dosed me good. I saw that new-hand Salty, I know I did. These sneaky Cordova girls are lying to me.

NODE: SUMMER SOLSTICE
DAY: 2

THE CORDOVA SCHOOL LIES JUST INSIDE THE FIRST PLAGUE RING OF Saltwater City, among our ancestral enemies, the normals who drove our grandmothers out of the factories more than a hundred years ago. The girls who live here are a dirty, thuggish lot. They have open sores on their faces that they try to cover with a flesh-coloured liquid. It gives their skin a sticky, tacky look. They rim their eyes with charcoal pencils, which only accentuates the pus leaking from their tear ducts. Juicy, translucent lice play happy hopscotch in their matted hair. And infected metal threads drip off them like lace fungus from diseased trees. If these are Saltwater City's strongest and fittest, then this city is not long for this world. I'll free my sisters, get me a new starfish, and get out.

If my mother double, Glorybind Groundsel, were here with me, she would make me eat upstairs with them. But I looked in on them yesterday. They chew with their mouths open and throw food and insults at one another like the barbarians they are. Two larger ones had a smaller one on the floor and were pounding the moonlights out of her. Imagine directing violence like that towards one of your own! And for no reason that I could see. I'd prefer not to eat with them, though I would gladly isolate one or two of the more civilized ones to ask what they know about the Saltwater City Grist Commune, the invading Salty, and a particular batterkite full of Grist sisters.

I wish I had my mother double to explain things and smooth

the way for me. She spoke to me once about a thing called "social skills," but I didn't know what she was talking about. I'm starting to get it now. If no one comes to see me, eventually, I'll have to brave that dining hall. I don't want to.

Calyx Kaki seems to have no trouble. She eats up there every night. But she also has no wits and can't be trusted with important things. Every night, when she's done exercising her social skills, she brings me a plate. I find their food unappetizing. I miss the dark leafy greens and rabbit stews of home.

When she comes with my dinner tonight, she says, "They aren't so bad. They just don't have anyone to discipline them outside of one very tired old teacher."

I've been here for seven nights—three under the influence of my own good forget-me-do, four able to think but swimming in my own private lake of loss. Calyx starts to prod me. "Can't stay down here forever, Groom Kiri."

I poke at the evening's offerings. There's a slice of some large animal, roasted. Some kind of vegetable too, in the form of little greenish-grey balls. The seeds of something maybe. They've been cooked so soft that there can't be any goodness left in them. Surely Our Mother does not consider such things food. There's sweet potato—a root we used to grow back at Grist Village. Rather than roasting it, they've boiled and mashed it and mixed it with rancid cow milk fat, which smells disgusting.

"They call it butter," say Calyx. "It's kind of good once you get used to it."

I guess I have that disease that Mother Glorybind taught me was called "homesick." She says Grandma Chan Ling used to feel homesick for Saltwater City. I can't imagine such a thing. To miss this mouldy, flooded, ugly place, crawling with barbarians, completely uncivilized. Where girls beat each other to make friends and there is nothing good to eat.

"Just try."

I eat a bit of the sweet potato and some of the greyish-green balls.

"Have a bite of meat."

The meat is hard and tasteless. I long to see Peristrophe Halliana's smiling face across the table from me. I long for a plate of her steamed pike and pan-fried greens.

NODE: SUMMER SOLSTICE
DAY: 3

A SMALL ONE COMES TO SEE ME. MAYBE IT'S THE ONE I SAW THEM pounding in the dining hall the other night. She says she hurt herself in the forage dance. I don't believe her.

Myra and Tania brought many of the herbs and tinctures that Mother Glory and I used at Grist Village back from the New Origins Archive. Needles too. The storeroom is also stocked with Saltwater City medications, including drugs from the time before, all expertly foraged by the barbarian girls. I know about some of them because Mama Glory told me their names, effects, and limitations, though I've never actually seen them, much less used them.

I check the girl for concussion and broken bones. Make a panax poultice for her black eye. Pop a few needles into the anxiety points for good measure.

"Do you know anything about the Saltwater City Grist Commune?" I ask her when she's feeling a bit better.

"I'm sorry, Doctor. What's that?"

It was worth a try.

ONE OF THE OLDER ONES COMES TO SEE ME AFTER HAVING BEEN caught and beaten for stealing shoes from a warehouse just north of the Eastern Night Market.

"It was a fresh shipment from the UMK. We've foraged there before and made a killing in sales. Such beautiful shoes! Made of real calfskin leather. So worth the risk. I know the dangers, but it's how we live."

This one gave as good as she got. Her knuckles are a mess, and she's got a broken rib. But she's strong. She'll be fine in a few weeks. I bandage her hand, give her willow bark tea and half a cup of forget-me-do. The rib will have to heal on its own.

"Do you know anything about a batterkite from HöST raiding villages in the Fourth Plague Ring?"

"I heard that HöST has been doing raids all through the third and fourth rings. Looking for some kind of animal or plant they need for some kind of technology. I'm sorry I don't know more. I'm just an ignorant Cordova girl. Chang knows the answers to such questions maybe. But he is locked from us. And no memory scale gonna give you those kind of answers."

"Ever meet a Salty that looks like this?" I ask after I've poulticed her swollen eye.

I show her a drawing I made of the invading Salty. She examines it with her good eye.

"Yeah," she says. "I think maybe that girl used to live here."

"Our Mother bless you," I say, like an idiot.

"Can I have an ibupro?"

"What?"

"An advil. It was a painkiller in the time before. I heard you have some."

"That is not good for you, little sister. The people in the time before, they were smart but in a really stupid way."

"Please, Dr Gristie. I don't know what you're talking about, but the ibupro works."

I give her what she wants. I'm all agitated by the thought that the invading Salty might have lived at the Cordova School. Maybe I'll brave the dining hall tonight to see what more I can learn.

In the afternoon, Madame Dearborn steps into the clinic. "I hear you've been doing a great job helping the girls."

"I have much to learn about Saltwater City healing techniques," I say. Mother Glory taught me to be modest.

"And I hear you've been asking questions."

"Yes. I'm looking for my mother double. And an ugly red-haired Salty who invaded our village," I blurt. Was that rude? I register Madame Dearborn's red hair streaked with white only now that the words have left my mouth.

"You must stop asking these questions if you want to continue working here," says Madame.

"Oh." More than rude, I've been naive.

"I'm not being inhospitable. It's for your own good."

"I have to find my mother double. I need that Salty, or my sisters will die."

"Then you have a hard choice to make, Doctor Groundsel. We cannot help you with those questions here."

THE RETURN HOME

25

KORA KO // SALTWATER FLATS

NODE: MINOR HEAT
DAY: 1

KORA AND K2 MAKE IT TO THE IRON GATES OF THE WOODWARD'S
Building. Kora punches in the ancient entry code, and the gates
buzz open.

"Did you know that we were the last family living here?" K2 says.

"Of course we weren't. There were the Singhs on the thirty-second
floor. And the Carters on the eighth."

"Carters moved to the Second Quarantine Ring. The Singhs
all died of the flu. We were so preoccupied with our lives we didn't
even notice."

The foyer is dark, except for the elevator area, which is lit with
expensive tungsten bulbs, the kind you can only buy in the Coast
Salish Timeplace. The elevators are new. That's strange. And there's
an odd smell in the air, like rotten fish. Kora presses the shiny new
button. Bright steel doors open, and they step in. The fish smell
intensifies. Are those fish bones on the floor?

They stop at the fortieth floor. Walk down the long dark hallway
to the apartment where the Ko family has lived for three generations.

A scale in her wrist lets them in. She calls for Charlotte. She
calls for Wai. "You won't believe where I found K2!"

The apartment is dark and quiet. Wings flap above her head. A pigeon. How did that get in?

"Charlotte! Uncle Wai!"

Still no answer.

K2 has gone all silent and docile. She takes his arm, sensing that he might run. Touches a light pad, but no light comes on. Why hasn't Charlotte been tending the solar panels? The flicker of unease she's been feeling intensifies to a churning fear.

She pulls K2 up the stairs one flight to the bedrooms. She goes to Charlotte's room first. The bed is neatly made. There is no dress hanging over the chair. A layer of dust lies over the vanity, but it is otherwise tidy. Too tidy.

She goes to her uncle Wai's room. The bed there is perfectly made too. There is no jacket hanging on the hook beside the door. She opens his closet. Inside hang his three shirts, all clean, though a little dusty. As in Charlotte's room, a thin layer of dust covers everything.

She goes to her own room. Her toy owls are lined neatly in a row on their shelf. Her bed is made. Her collection of scavenged machine parts, gathered for their beauty and strangeness, not for any use, are also laid out more neatly than she ever would have laid them.

She checks K2's room. It is similarly well ordered. He follows her, uncharacteristically quiet.

She ascends the steps to the rooftop garden. The stairs are dark and she doesn't see her uncle's boots placed tidily at the top step until she trips over them and has to catch herself with her bloody right hand. If he's not wearing his boots, he can't be up here working. She pushes open the hatch. Everything is there: the half-collapsed goat shed, its bloodstained floor, the jars of depleted earth, the raised beds, and the rain barrels. The garden is unusually neat. But nothing is growing. All the cabbages and carrots have been harvested. She stares for a long moment.

"Do you think they moved?" she asks her brother, stupidly.

"I don't think so, sis."

"Were they abducted?"

He says nothing, but his pupils shrink.

"What happened to them, K2?"

He gazes at her, a long gaze full of grief. He opens his mouth. Closes it. Turns and runs down the stairs with only the slightest limp.

"Where are you going?" She tears after him, through the apartment and out the door. His legs are much longer than hers, and he is down the hallway and in the elevator before she's even halfway there.

She doesn't pursue. She returns to the roof. Minutes later, she sees him run across the courtyard below and out the iron gates. She watches the tiny figure run down Hastings Street until it disappears into a covered alley.

She sits down on her uncle's resting bench and stays there for a long time.

Under the cool and mournful light of Eng, she smooths the already smooth dirt of the raised beds. Chang rises and turns the grey light gold. She puts her uncle's boots in one of the potato jars and covers them with depleted earth, though it's hard to shovel with her bitten, throbbing hand. She ought to pray, or chant, but she doesn't know any prayers or chants. She doesn't worship Our Mother, as Charlotte did. Does.

She sits with the dirt and watches Chang rise and set four times. The sky grows light, and Eng too disappears over the horizon. No amount of sitting is going to bring them back. The stuck stone feeling she's had since she left them intensifies.

She goes down to the kitchen for a glass of water. There's a thin film over the water in the barrel and some kind of bug swims in it. On the counter glints an open scale—the old-fashioned, non-implantable kind. It looks like a large fish scale. What's this doing here? She picks it up and puts it in her pocket. She casts a final lonely glance at the stairs leading to the rooftop garden. Above the stove, Charlotte's figure of Our Mother gazes at Kora without judgment. Kora clicks the door shut behind her and heads back towards the Cordova Dancing School for Girls. She has nowhere else to call home.

It's then that she remembers the catcoat, dropped by the roadside hours ago so she could rescue her spoiled brother. She hurries back to the spot. There is no sign of the catcoat anywhere. Madame's going to be killing mad. And the Cordova girls will have a field day.

26

MADAME DEARBORN'S KITTENS

NODE: SUMMER SOLSTICE
DAY: 9

I WAKE EARLY, WIRED. THE DANCING GIRLS HAVE BEEN OUT ALL NIGHT, thieving and mugging. The whole building seems to slumber. Perhaps Our Mother woke me so I can leave my clinic to go greet Chang and Eng. I slip out and find the stairs to the roof.

The whole city lies at my feet. The sky is hazy, but I can still see the Pacific Pond stretching to the west and the endless crumbling suburbs and low mountains to the east. All the houses on the North Shore are dark. Silhouetted against them stands what must be the collapsing ruin of the old sulphur refinery my mother double once told me about. Although the polluted air smells foul and rotten, there's a damp sweetness beneath it, the rich undercurrent of life trying to fight its way through all the nightmares laid over the land in the time before. Several sturdy gulls careen overhead. Like these dancing girls, they are good scavengers. And above them, distant Eng looks down benevolently, casting her blessings on me. It's the first time I've stood alone in her pale light, without Glorybind and Peristrophe beside me. I raise my arms to better absorb her grace.

Chang rumbles up over the horizon and begins his rapid path

across the sky, large and ungainly. The sky changes colour from pale blue to orange-grey. The gulls scream away from Chang's shadow.

"Dr Groundsel, you have to come to the lab." It's Tania.

"What lab?"

"Madame Dearborn's lab. Where she makes the catcoats. Bring your bag—and hurry."

The lab is at the other end of the basement. In all these days, I've hardly left the clinic. I've been too afraid of what I might see.

Tania takes me to where Madame Dearborn lies on the floor. Around her swarm more than thirty kittens, all emaciated and mewling. She's covered in blood and scratches.

I kneel beside her, draw a clean cloth out of my bag, and begin wiping away blood so I can see what's going on underneath.

One of the kittens leaps at my face. Makes a flying swipe at my eye. I swerve away. It misses and tumbles to the floor.

Tania picks it up, and it begins to mewl mournfully.

"She was rushing, trying to make catcoats for all of us. She's bred too many in too few generations. Their genes are not as refined as they should be," says Tania.

The kittens yowl, dismayed at the violence they've wreaked upon their beloved caretaker and tormenter.

"What happened?" I ask.

"They attacked me," whispers Madame.

She's covered in gashes—deep ones. These kittens she's breeding have inordinately long claws. She will need a lot of stitches.

"Help me get her to the clinic. The wounds need to be cleaned well before I can stitch her up. I'm glad you brought back lots of moonshine from the NOA," I tell Tania.

Calyx comes to see what's going on, and the three of us gently carry Madame to the clinic. As we leave, the kittens slink around us, yawping their sorrow and confusion. We kick them away and close the lab door on them.

I send Calyx to brew herbs for pain.

"There's morphine," says Tania.

"What's that?"

"Strong painkiller from the time before, works great."

"You can just inject me with it," says Madame. "You're good with needles, aren't you?"

Through her pain, she explains how to measure it, and I administer a Saltwater City drug by needle for the first time. I clean her wounds thoroughly with mother moonshine, even though there's also something they call "disinfecting alcohol."

She's so badly gashed, it takes more than an hour to stitch her up. Although her cats knocked her over, no bones are broken. But there is a danger of infection. I'll keep her down here and keep brewing cicada molt. I'll dose her until the danger passes.

Myra and Tania come downstairs every few hours to ask how she is doing. However wild and vicious these girls are, they care about their old teacher.

NODE: SUMMER SOLSTICE
DAY: 9

I'M DREAMING OF A VILLAGE IN THE MOUNTAINS WHEN THERE'S AN urgent knock at my door.

"Dr Groundsel! Wake up, hurry!" Tania's voice.

I drag myself out of bed, pull on my old, soft spider-thread tunic.

"It's Madame. She's taken a turn for the worse."

Her favourite girls are gathered around her as she lies, breathing roughly on her bloody sheets. The candles they've lit cast a pale yellow light over her sharp face. Her neck looks swollen. I press my hand against it. It's hot. Her forehead too is warmer than it should be.

"She can't see," Tania says. "Her vision is blurred."

"Is that right, Madame?"

"My head hurts," she says.

She looks old and frail. The hair that was bright red yesterday has gone ashy.

"The brain can swell," I tell her. "It's rare, but you were scratched very badly. I could cut? I'm a good surgeon."

"I know what you want to know, Doctor Groundsel."

"She knows, but she'll never tell," says Tania, moving loyally to Madame's bedside.

"Never," says Myra. "Don't you dare ask."

I prepare morphine as Madame taught me, find a place in her leg that can bear a needle, and inject her.

"I'll tell you, but you must promise to keep it secret."

"I have no one to tell." Of all the times to get what I want.

"Let her save you, honoured teacher. You can tell her then."

Madame speaks slowly through her pain. "You've landed right at ground zero of the Grist Commune."

"I don't understand. There are no Grist sisters here."

"The Cordova School was the Grist Commune. It's where Grandma Wun Ling came after the purge, and after her sister, Chan Ling, fled with many others to the quarantine rings. The school was a cover for it, so we could hide and survive. As our numbers dwindled, we brought in orphans so we could pass our history and survival techniques on to them. But it was to no avail. We lost our last doubler three years ago."

"I don't believe you." I begin to shave away the ashy red curls.

"Please, Madame," says Myra.

"The girl who came to look for you was our last starfish."

"Enough, dearest Madame. You must stop." Tania. "Just let the doctor fix you. You can tell her whatever you want later."

"It can't be so," I say. But my heart knows it's true.

Madame Dearborn says, "Why would I lie to you? I am the Grist Commune's last groom."

"Not possible," I breathe. I know I should stop her from talking if she's to make it.

"When I die, the Saltwater Grist Commune will be over. That's why Carmela Sweetwater came to look for you. I advised her not to. We needed her starfish abilities, and Myra and Tania were already looking for the mythic Grist Village. But she was stubborn, said only she knew where to look. She was a half sister, descended from Wun Ling through her mother's line. She found you, though she paid with her life." Her eyes brim with tears.

"But my sisters ..."

"Miss Sweetwater got there before any army, and she lost her hand to you. We heard you were attacked, though we don't know by whom. Most likely Isabelle Chow and the HöST army. I sent Myra and Tania to look for remnants. That's you and your sister Calyx Kaki. I'm so grateful you are with us. It means my dearest Carmela Sweetwater did not die in vain. Please look after the girls when I am gone. They are not Grist sisters, but they carry all the knowledge we were able to leave."

"Now you believe that she's dead?" says Myra.

I nod. "Is Isabelle trying to complete the extermination her grandfather began?"

Madame's voice is growing weaker, but she insists on telling her story. "Isabelle Chow has created a new technology said to cure the mind of the body. But to us Grist sisters, it is simply a death machine. It imagines the mind can be separated from the body. We don't believe that. And it needs Grist sister DNA to feel real. It is why the Saltwater Grist was destroyed—through her relentless kidnappings and experiments. Before she murders you, she'll extract your cultivation techniques for forget-me-do so she can make more and better N-lite. You are in grave danger."

My head reels with the twistedness of it all. Isabelle Chow is responsible for the attack on Grist Village. And indirectly for that Salty—Miss Carmela Sweetwater—coming to warn us, and bringing the flu that killed my Peristrophe Halliana. There are different kinds of Salties, with different interests. Will Our Mother's wonders never cease? I flush red and hot as my old rage seeks a new target.

"So I'm not here by coincidence."

"No, Groom Kirilow. You are here because I asked Myra and Tania to dance the connections dance. As they are also doing for the purveyors of tiger wine. You see why I love my girls, even though they are so far from perfect."

She sighs deeply. She closes her eyes and doesn't open them again.

I begin to prepare my scalpels.

"Dearest teacher," Tania breathes.

"Don't leave us," Myra whispers, choking in terror and sorrow.

"My best girls," Madame says, so softly we can hardly hear. "Look after them, Doctor."

Her breathing grows softer.

I look to Myra. "Should I cut? The morphine is affecting her lungs."

"It's not the morphine," Myra says, her eyes brimming.

"Dearest Madame ..." says Tania.

And like that, she is gone.

CASCADIA YEAR: 127 TAO (TIME AFTER OIL)

UNITED MIDDLE KINGDOM CYCLE 80, YEAR 42 (WOOD SNAKE YEAR)

GREGORIAN YEAR: 2145

NODE: MINOR HEAT
DAY: 1

THE CORDOVA DANCING SCHOOL FOR GIRLS IS THE LAST PLACE KORA WANTS to go, but she has nowhere else now. Her heart is so full of dread and mourning, she thinks it might burst. But she still doesn't cry. Why would her family leave her without a sign of any kind? What does K2 know that she doesn't? She scuttles along the broken sidewalk, past two locked plague houses, a lady with a dog, six shivering girls huddled together, a side street crowded with N-lite junkies, and the long row of scale workshops that both manufacture and implant any kind of scale you want for the price you can pay.

Dark clouds are gathering for the evening rain, but she's almost there. She wedges her hands into her pockets. The uninjured one finds the open scale she picked up from the kitchen counter.

She turns it on, and a vision rushes up into the space before her eyes, fiery orange and red.

Deep Scale Commune
Pacific Pearl Parkade
Gallbladder Hour

2nd Day, Minor Heat
Wood Snake Year 2145

Two squelchy oblong figures with dangling tentacles, not unlike the squid she saw in her dream, pulse through the flashing letters. Gold and yellow flames chase and lick at them. The flames burn bright as real flames, though they shed no heat.

Her heart fills with curiosity. Why would K2 invite her to the tiger parkade? She stares at the flickering projection, lost in thought.

She's so mesmerized that she doesn't see or hear the procession coming up the street until it's right there. Who are these sorry, wailing people, all dressed in grey? Through the flicker of the invitation she realizes it's the girls of the Cordova School. They bawl and howl, some of them sincerely, others in ritual tones. Many of them have instruments—drums, kazoos, rattles, and horns—that they blow, bang, or shake in a deafening frenzy. Myra marches at the head of the parade, turning an airy grey pennant in a figure eight so that the fabric undulates above the motley crowd like the tail of a sorrowful dragon.

Velma is at her arm. "Come on, Lady Kora! Don't stand there like an idiot. Madame Dearborn is dead. We are marching her to the crematorium. What's that?"

Modesta is beside her. "Yeah, what's that, Lady Kora?"

Kora shuts the scale off fast. "Nothing."

"Doesn't look like nothing. Looks like a fancy scale vision," Modesta says.

"Leave her alone, Modesta," Velma says. "Obviously, it's private."

"Give it here," Modesta says. "Myra will want to know about it."

Kora closes her fingers tightly around her brother's gift.

"Come on, hand it over." Modesta lunges at her.

Kora steps back, then quickly forward, takes a swing at Modesta's face with her already closed fist.

"No point getting all belligerent." Modesta comes again.

Kora dodges to the left, and her bloody right hand comes up and out of her other pocket and flies at Modesta's chin before she even thinks of it.

Modesta ducks, and Kora misses.

"Stop that, Lady Kora! It's not a day for fighting. Madame Dearborn is dead," says Velma.

Modesta laughs. "What is it, Kora? Love letter from a tiger man?"

"Shut up," Kora says, mean as she can muster. Her injured hand throbs inside its wrapping, indignant at being put to work so soon. "It's just something from my brother."

"Ooooh, family girl, is it?" Modesta's hand darts out to grab Kora's wrist.

Kora swerves out of the way. The last man in Modesta's family, a distant cousin, died last year. Kora contemplates *At least I have a family* as a retort, but this has become only dubiously true. "None of your business," she says, too softly.

It's a stalemate in the battle of psychic pain.

"Feast night tonight," Modesta says, as the first drops of rain begin to fall. "To mark a death that might mean the end of us all." She leans back against a solar lamppost, no longer interested in punching Kora. "Me, Tania, Soraya, and Myra got real meatballs. And chocolate."

Cocoa beans have been extinct for eighty years, wiped out in a single cocoa plague. Jemini has been promising for more than a year to bring them back, but they're holding off to increase their value. If you're really rich, you can buy chocolate from Gupta-Anderson, the only supermarket chain to stockpile it en masse before news of the extinction spread.

"We did it with only three catcoats to share among four of us," Modesta says, almost a dare. "Someone stole the new tortoiseshell one that Madame Dearborn made before she died. Her last catcoat."

Kora takes a sharp inhale, then immediately tries to disguise it as a cough.

"You wouldn't happen to know anything about it, I don't suppose?"

"No," says Kora, "Did Madame Dearborn successfully make another one? I heard it was in the works, but ..."

"We'll catch you out one day, Miss Sly. Everyone already knows what a traitor you are."

"Oh, you mean frame me," Kora snarls back. She's getting better at holding her own.

Modesta says, "What happened to your hand anyhow?"

The bandaged right hand throbs harder, as though in response to the question. Kora sticks it back in her pocket. "Know how much info you have rights to? Exactly none, Tin-Can Stan! Zip, zero, zilch. Because you have no family, and no one cares about you."

"It'll all come out, Our Lady of the Flu. Then we'll see how tough you are."

They have to run to catch up with the procession. Once they're at the Buddhist church turned crematorium, it's a long wait behind thirty other families bringing their loved ones dead of the flu to the nuns who run the operation. The air smells of smoke and incense, with an undercurrent porky odour of charred human flesh. Chang rises for the ninth time today when they give the makeshift coffin to two sturdy sisters in saffron robes. The nuns place the coffin on a dais, and the girls line up before it to kiss Madame one last time and say their farewells.

Myra's face as she approaches her beloved teacher is grim and pinched with grief. Tania's eyes stream with tears. When it's Kora's turn, she gazes for a long time at the closed eyes of the old woman kind enough to take her in. "I'm all kinds of asshole," she tells the dead lady. "I'm sorry. I'll try to do better." She leans forward and presses her lips to Madame's gashed, cold cheek.

The nuns make them step over a bowl of water on their way out, to be cleansed of the bad luck. Outside, the line of sad families with their cargo of the dead is even longer. The nuns will be working all night.

The girls get back to the Cordova School just as it begins to rain. The ones whose turn it is to serve lay spaghetti and meatballs out on large platters.

Myra rises. "No one touches the food until speeches are said."

Too late. The girls are ravenous, already stuffing their faces.

Tania gets up. "Did you not hear our new leader speak? Dear ones, we must not descend into chaos! If we are to survive the changes that are coming faster and faster every day, we must maintain discipline!"

The girls don't stop gobbling, though a few slow their pace. A large cockroach scuttles over the head table.

Myra stands. "The food you are enjoying was obtained by Tania, Modesta, Soraya, and myself, with the use of only three catcoats. We have a fourth—Madame Dearborn's last catcoat. But it has gone missing. Tomorrow, we will have a group assembly until someone fesses up. Whoever does not come will be suspect and subject to beating. Times now are not what they were. We can't afford to be soft. May Madame rest in peace."

Kora can hardly eat. Although the meatballs are delicious, her throat refuses to swallow.

Her neighbour, a sickly thing called Amanda, leans over and whispers, "Tiger party tonight at the Pacific Pearl Parkade. Modesta's intel. You coming?"

Kora's stomach turns over. She swallows the acidic, half-digested spaghetti and tries to look calm. As though with a mind of its own, her injured hand begins to pulse with a strange new pain.

"Something's wet," Velma says. She looks down at Kora's hand, resting on the bench beside her. "Lady Kora, you're bleeding bad."

Kora lifts her hand and examines it. The old stains of the bandage are soaked through with bright new blood.

Velma says, "Did you know the Cordova School has its very own doctor? She can help you."

Kora's been ignoring her screaming hand, but now that Velma has pointed out all the blood, it really hurts. She allows the young girl to lead her to the basement, where the Cordova Dancing School for Girls houses its clinic.

GIRL WITH AN INJURED HAND

28

NODE: MINOR HEAT
DAY: 1

GRIM WITH GRIEF AT THE SUDDEN GAIN AND LOSS OF ANOTHER GRIST sisterhood, Calyx and I fit together a medicine cabinet we've cut and jointed from salvaged boards the Cordova girls brought us. Madame's revelation and her sudden death three days ago have made my homesickness worse. And my chance of finding another starfish has just dropped. But I can't leave without one. Until that fine day, we must make this alien place as much like home as possible.

A young student with sad eyes and a snotty nose brings in a girl with an injured hand.

"She got attacked by feral dogs," the young one says. "She got bit."

She takes her older companion's hand and holds it out for me to see. The hand is wrapped in a dirty scrap of T-shirt. Fresh blood seeps into old, crusty bloodstains.

Thin as a winter rabbit and pale as fog, the girl seems barely there at all. The smeared remains of charcoal pencil applied around her eyes only add to her haunted look. Her eyes dart back and forth. Her hair's been cut short—a feeble attempt to stop lice. A tangled mass of scales falls thickly around her. They aren't very clean. Large black insects scuttle through them. I don't want to imagine the condition of her brain with all these dirty twigs plugged into it.

"Lie here," I say, patting the examination table that Calyx Kaki and I built a couple of days after I woke from my forget-me fog.

The girl lies down, and I think I see a resemblance. The high forehead, the curve of jawbone. She looks a little like a Grist sister. My heart leaps.

"Are you going to help her or what?" growls her small friend, surprisingly fierce. Her breath reeks of old cabbage.

I unwrap the hand. The wet stench of pus fills the air. I hold my sleeve to my nose. The wound at the side of her hand pulses scabby and purple-black. Dirty, ragged skin and torn flesh hang off it. There are multiple puncture wounds, four of them deep. From one of them, blood spurts in intermittent red globules.

At the sight of her injured hand, the girl grits her teeth like she's going to cry. But she doesn't. I'm impressed. It's a nasty wound, and it must hurt like a knifed rabbit.

"Not sore?" I say.

She nods. A single tear falls now, and she sucks a great wad of snot back into her nose.

"How long ago did this happen?" I ask.

The short one shrugs. "I don't know, ma'am. Lady Kora came back like this. She's new, and she runs a bit wild."

"Don't you all?" I blurt.

The short one gives me a hurt look.

"This morning," says Lady Kora.

I flush the wound with water and wipe it down with a few drops of mother moonshine.

The girl's eyes bug wide. I give her a precious two shots to drink.

"Any other symptoms?" I ask.

"She was a bit nauseous at dinner," says Shortie. "Can you help her? Her hand's gonna be okay, isn't it? She's the one with the touch, you know, for locks and stuff."

"I'm going to give you something to make you a bit sleepy," I tell the girl.

Shortie says, "Do you have any vaccine for tetanus? And maybe rabies?"

I pause to remember what these are. Tetanus is lockjaw. Rabies is bat-bite sickness. I ask Calyx to make a decoction of cicada powder, scorpion powder, heart-of-earth, skullcap, woad, tree peony, and coin grass to clear heat, cool the blood, and expel wind-phlegm. There are small amounts of all these herbs in the meagre supply we brought from Old Grist Village, already steamed and powdered. I don't know how I'll get more when they run out.

Shortie says, "No vaccine? Madame hoped you might have brought some of those things with you. She said you like needles."

"My people don't dance, scavenge, or steal," I tell her. "We also don't use poisonous medicines from the time before."

That hurt look again.

"I'm sorry, I'm sorry." Our Mother of goats and atonement, without Peristrophe Halliana at my side, I'm all foot in mouth. "The wound is very dirty. Whoever bandaged it didn't clean it first. I don't know how your friend is going to fare."

Calyx brings the bitter drink, and I make the girl swallow it.

One puncture wound won't stop bleeding. I'll need to suture it. I begin to prepare a needle of precious poppy.

"No sleepy stuff," the girl says, pulling her arm away. "I need to work tonight."

"Doesn't your hand hurt?"

The short one laughs. "Work schmerk! She wants to go to a party, don't you, Lady Kora? She's in love with a tiger man!"

The injured girl hisses at her.

"Love is a drug," I say. I pop a needle into her arm before she even guesses I might do it.

She opens her mouth to scream bloody murder, but her eyelids droop, and in another second, she is asleep.

"Show's over," I tell Shortie, and urge her out the door. "I'll send word when she's ready for visitors."

The little one looks reluctant to leave, but when I pull out my suturing needles, she goes.

Calyx swabs at fresh blood welling from the puncture site, while I sew the hand up quickly. The wound isn't such a big deal. It's infection that concerns me.

Sure enough, when I go back to check my work a couple of hours later, I notice the flesh of the hand turning red in a disconcerting way. Some of the fingers are brown, and the thumb is turning black at the tip. I press it and the flesh crackles slightly. Not rabies after all. Wet gangrene. The girl is fast asleep.

I leave her for an hour. When I check again, there are blood blisters all over the hand. It could get better, but it's not likely. A wicked thought crosses my mind. What if she is like the Salty that came through our woods? What if she is like Madame's lost Carmela Sweetwater? Her hair is black like that of the Fourth Plague Ring Grist sisters, not red like the Cordova School ones. More than any other Salty I've met so far, she looks like she might be related to us. In any case, I have a duty to stop the gangrene from eating up more than the hand.

I take a tea break to consider the right course of action. Sip a little cerebral tonic in hot water, as my mother double used to do when facing a crossroad.

When I come back the girl is dopey but awake. "What are you doing, Gristie doctor?"

"Are you going to hurt me?" she groans, her voice sleepy and low.

I begin to sharpen my bone saw.

"No, no, no! Charlotte! Uncle Wai!" She croaks the words out, throaty and creepy.

I don't want to be alone with her. I give her a double shot of precious poppy and more needles into the meridian of calm.

"Delphine," she moans before she drops back into sleep.

I heat a large flat knife until the metal glows red. I prepare a cup of forget-me-do for her to drink as soon as she wakes.

My sharp saw cuts through flesh and bone as through water. Blood spurts in purple gouts. With the hot flat knife, I cauterize the wound. Then I bandage it and leave the girl to sleep.

Any amputation is a big deal. My Peristrophe Halliana died of one—well, that plus tiger flu. I carry the girl to the small convalescing room that Calyx Kaki decorated with images of Our Mother in all her forms—human, animal, and vegetable. At the head of the bed she's also placed a large watercolour of Eng. I put the cup of forget-me-do on the night table.

Then, exhausted, I retire to the small but private living quarters at the back of the clinic, which Madame so generously had a few of the girls set up for me and Calyx Kaki.

I try to sleep, but sleep won't come. My head runs with memories of the eye surgery that was Peristrophe Halliana's last, visions of Grist Village on fire, and the nightmare of enmeshed sisters swallowed by HöST's batterkite. When I can't stand it anymore, I push the blankets aside, drop my feet to the floor, and tiptoe out the back door, down the hall, up the back stairs, and out into the night.

POTATO DREAMS 29

NODE: MINOR HEAT
DAY: 2

KORA DREAMS OF POTATOES. SHE SPILLS THEM FROM AN EARTHENWARE jar, and they tumble from its lip, round and juicy, along with a flow of earth that smells sweet as clean rain. With her right hand, she picks up a particularly plump one, and with her left, begins to brush the dirt from it. The dirt feels moist, and its particles vibrate with subtle life. The surface of the potato glows smooth and healthy. It is a pleasure to touch it, even after all the dirt has been brushed off. She strokes its velvety surface as though it were a live animal, tender and quivering. She thinks she hears it release a faint mewl. Its very softness makes her fingertips itch, just slightly at first, then more intensely. She strokes the potato harder, seeks a rough spot on which to scratch, but the skin is smooth, so smooth. The itch spreads down her fingers to her palm. She rubs her palm against the potato, but its shiny surface offers no relief. She grasps it with her itchy right hand and squeezes this lovely fruit of the earth until its skin breaks and the white flesh is crushed to a pulp. Potato juice drips between her fingers, but still, the hand itches to the point of pain.

Her eyes blink open then, and she realizes she has been

dreaming. The hand continues to itch like a demon. What drug did that strange doctor give her? Her left hand is so heavy it takes all the will and strength she's got to move it to the right side of her body to scratch the itchy hand. When her left hand arrives at the right, the right is not there. Heavy with sleep, she fumbles. Is she still dreaming? Wake up, Kora! She pinches the arm above the absent hand. The pinch hurts. She feels again for the hand. Still not there. Sleep more, Kora, it's a bad dream. When the drug wears off, you'll find your hand again—bitten and infected, to be sure, but well on its way to healing. She closes her eyes and dozes.

The hand begins to itch again, just a little, but then it offers up a screaming, searing itch, as though it is on fire, as though it is dry wood, crackling and sparking in a mid-autumn bonfire. She sits up, pulls her hand from beneath the covers.

She looks at it.

It is not there.

A scream erupts from deep in her lungs and pours out of her. She screams and screams and can't stop screaming.

At Kora's bedside, Tania slaps her palm over Kora's mouth. "Shhhhhhh! You'll wake the whole school."

Velma's there too.

Kora shakes and drools and points with her one existing hand to the place where her absent hand should be.

"The doctor took her hand," Velma tells Tania. "There was gangrene."

"Took her hand!" Tania stares incredulous at the absence. "I've heard that Grist sisters do that. I didn't think it was true. How barbaric! I wonder if the doc—"

"Don't be foolish," Velma says. "There's no such thing as Grist sisters. That's an old wives' tale. It was gangrene, that's all. The doctor saved her life."

"Of course there is," Tania says. "Madame—" She stops herself. She and Myra are the only ones who know the truth about Madame Dearborn, Miss Sweetwater, and the burnt village in the Fourth Quarantine Ring. Madame had said there was no need for the young ones to know.

Kora is sobbing now.

"Don't cry, Lady Kora. You don't want Myra to catch you like this, do you? We're going to a party. Why don't you come? You'll forget all about your silly hand."

"She's not going to forget," Tania says. "Would you forget, Velma, if someone took your hand?"

Kora still sobs. Tries unsuccessfully to bite the palm still clapped firmly over her mouth.

Tania says, "Look, you have to calm down, Kora. If I let go of your lip, will you promise to stay quiet?"

Kora nods.

But even though she doesn't want it to, when Tania takes her hand away, the scream keeps coming.

Tania claps her hand over Kora's mouth again. "Where is that good-for-nothing doctor anyhow? This girl needs a sedative."

"Lady Kora wants to come to the party, don't you, Lady Kora?" Velma persists. "It was her invite to begin with, not Modesta's. She's in love with a tiger man."

"Don't talk nonsense," says Tania. "How would she get an invite? Kora Ko is getting good at some things, but she's no diplomat."

"Maybe she's good at more than you think," Velma says. "It was her invitation." She nods her head up and down, as though insistent affirmation will make it so. "Lady Kora, don't you want to come to your party? And see your tiger man?"

Kora opens her throat, makes a rasping affirmative sound.

Tania removes her hand from Kora's mouth, and this time Kora does not scream. She wishes herself home in the family apartment, lying in bed in her room. She wishes she could hear the sound of Uncle Wai on the roof above, hoeing, raking, and watering his garden. But she knows she never will again.

Her phantom hand still itches like a mother. "Where is the doctor? And her assistant?"

"Probably gone to the party," says Tania. "The whole school is buzzing about it. But I don't think you should come. You've just had a serious surgery."

"But she wants to, so bad," says Velma.

Tania says, "She's in shock. Look, the doctor left you a cup of tea, Kora. Smells like medicine. Maybe for your nerves. You should drink it."

Kora shakes her head. "She took my hand. I've had enough of her medicine. Please don't leave me."

"Everyone's going," sings Velma. "Everyone. The tiger men *never* open their garage to outsiders, *ever*."

"Don't bait her," Tania says. "I'm not so sure this party is a good idea. We know nothing about the tiger men except that they're sick with flu yet still live."

"Cordova girls are tough," says Velma. "And we've never been inside the Pacific Pearl Parkade."

"We're too curious for our own catcoats," says Tania. "But let's not bring a wounded girl to a place we don't understand. Anyway, look at her. She's in no condition to leave her bed."

"I want to go to the Pacific Pearl Parkade," Kora says.

"It's a bad idea," says Tania. "Kora, I came down here because I wanted to say something to you." To show her sincerity, she holds out half a biscuit, spread with a rich-smelling oil.

"She's drugged to the hilt," says Velma. "She won't remember a thing."

"I'll remember," Kora says. She takes the biscuit and crams it into her mouth.

"Myra is cruel to everyone when they first come and extra cruel to those who pose a threat. She riles up the other girls to match her too. She was the same to me when I first arrived. Because of my connections at Cosmopolitan Earth."

"Oh," says Kora, perking up through her drug fog.

"It's how I lost my tooth." She grimace-grins so Kora can see the space. "It's how she keeps control."

Kora nods, still stunned.

"She hurts us to save us?" says Velma, squinting as she tries to wrap her head around the twistedness of it.

"Yes. To keep us in line and so keep us together. She was so afraid of losing Madame Dearborn. And now we have. So we're all scared, but Myra most of all. I'm sorry for my part in the hazing."

Pushing through the strange doctor's sedative, Kora attempts to gather her dignity. "Hazing? While you were away, I killed an old man. I would have left you all, if I had anywhere else to go. And now my hand is gone. You are all cursed." Her eyes flicker with realization. "And I'm cursed with you."

Tania gives her the other half of the biscuit, spread with more of that delicious oil. However angry she is, the oil is too delicious and Kora is too hungry not to eat it.

Tania says, "This won't bring back your lost hand. But it comes from a care package my mother sent me. It's real food, not from a nasty plague house. Oolichan oil."

Kora is as surprised as Velma and Tania when her tears begin to flow again.

Velma feels sorry that Kora can't go to the party. She doesn't really grasp Tania's words or gift, but she wants to do something. So she gets Kora a shot of whisky from the time before, from the upstairs kitchen. Tips it into the cup of forget-me-do that Kirilow left by the bed.

Kora drinks.

To Tania and Velma's surprise, Kora's eyes go faintly green.

"By Our Mother's holy hair!" says Velma.

In the light pouring from Kora's eyes, a flickering green figure appears.

"That's Isabelle Chow," say Tania. "Holy crap."

Isabelle kneels. Kora has seen her kneel this way before. Her face is wet with tears. Kora has seen these tears before too.

I guess you chose her after all. I can't believe it, after all we've been through together. What was I thinking? I guess I'm a girl and stupid ...

Tania and Velma gawp.

Kora wills the vision to stop playing, but it rolls on. *I'm not even talking to you. I'm talking to the ghost of you I keep in my moronic little heart, like an idiot, like a chump ...*

"What is this?" Velma says.

Tania looks at. "Where did you get this?" she asks, flicking the red filigree scale with her finger.

LiFT is still only at eighty-five percent verisimilitude, you know. And neither you nor that little bitch—how could I have ever called that charity case my best friend?! ...

"I don't—I don't know ..." Kora stutters.

"By Our Mother's milky left boob, of course you do!" Tania's tenderness has left her. She's panicked and angry. "Tell me now, Kora. This is not a joke."

"At the Isabelle shrine—" Kora squeaks.

"What Mother-smacking shrine?"

"Down by the water ..."

"Myra is going to be livid."

I'm amassing an army, do you hear me? You don't get to treat me like this and live!

When the vision reaches its end, it starts again. On the second pass—the third for Kora—Isabelle's tears seem even more pathetic.

I guess you chose her after all ...

Tania becomes reasonable again. "The gossip is everywhere. Someone is moving against Isabelle. Her lover betrayed her. We think someone is selling her projections, to make money and undermine her credibility when she releases a new technology to save us from the flu. We don't know more. We're monitoring. Even though Isabelle has caused us terrible harm, whoever is working against her could well be worse. Don't show this to anyone, Kora. I mean it."

"I wasn't trying to show it."

"I think the forget-me-do or the whisky might have triggered it."

So you're going to sell a defective product to the desperate. I'll make it again, and I'll make it per—

"This should do it." Tania yanks the red filigree scale out of Kora's halo.

"Ow! That's mine."

The vision comes to an abrupt halt.

"Not anymore it's not. Will Our Mother's tech variations never cease?"

Tania takes the red filigree scale upstairs. Velma trots after her.

"Bring that back! It doesn't belong to you!" Kora yells.

But the other effect of the drink is a drowsiness she can't fight off. She tumbles into a bottomless sleep. She wakes once after several slams of the main door, directly above the clinic, as Cordova girls head off to the party.

KORA WAKES SOME HOURS LATER. SHE LIES IN BED SURROUNDED BY images of Our Mother, with a large watercolour of Eng at her head. She's groggy and confused. Her phantom hand itches like the dickens. What if the doctor is a Grist sister? One thing's for sure—she's not from Saltwater Flats, so she must have come from one of the quarantine rings beyond, or somewhere even farther afield and even stranger.

Eventually, she dozes again. She finds herself once more in Uncle Wai's garden on the Woodward's rooftop. She dreams of rows of jars brimful with fresh earth and potatoes glowing with life beneath the soil, so palpably she can almost hear them breathing. She grasps a jar to tip it out, but when she looks inside, she sees her uncle Wai lying curled there, dead or asleep, so fragile in his stillness. She wants to get him out, but the jar is large and heavy. She leans against it and pushes. The jar seems to have become even heavier. She stands on tiptoe and peers in the top. He seems so far down now, at the distant bottom of a well. She drops down to flat feet again and pushes, throws her weight into it, heaves with all her might. The jar will not budge. Then, just as she feels the slightest movement, she hears a plaintive mewl coming from the adjacent jar. She ignores it and continues to heave and shove. The mewling becomes a thin, persistent yowl. Still she ignores it, pushes harder, finally manages to give Uncle Wai's jar a good jostle. From the mewling jar emerges a fearsome, unearthly croak. She stops and goes to look. A massive tiger leaps out, teeth sharp and glistening with saliva. It comes straight for her face.

She bolts awake. Her hand itches furiously. And a pitiful mewling really is coming from beneath the bed.

Although her arms and legs are still heavy, she can move them now, at least enough to climb off the bed and out from under the unsettling watch of the watercolour Eng and the many beatific gazes of Our Mother. She crouches on the floor and pushes aside the ruffled curtain that hides the doctor's under-bed storage. Laid out neatly on top of packed boxes of medicine, needles, bedsheets, and who knows what else is the lost catcoat. It quivers when it perceives her presence, and the mouth part stretches into a wide, lazy yawn.

"You," says Kora accusingly. "How did you get here?"

Pinned cruelly to its ear is a note that says, *I dare you*. Blood drips unseemly from the pinprick. Whoever did this is not very nice.

Kora contemplates the nature of the dare. Who has issued it? Velma, wanting her to come to the party? Myra, letting Kora know she knows? Or her misguided, clue-leaving brother? Although she thought she knew him like the back of her vanished hand, he's jobless and sick with a death-dealing flu—and now part of a large group of men all suffering the same indignities. These are conditions that might have driven him to things he would never have considered before.

She picks up the catcoat. A little mangier than it was yesterday morning, it is nonetheless very much alive. It begins to keen. She seeks its seams and shoulders, gets it upright, lowers its feet to the floor, then steps in, and zips it up. Soothed by the companionable warmth of her body, the catcoat stops mewling, and begins to vibrate contentedly. Kora takes a deep inhale, lets it out, relaxes into the purr.

INVITATION 30

NODE: MINOR HEAT
DAY: 2

I'M OUT ON THE WIDE BOULEVARD FOR THE FIRST TIME SINCE MY arrival. Although not a captive, I've been acting like one. I'm restless as river water aching for the sea. But the source I come from has been dammed with dirt, and I can never go back. If I'm really ~~clever~~ bright, I could make a new source. But I need to find my true sisters, the ones that were taken up, up, up in that hideous batterkite.

Two solar nodes—more than a full cycle of the moon—have passed since the death of my Peristrophe Halliana. Here I am, a stranger in alien territory, home of my grandmothers, though I feel as much at home as a fox would in a bear's den. Could Madame Aurelia Dearborn really have been my long-lost auntie? The red hair was so ~~foreign~~ weird. My mother double told me there were other kinds of sisters, germinated by Jemini from the seeds of other individuals. I didn't know what that meant. All the sisters I ever knew were part of me. But now I think I see. There are kinds of cousins that only seemed possible in dreams. Aurelia Dearborn was a dream come true.

That's not what the expression means, Kirilow sweet, the mother double in my head says. *One day, I will take you to Saltwater City and you will learn more.*

Here I am, Mama, but not under conditions of my own choosing. Oh, you taught me well, from your dearest and most beloved head. But now I'm among them, and no Inglish could be more alien.

What a gutless fool I've been to stay trapped down there with these strange and terrifying Salties, as though they are the only kind of Salty that exists. I'm gripped now with the thrill of finding what other kinds there are. *Because, Kirilow, they don't double. They are all individuals.* She told me this a hundred times, but my brain can't grasp it.

Along the wide boulevard, durian trees grow. Right outside the door! At Grist Village, we cultivated them in cold frames, transplanted them outside when they were strong. We fed them good. With droppings of elk, bear, and sometimes even revived Caspian tiger, if an escaped one happened to roam through our beautiful forest. Here, the trees grow well, seemingly without assistance. Their trunks expand like the waists of well-fed Salties, like the two walking towards me in shimmering fabrics. How sleek and fat! Handsome in a barbaric way. The branches arch out, curve away from the trunks and sprout luxuriant leaves. And fruit! Already it's time for the first flushing. They hang heavy from the branches, precious eggs for Our Mother's babies.

Chang rides high in the sky like a ripe durian, begins his descent into his own night. Eng rises in the southeast, distant, slow, and round. Tonight is ceremony night, the night we would feast Auntie Radix on the richest roots, the darkest greens. There would be medicinal soup I simmered myself with the juiciest ptarmigan and a secret combination of fertility herbs that old Glorybind taught me before she became forgetful. We'd decorate Auntie Radix with precious leaves from our most fertile durian tree and feed her fruit of the first flushing, ripe and fragrant.

I wonder if the little groom Bombyx Mori carries these rites out tonight for Corydalis Ambigua at New Grist Village, in the clearing where I killed an elk last summer, deep in the mountains. I imagine Bombyx and Corydalis fixing up the caves and planting fresh gardens.

I pause where two roads called "Main" and "Hastings" cross. (My mother double taught me the Salty technology of text, at least enough to sound out simple words and read these worn signs.) Here, the biggest durian tree has burst up through the asphalt. It's an old tree. I suppose it burst through many years ago, maybe even at the time of the great-grandmothers' expulsion. Its trunk is thick as a house, and its branches curve so high they block the pink light that Eng sheds down on us. The limbs arch back to earth, cascading fruit. Many people stand to admire as tree priestesses gather the fruit. Spectators and officiators are mostly women. The flu keeps men indoors, I suppose. Or else they can't stand the cat shit and lilac smell. It makes me homesick. I find a spot beneath a dense waterfall of leaves and fruit and draw the rich odour in, peer through the shivering blossoms at Eng's distant glory.

I watch Eng chase Chang, though her orbit is so distant and wide now that she will never catch him. Chang, in his ruined orbit, dances away too fast on a different path. He is so close that I can see the ports where shuttles used to dock in the last days of oil. If the Cosmopolitan Earth Council won't boost him back out with one of their rockets, it is only a matter of time before he crashes into Earth and kills us all.

Eng pauses at her zenith, then swells, rounds, and tumbles towards the northwest horizon. The heavy odour of fruit permeates my brain and limbs. I walk like a drugged person back towards the Cordova School, dreaming of the aunties back home, and Saltwater City at the long-ago launch of Chang and Eng. Beneath a young durian tree stands a man with eyes bright green, like he's drunk too many cups of forget-me-do.

It takes me a few seconds to realize the man has fallen in step beside me. "Do you mind if I walk with you?"

I become aware of my own beauty in a way I had never considered before. We Grist sisters come from the same DNA. Only our ages and the differences of scars, haircuts, or minor mutations mark us as distinct from one another. We don't think about beauty, because there's no competition to be had. I never thought about my looks until this particular man looked. Is that how it's done in this decaying city?

I imagine two slugs slip-sliming over one another on a log. The rage I was born with, that I've worked so hard all my life to contain, rises in my throat. "No thanks."

"I just want to talk to you."

Old Glorybind taught me what women are. I know how humans doubled in the time before, how they still do in Saltwater City. Technically speaking, we Grist sisters have the same bodies they do. He touches my arm and an unexpected electricity runs through me.

"Go away, or I'll hurt you." I walk faster.

He follows me.

"I mean it. Go away."

He keeps coming.

I turn, grab his arm, press my thumb hard into the meridian of vision. He yelps, claps his free hand over his eyes. I've seared him. I let go.

"It isn't friendly if I don't want your company," I tell him. We pass a heavy-laden durian tree, and my head fills with its jasmine and vomit odour.

"Maybe you do," he says. "Your sister is already at the party. You know, what's her name ... Alex Coady ... or something ... Black hair and purple dress?"

Calyx Kaki. Our Mother watch over us. "What have you done with her?"

"Interested now?" He presses something into my hand, then springs away into the darkest hour before dawn.

WHEN I GET BACK TO THE CLINIC, SURE ENOUGH, CALYX KAKI IS GONE. The girl with no right hand is also missing. From the head of the bed, the watercolour of Eng seems to beam at me knowingly.

I take out the green-eyed man's gift—a small disk the size of a peach pit. There's a little button on it. I push it. A vision in gold and yellow flashes up into the air. Two batterkites with long tendrils fly up from either side, and some text glimmers, wavers, then solidifies at the centre.

> *Deep Scale Commune*
> *Pacific Pearl Parkade*
> *Gallbladder Hour*
> *2nd Day, Minor Heat*
> *Wood Snake Year 2145*

I sound the words out slowly, as old Glorybind taught me. I grab my hunting knife and a sleeve of all-purpose needles and hurry out into the night.

DEEP SCALE COMMUNE

31

KORA KO // SALTWATER FLATS

NODE: MINOR HEAT
DAY: 2

PROTECTED BY THE WARMTH OF THE CATCOAT, KORA GOES OUT INTO the cool evening. All along the road that leads to the entrance of the Pacific Pearl Parkade hawkers sell onion cakes, red bean buns, and chicken skewers from small carts with built-in burners for bamboo charcoal. There is a woman selling disposable clothing imported from the UMK, two years out of fashion by the time it arrives. And another from St'át'imc territory selling oolichan grease rumoured to have been traded down from Haisla shores. There's a bicycle repairman with chains, pedals, gears, and pins, all from the time before, laid out on a blanket. The ubiquitous scale artists have set up satellite stalls with a selection of their wares. They will do minor installations on the street. There are touts to guide customers to flagship clinics for larger operations and greater choice. But more than half of the stalls flog a substance that Kora has heard of only in half whispers on the street late at night, a drug called N-lite.

"See the present as you've never seen it before," shouts one seller. "You know you want to!"

"Life after life!" promises the next.

"After life after," croons a third.

A fourth sings a little tune:

chang high day nigh
gang sang sky hang
up sup you glue
left brain sync same

The third sings back:

eng low soul bowl
fool pool true who
low load new you
right brain crime scene

And the second answers them both:

auld syne small game
main frame brain drain
old sign self same
true fool goon you

Kora's heart fills with curiosity. Her phantom hand burns like white fire. She blocks it from her mind, as though it is separate from her, as though it doesn't belong to her anymore, which of course it doesn't. It belongs to that creepy doctor. She needs to concentrate. This is her one chance to find out what her brother did to Charlotte and Wai.

Near the entrance to the parkade, she comes across a contingent of girls from the Cordova School, dressed up in feathers and crinolines, masks and makeup.

"You have to take it, or you won't experience a thing," says Soraya.

"Isabelle Chow captures everyone on it and takes them away for medical experiments," says Modesta.

"No," says Mirabelle. "She uses it to kidnap you and sell you as a sex slave in the UMK."

A young one called Anna says, "It's nothing, people. It feels good. Just take it and enjoy the party."

Kora squeezes past them.

The entrance to the parkade is a massive sculpture made of empty food cans from the time before, variously bolted, screwed, glued, welded, and strung together to form the shape of a giant tiger's head with a gaping maw. Flashing back to her dream, Kora shudders. The tin-can head is bathed in a flickering yellow and orange light.

Kora's hand throbs. *I wonder if it takes away hand pain.* She senses a presence beside her. Turns her head. Facing the other directly, she can see who it is. Myra, in her catcoat. "Found your old friend, I see," she says, knowingly. "Don't be so careless next time."

"Did you—?"

Myra holds out a vial. "Take this, Lady Kora. In for a penny, in for a pound."

Kora eyes Myra and thinks about what Tania said. That she's not mean, only scared. Myra looks pretty mean to Kora. And Kora is suspicious of this drug. The Gristie doctor's drugs were bad enough. But she's also burning to find answers.

Myra's dark eyes inside the catcoat turn and churn, deep as ocean tides pulled by the true moon. Kora hears voices behind the singing voice:

chang high day nigh
gang sang sky hang
up sup you glue
left brain sync same

Myra says, "If you don't take the N-lite, the parkade is just a useless ruin from the time before. To see the truth of this place, to see the Pacific Pearl, you need the drug. It's the first step of the upload."

This idea is weirder than the N-lite sellers' strange chant. But lots of weird things have been happening since she left home. Should she, or shouldn't she?

"If you don't take it, I'll see everything and you'll see nothing," Myra says. "Is that what you want?"

Kora knows Myra is baiting her.

"How about I take half and you take half? The stuff is pretty strong anyway." Myra pops the cork, raises the vial to her left nostril, and inhales deeply. Passes it to Kora. "Come on!" The green gas wafts out, escaping to the air. "Hurry, or it's wasted!"

Against her better judgment, Kora takes the vial and holds it up to her nose. She and her catcoat draw the green vapour in. It has a powdery candy smell, a bit chemical. Kind of like the cream soda Uncle Wai gave her once as a New Year's gift. *Have the manufacturers accounted for one-handed girls in catcoats?* she wonders. The green vapour goes straight to her head, three times as strong as any of the strange doctor's teas. Her eyes cross and her brain floods with an alien consciousness that both is and is not her own. Our Mother which art artful. Remember? Forget? Remember, forget, yet yet yet ...

The tin-can tiger gapes its maw, and its tin-can teeth rattle and shake above her like wind chimes from the world inside the world. Did she just think that? She grabs Myra's hand. They enter the cavernous cathedral that was once the Pacific Pearl Parkade.

Men sick with tiger flu have lived here for a hundred years, since the first resuscitated Caspian tigers leapt their own extinction and burst from the DNA extracted from an old tiger-skin rug in the living room of a once revered and then denounced party official from the United Middle Kingdom, or whatever it was called before it expanded and swallowed all the smaller countries around it. The People's Pub of ... something. She had the scale, but traded it to K2 for one about medicine before the privatization of Chang and Eng. Now that the flu has intensified against human males, the tiger men have become insular to the point of reclusive. Other denizens of Saltwater City have not entered the parkade in a generation.

The tiger men have retained part of the original parkade structure, so it is still possible to follow the path of so many ancient automobiles to the parkade's sky-piercing pinnacle. But they have also removed half of the ascending lanes, so from the foyer in the tin-can tiger's throat Kora can look up up up, as though up to the spires of an ancient church and into the eye of a wrathful old god determined to damn all denizens to the very depths of an ancient, half-forgotten hell that for centuries ruled the actions of men—yes, men—through an even more ancient fear and brought the world to its knees.

Whoa, Kora thinks. *This N-lite is one heavy drug.* Its hell pulls, pulsing beneath the soles of her feet. It rumbles and shudders, hums with the deep glottal growl of an old tiger twice the size of the massive parkade, lying just below the surface of the earth, half-asleep but vibrating into wakefulness and waiting to pounce.

face place grin fine
small game goon tool
soon rule soul bowl
kow tow know how

"What is that?"

"Devil's revel and memory share. That's what the invite said. Didn't you read it?" Myra responds.

Denizens of Saltwater Flats rush past them, feathers shaking, bells jingling. In their midst, tiger men also rush by, streaming long white hair and tendril scales, which writhe vigilantly above and behind them, three times the length of any Kora has seen in the streets. The press of bodies eager to get to the place from which the rumble rolls, expands, and deepens. Kora and Myra skirt its edges and so progress slightly faster than those at the thick, dense centre. Down to the rumbling, vibrating place they go, in a slow spiral.

P2A has been opened up to make a wide hall. At one end is a stage. On it, a large and ancient man sits on a stone dais, long white hair flowing all around him. A massive skull rack halo of the kind popular sixty years ago crowns his head like the antlers of a winter bull elk. Every terminal is jammed with scales. Some are the small sleek kind of a decade past; some are the fine, filigree kind so thin you can barely see them unless they catch the light as they writhe and wave. Scales flow from his thick white beard too, and his face and neck shimmer with the flat metallic type. His closed eyelids are covered with them, and in his slightly open mouth, Kora can make out neat rows of scales implanted on tongue and teeth. They extend beneath his algae-cellulose shirt too—it is likely that every nerve ending in his body has been tapped. He is like an old tree with scales for leaves and bark. Since HöST's privatization of Chang and Eng, Marcus Traskin, lord and CEO of the Pacific Pearl, has become the largest public mainframe in Saltwater Flats.

> *brain frame face drain*
> *rain same main game*
> *pin time raw wine*
> *crane brine sync line*

A circle of initiates surround him. All sport a dense array of scales. Their heads, necks, and shoulders are matted with the kind that emit a flickering yellow and orange glow, more heat than light. But these are younger men, born after the tiger flu's great third wave cull. Thin and ethereal, they look too much like Lewis Lai, whose seven fertile sons all but saved heterosexual reproduction in Saltwater Flats after the third wave.

The music quiets. The low rumbling sound of history itself intensifies and enters into the men through the massive dose of N-lite they took an hour ago.

> *blew through you who*
> *flesh dress dross floss*
> *brain boss cleave meat*
> *fish dish kiss this*

The men's eyes project the vaporous green glow of their N-lite high. Deep within her fog, Kora understands something of the forget-me-do vision she projected in her sick room hours earlier. But the light the men pour out is infinitely denser and dead steady. The room sighs in collective wonder. The light gathers and coalesces in a viridescent haze that surrounds them and expands to a billowy cloud above. Everyone shudders. Their bodies jerk into the N-lite dream.

Kora sees in vivid detail the things her own poor scales teach her as flat information. She sees the launch of Chang and Eng on rockets trailing magnificent fire. She sees a tiger-skin rug, a UMK official in prison, an incubation jar with a tiger fetus inside, then millions of jars row on row, and the first of the new Caspian tiger kittens, cute and fluffy. Massive adult tigers prowl through the vapour and curl into sleep above their heads. Their fearsome purring makes the rumble of the past resonate deeply, below the level of audible sound. And then the slaughterhouse—a stadium-sized abattoir where dead tigers hang from their hind legs, bellies slit and bloody. She sees a crew of grim vintners pile roasted tiger bones into large earthenware jars, just like the kind in which Uncle Wai grew his potatoes. In her stoned haze, she seeks familiarity in the faces of these vintners. Is she really related to them? The images spiral and turn too quickly for her to see.

She sees the jars in red velvet rooms, with spigots at their bases to release the precious liquor. Happy revellers drink from crystal glasses at first, then later, mouth to spigot as addiction deepens. Then the same vintners and revellers waste away in overstuffed hospitals and clinics from Albuquerque to Seoul to Kinshasa to New York City.

The tigers pad softly into the night, and the room fills with the roar of another crumbling. Vast cliffs and towers of polar ice calve into the warming sea. A parade of long dead animals—wolves, mammoths, bear, and oxen—find their way into the wombs of their contemporary cousins. In white rooms, giant bellows expand and contract, to help those in the throes of the third wave breathe longer than they otherwise might. Oceans swell and rise to engulf whole cities. The denizens of Saltwater City construct a massive wall of earth to protect themselves. The earth's angry maw gapes to swallow those outside. The wall falls, and the people build canals instead. The ocean swells through them, recedes, then swells again. The fourth wave of tiger flu comes. Men vomit and shrivel in dirty hospital beds, their bodies refusing to hold water. Lineups the length of city blocks for the Seven Houses of Lewis Lai, the last fertile men at Saltwater City, grow ever longer. Cassandra Chu, the four-breasted parthenogenic woman of Saltwater Flats, runs through fields of daisies, followed by an endless stream of little girls who look too much like her. Then, to Kora's shock and horror, she sees a girl lifting cans of tuna and soup from a plague house on the edge of the Second Quarantine Ring. The girl turns her head, and Kora recognizes her own gaunt and pimply face. She inhales sharply. The catcoat suddenly feels much too thin. She releases her breath, and a dry mewl rushes from her lungs. She turns to look at Myra, who looks back, horrified. Kora glances around the room, not trusting the catcoat to keep her covered.

On the lightest of feet, she scurries from the thick of the crowd, back towards the wall, and then sidles towards the entrance. But then, at the far edge of the room—is it? Yes, it is! Her Mother-cursèd brother. He raises his hand like a traffic cop, seems to beckon her and Myra to follow him. Can he see them? Kora's head swims with N-lite wooziness. How does he know they're there? *Because he knows.* Will he help them? *Trust him,* says the drug. She takes a last glance towards the exit. Hears his wolf whistle. Myra grabs her arm and pulls her through the dancing, shivering crowd still watching the flow of images. They trail him as the parkade curves lower.

There is a thick press of tiger men blocking the way to the lower levels. Kora pulls her catcoat tight and squeezes through a gap, but just as she does, the guard nearest her takes a step backwards as he laughs at something another guard has said. He bumps right in to her.

"Hello?" He seems to look her right in the eye. "What the—?"

Her own eyes bug wide. It's K2's grabby friend Stash. She gasps, then darts out of the way. He reaches for the spot where she was but misses. As long as they don't see her face to face, the catcoat works.

She scampers after her brother, who moves quickly now, down and still farther down seven layers of the old parkade, past the men's sleeping stalls, past dark corners where rats and other rodents gather, squealing, chittering, fighting over empty cans and scraps of rotten meat. There are burn marks on the walls, and the hazy darkness reeks of ammonia, sweat, and rotten onions. Biological and chemical agents moulder together, the smell of an ancient police force that used to amass here, preparing to quell the terrified city above in the wake of the first wave of tiger plague. The vaporous green light that filled the upper hall intensifies the deeper they go. The smell of ammonia, sweat, and onions intensifies too, to the point where Kora, Myra, and their catcoats choke on it. Kora's eyes water. She can hardly breathe. Was this a biochem weapons storage depot, rather than a staging area? Between the rank odour and the N-lite, she feels very woozy and not at all herself.

Seven spiralling floors below the great hall where Marcus Traskin, his men, and the crowd of revellers project the making of the new world from their eyes in green gas, Kora and Myra arrive in a very different kind of room. It is laid out like the lobby of an office building from the time before. A nice lobby, with white tile floors trimmed with a border of little black stars. There is a bank of elevators in front of them. Above each one a dial spins and flaps, running up and down a set of numbers, one to thirty-six.

Lined up in front of the elevators in a neatly cordoned zigzag are at least a hundred women, with identical glazed eyes, black hair, sharp faces. They are all around the same height, except a few who are clearly not yet fully grown.

"They look like you," Myra whispers to Kora, her voice full of wonder.

At the front of the line, six tiger men usher a group of women into an empty elevator. Docile as sheep, eyes emitting green vapour, the women step unquestioning past the sliding doors. The doors reel shut behind them. The numbers of the little dial begin to ascend.

Then the doors of the elevator beside it slide open. The foul odour of ammonia, sweat, and rotten onions fills the room, and water gushes out the elevator doors. There is something in it. A writhing, flapping mass of fish, interspersed with clots of red. Blood? The water floods away into a deep gutter at the elevators' edge.

"See that?" Myra whispers.

"Fish ..." says Kora.

"Yes," says Myra. "And?"

"And roses," Kora says, astonished. Luscious blossoms glisten and shimmer among the bucking, desperate fish.

A crew of tiger men with wheelbarrows emerges from behind the bank of elevators. With practised hands, they gather the fish and roses and expediently cart them away. Did Myra nod at one of them? She's got her hood off. What is she doing?

Kora watches the loading crew usher the next group of women into the empty elevator.

Myra is on her then. "She's here!" Yanks the hood of Kora's catcoat from her head, exposing her to plain view.

"Get your hands off me!"

It's too late. The tiger men are there, pulling at the parts of Kora they can see, as Myra grips the catcoat, tears it at the shoulder, and peels the sleeve from Kora's arm.

"Let go of me, you traitor!"

The catcoat yowls a terrible heart-wrenching yowl as its deformed body is torn asunder.

"You're killing it!"

The coat emits an unearthly shriek. Kora shrieks with it, but to no avail. They pull her free of her cover. It howls like a thousand dead people, all rage and pain. A gunshot. Then silence.

Kora regains herself and begins to yell, "Murderers! Get off me!"

Someone slaps a hand over her mouth. It takes six tiger men to drag her towards the elevators.

"You get to jump the queue, lucky you," one of them sneers.

They toss her in, all on her lonesome. In the moment it takes her to realize what has happened, the doors roll shut. She dashes for it way too late—just as the last inch closes. Thinks she hears her brother's voice now, "This isn't what you said ..."

The elevator clocks its way smoothly up to who knows where. It smells faintly of fish and salt water. She should never have trusted Myra. That's on her. But her brother. How could he betray her like this? She's so mad she forgets to be scared. Her brain swims in N-lite waters.

The doors open. She steps out. It can't be. She's on the rooftop of the Woodward's Building, in her uncle's garden of earthen jars. The goat hangs by its hind legs from the roof of its shed, belly slit wide open. Blood drips from the exposed intestines to its straw bed, and flies buzz around the steaming cut.

Charlotte and Wai stand in front of the dead, swinging goat.

"How could you? She's suffered enough!" shouts Charlotte.

"I should never have answered Father's call. I could have had a happy life in the UMK!" Wai responds.

"You should never have betrayed your brother!"

"Father left the Jemini Group to me, but Kai Tak just took it. And because of you, I didn't fight back. He even took Tiger Wine. Not that I care. I didn't want it anyway, but I never owed him anything—"

"We are cursed for your father's ridiculous project, as though he had a right to play God, release those baby tigers from that dead rug."

From thin air, Charlotte produces a giant undulating fabric of orange and black, whirls it above her head, then throws it to the ground. It is an ancient tiger-skin rug full of moth holes and torn at the neck. The head hangs at an awkward, broken angle.

"Charlotte! Uncle Wai! Stop fighting. It's me. I'm here."

"Kora!" her uncle calls. "Don't come out! Get back in the elevator now! Go! Everything we sacrificed—it's not for you to end up here!"

"Leave us—go!" Charlotte yells.

The doors have slid more than halfway shut. Charlotte runs to them, jams her hand into the narrowing space.

"Charlotte, your hand!"

Charlotte pries the door open with sheer strength. Uncle Wai pushes Kora towards the door, and half lifts, half shoves her in.

Charlotte lets go, and the doors slide rapidly shut.

The elevator reeks of fish and vomit.

"Charlotte! Uncle Wai!" Kora screams, her druggy voice all thin and high.

The dial on the inside, identical to the one outside, a half moon with numbers rimming its edge like an aura, shows the elevator descending.

"Charlotte," Kora sobs. "Uncle Wai—"

Before it gets to minus seven, the elevator bumps. Right at zero. Is she to be set free? Her tight heart leaps.

"Is there anyone there? Let me out!" She yells at the top of her lungs and thumps on the cold and heavy doors.

They slide open. In the doorway, wearing a gorgeous blue robe, stands an astonishingly tall and beautiful woman. It's Isabelle Chow, chief executive officer of HöST Industries, the power behind the glass city, inventor of scale technology and the batterkite. And this strange elevator too? Isabelle seems to glow from within. Behind her, a thick darkness gathers. The air smells salty and damp.

"Did you see them, Kora Ko?" Isabelle's eyes burn animal dark. Her voice is rich as oolichan grease.

"What?"

"Did you see them?"

"Who?"

"Your mother and father."

Kora's voice cracks and wavers. "I saw my mother and uncle."

"Do you understand what you saw?"

"I don't understand a thing."

"They have left their bodies and are held captive."

Kora's mouth flaps open. "By that nasty Marcus Traskin? Is it about that plague house? Those cans I stole?"

"No, Priestess Kora, it is not."

"Priestess?"

"A priestess of Our Mother of Light is what you will become, once you have done your duty. Our Mother does not care about cans or plague houses. Neither will last."

"I'm a non-believer. Ask that weird Gristie doctor about Our Mother. My family is innocent. You've made a grave mistake."

Isabelle Chow's blue robe flutters in the salty breeze. "I never make mistakes, Priestess Kora. Your parents have uploaded to Quay D'Espoir, my little paradise on Eng. Marcus Traskin has taken Chang from me, and all the virtual cities I built there for people like you and your family. But don't worry, your mother and father are safe."

"Wai is my uncle," says Kora.

"They remain under my guard at no cost to you. If you want them to stay there, you will do me the smallest of small favours, and then you can join them in the most beautiful place you have ever seen. Or live out the rest of your organic life here on this decaying Earth and join them just minutes before your natural time."

The whispers of the vendors along the road to the parkade make fresh sense.

Life after life
After life after

Kora's scales click and writhe to follow Isabelle Chow's logic. Kora's natural flesh trembles. "What favour?"

Isabelle smiles, revealing her small white teeth. "I thought you would never ask."

The elevator doors shudder, then begin to slide shut. Kora's hand darts out, and the doors slide open again.

"You will remove Marcus Traskin for me," Isabelle says.

"Remove?"

"Don't they train you? As thief and assassin?"

"They teach us all the old dances," Kora says. "Mambo, tango, cha-cha-cha."

Isabelle waits. She knows better.

Kora stares. "All right. As a thief. But not an assassin."

"You have killed before. You will find a way to again. Go back to the Cordova Dancing School when it is done," says Isabelle Chow. "Make friends with the doctor from Grist Village."

"That weirdo Gristie doctor? No way, no. She took my hand."

Wind rushes behind Isabelle, and Kora can hear a large body of water surge. Is Isabelle even actually here? Or is she a drug effect, a projection? Kora reaches out to touch her, but the elevator doors begin to slide shut again. Kora pulls her hand back before she loses that one too.

The elevator descends again. It stops at minus three, and the doors slide open. There, just as Isabelle would want, stands that creepy Gristie doctor, the inimitable Kirilow Groundsel.

RED RIGHT HAND

32

KIRILOW GROUNDSEL // SALTWATER FLATS

NODE: MINOR HEAT
DAY: 3

THE ELEVATOR DOORS SLIDE OPEN, AND A GIRL STANDS THERE. HER scales make a moist rattling noise as they writhe and shudder. Her eyes emit a green gas, like she's drunk six cups of forget-me-do in succession. Did these vile Salties sneak into our Grist gardens unbeknownst to us? Or perhaps this one was involved in that raid and fire in our forget-me fields last year. How can they call us witches when they go out in public looking like this? I smooth my hair as though it will help.

"Lady Kora?" I'm astonished to recognize her.

Her arms hang slack at her sides. The bandage over her stump is filthy brown and red. I could turn around and just leave her here. Who needs this mess?

I've been exploring the Pacific Pearl Parkade all night, seen things Our Mother would curse with pox and socks. No sign of my little Grist sister Calyx Kaki and no sign of my mother double, Glorybind Groundsel.

But I can't abandon Kora. Although the sight of her doesn't exactly cheer me up, she could be the one to save the Grist sisters and everything we hold in our bald brains from the time before. I need to know about the hand, in case somewhere in her is a bit of me, a bit of us, the deep blue genes of the grandmothers who did not make it out of Saltwater City.

I hear boots tromp in the hallway, louder with each step. I take a deep breath. I reach in to grab her good left hand, but she darts out of reach.

"Freaky Gristie doctor. Get away!" She punches furiously at the buttons. The doors begin to slide shut.

The boots click louder. I hurl myself into the elevator, hit zero, and grab her arm.

"Let go of me!"

"I'm not going to let them take you. Whatever they're doing here, you'll be fodder for it."

Kora's eyes grow round. "I saw them," she says. "I saw my mother and uncle."

The short girl who first brought Kora to me told me that her family were all dead, except her brother.

"Impossible," I say, and grab her arm now, while her guard is down. The elevator comes to zero, and the doors slide open. I can still hear the boots from three floors below, tromp tromp tromp. "Come on! Do you hear those boots?"

She whimpers. "I don't understand."

"I don't understand either. But this is not a good place." I continue to pull. She digs the spikes of her nasty boots into the elevator floor. She might look sickly, but she is strong.

"Come on! I know you don't trust me, but believe me, you are better off with me than you are here."

"Let go of me. You creep me out!" She yanks her left hand away from me. Grabs the rail at the back of the elevator.

I lean in and snatch her injured right. She howls. It must hurt like the dickens. I don't care. I keep pulling. "Come on!"

"You've helped me plenty, thank you very much. I saw them. I have to help them. Let go of me, you horrible Mother-cursèd Gristie!"

"Don't speak about Our Mother like that!" If she's not the one I need, then to hell with her. I'll find out right now. I unpin the bandage and give it a yank. It unravels in one long reeking piece.

There, at the end of a slimy grey stump, grows exactly what I'd hoped. A new hand. Small and raw, it is nevertheless perfectly formed. Praise be to Our Mother! A new starfish. My heart aches for home.

Kora Ko stares too. "What have you done to me, witchy Gristie! What hideous Grist magic is this?"

Hope makes me twice as strong. I grip her wrist tight. "Come with me and I'll tell you."

"Let go! I'm not coming with you!"

The boots tromp louder.

"Come with me—"

"Never."

"Anything you want, just name it and it's yours."

"Can you bring Wai and Charlotte back?"

I grip her wrist tighter still.

"No? I didn't think so. Can you kill Marcus Traskin for me?"

"Who's Marcus Traskin?"

"That crazy, scaly old man up on the dais."

The boots have arrived at ground zero. They are so close now. "You want Marcus Traskin's head, Kora? Why?"

"His death will bring my mother and uncle back. So I'll do it. With this weird monster hand you put on me."

"What are you talking about?"

"Let go of me, you hideous, disgusting Gristie!"

I don't see it coming.

She leans in and bites my arm.

"Little mother!" I thump her head so hard.

But she doesn't let go.

I feel the skin break. I feel blood gush. "Stop biting me!"

Still she digs her teeth in.

"Look, I'll help you, okay?" I hit her again, but the teeth go deeper. "Whatever you want, I'll do it. Just—teeth out!"

She raises her face, mouth all bloody, like a Mother-cursèd vampire from stories of the time before. "Whatever I want?"

"If you come with me after." My bitten arm hurts like heck, and blood seeps from the wound, but I don't want to let go of her wrist to staunch it.

Tromp tromp tromp tromp. The boots are at the corner. I'd rather not get involved, but I need my new starfish.

"Say it."

"I'll help you kill Marcus Traskin. Okay? Now can I let go of you without you running away from me?"

Tromp tromp tromp tromp.

She shrugs, then nods.

"All right then." I look her in the eye.

She looks back and keeps nodding.

I let go.

She releases the rail and we run run run, fast as our short legs will carry us. Behind us, the boots tromp faster and louder. We hear them turn down another corridor and their noise diminish. There are voices ahead. We duck into a side corridor and wait for them to pass. Somehow, we make all the correct turns. Hustle quick as winter rabbits, straight to the tin-can tiger's mouth.

THE MOUTH OF THE TIN-CAN TIGER IS PACKED WITH MEN—ALL WEARING the dark blue uniforms of Arm-a-Gideon Security. But the men's heads are shaggy and jammed with scales. This is not the return of Arm-a-Gideon.

"Form a line! Form a line!" I hear their marshal shouting.

Outside, it's raining, windy, and brutal dark. The people look miserable. Above the clamour, coughing, and hawking, a woman's plaintive voice: "My husband has no time to form a line. He's got mere hours. Please ..."

Three young women—her daughters, maybe—raise a plank above their heads, atop which lies a thin and wasted creature covered with a tattered blanket. The rain falls without mercy upon the gaunt shape.

"Form a line!" the marshal shouts. "Form a line, or he has mere minutes!" The tiger soldiers raise rifles from a stash perhaps belonging to the militia that used this parkade as a staging area a hundred years ago.

The motley mob stretches back down the road as far as I can see. We are not going to escape out the tiger's mouth.

The boots are almost on us. Tromp tromp tromp tromp.

I pull my new starfish into the shadows. She's fiddling with something. "We have to go back," she says.

"What you got there?"

"An open scale."

"I have one of those too." I reach into my pocket to see if it's still there.

"It was my brother's invitation to this place. Now there's a message. Or something. There's just a point on a map of the Pacific Pearl. It's blinking. I think my brother needs help."

"How do you know it's from your brother?"

"He gave me the scale. This kind only works from one person to another in a single direction."

"Didn't your brother just try to kill you?" I don't understand fully what that awkward boy is up to, but whatever it is is not nice.

She hesitates. "He tried something strange and not entirely loyal."

"So to hell with him! Let's go."

She follows me, out of the shadows again, but her feet drag. "He might be in danger." She casts a map from the scale into the air—very pale so as not to draw attention. It shows precisely where her brother is with a blinking orange dot.

"Looks like a trap to me," I say flatly. "Forget about him. He doesn't love you. Let's go before it's too late."

"Of course he loves me, you ignorant Gristie," Kora says.

"Don't call me that."

"Okay. But we are going to find him."

"By Our Mother's feet, why?"

"He's the only family I have left."

The hallway is impossibly dark. We scuttle down it like crabs, feeling our way. My hand brushes something and there's a clattering noise. I hurry farther, not wanting to know what toxin or danger I've unleashed in Traskin's unsettling hellhole.

"Wait, wait!" calls Kora Ko. She presses one of the fallen objects into my hand. "These are infrared goggles. We learned about this in Dark Spaces dance class."

What is this place? I pull them over my head, and Kora does the same. A rabbit warren of back passages lies before us.

In the distance, I hear groaning. I don't want to know about it. I choose a passage that moves away from the noise, one that might lead to a quieter exit. But Kora pulls me towards the noise.

"That's where the map points. It must be him. He's in trouble for letting me go."

"By the sweet blue light of Eng. We can't help him."

The groaning grows louder.

"We have to try," the girl says.

I allow myself to be led down a very narrow hall. Halfway down, there's a door on which, somewhere in the mists of time, the word "Electrical" was painted. I help the girl pry it open. In the small, dimly lit space, tied to a chair and firmly gagged, sits a young man, a boy, really, who looks very much like Kora Ko—at least, as much as any Salty breeder can look like another.

"K2," she whispers. Then she turns to me. "I told you. My brother."

He continues to moan, but softly.

We untie him, pull the gag off, attempt to help him up. He doesn't budge.

"Okay, let's go," I say.

The boy says, "I'm staying. I'm thinking."

"K2, have you lost your mind?" Kora says. "Let's please get out of here!"

"What are you doing here anyway?"

"You signalled me."

"I did not signal you. Remember we said we'd go our separate ways? You're interfering."

"I'm helping you!"

"I have a decision to make."

Kora says, "You're not making any sense, big brother. We need to get out of here now. Isabelle Chow has Charlotte and Wai at a place called Quay D'Espoir on Eng, and we need to take out Marcus Traskin to keep them safe."

The boy chuckles, too bitterly for one who has seen the new monsoons only twenty times. "Marcus Traskin has a cure for the flu. He is going to save Saltwater City. He is a hero, and you should want him to live. We all should. I'm a tiger man now. I have a direction, a place, a way to live now. Don't you see?"

"Tiger man, my eye. If you're a tiger man, how come you're tied up and screaming? You're a child. You have no respect. Didn't you hear me? We need to help Charlotte and Wai. So can you please forget your silly boy delusion and come with us now? Or we'll tie you back to the chair, I swear we will."

"Charlotte and Wai would be okay if Marcus took control of Eng ..."

"Is that what you think? Marcus Traskin is not a good man."

"Marcus Traskin is a victim of our family's greed. If they had stopped breeding those tigers, if they had stopped making that wine ..."

"What tigers, what wine? Grandpa's time is over." Kora throws up both her old left hand and her new right one.

"Where do you think all of Uncle Wai's precious jars came from, Kora? You think he was just some sweet old rooftop gardener growing cabbages and potatoes to survive the coming apocalypse? You're naive, you're a child—no, you're wilfully ignorant. You see only what you want to see and close your eyes to all the rest."

"What rest?" Her eyes bug wide, and so do mine.

"Tiger farms, Kora. And tiger-bone wine factories, hidden all through Saltwater City and the quarantine rings. All operating smooth as silk. You think I was working at an elk farm? Why do you think the flu epidemic keeps getting worse? They are making it worse and trying to export it to the UMK. It's not just hangover trauma from some time long past. It's happening over and over again, right now. For the love of Chang, how could you not know?!"

The girl stares at him. "It can't be true." Her tendril scales writhe atop her head, cogitating.

"You know it's true, or you wouldn't deny it so hard, sister. You know it's true."

The scales quiver. Kora doesn't know what to think. She closes her eyes, then draws in a great breath of air. "Please come with us."

"Not a bad idea, boy," I say. I want out of here, and I want the new pink hand to come.

"Can't. You just helped me make up my mind. Tie me back up. Marcus has made me a wonderful offer. I have a debt to pay and a gift to receive. I'll take my chances with the tiger men."

"You're a fool," I mutter.

"We're not going to tie you back up, you idiot!" she wails.

He sits back down in the small wooden chair, so hard that it scrapes back several inches along the dry floor. "I'm waiting," he says.

"I'll do it," I say.

"Don't hurt him, please, Dr Gristie," says Kora in a very small voice.

"Kirilow," I say. "Call me Kirilow."

PERFECT MONEY MACHINE 33

NODE: MINOR HEAT
DAY: 3

THE LOCKSTEP CLIP OF BOOTS IN THE HALLWAY INTENSIFIES, LEFT right left right. Kora watches the hands of the Gristie doctor wind rope around K2 and his chair, tie an elegant and practised knot, then wind again.

Tromp tromp tromp tromp.

"Hurry up, or they've got us for sure."

Kirilow's hands fly.

Left right, tromp tromp. But which direction is the noise coming from?

"I'm outta here," says Kora.

She makes for the door. In an instant, the Gristie doctor is behind her. Kora pulls on her infrared goggles, opens the door, looks left. Already, Traskin's police are rounding the corner. She turns right. Oh no. The men are coming from both the left and the right.

"Shit, shit, shit!" says Kora. Now what? They pull back into the electrical room. There is nowhere to hide.

"Filthy, traitorous Salty," Kirilow hisses at K2.

Kora just stares at him, not comprehending.

K2 says, "I'm sorry, I had to make a choice."

Kora's tendril scales shudder and undulate. The flat ones vibrate and shimmer a horrified blue. "You sold me out? My own brother?"

K2 shrugs. "I'm saving your life. What more do you want from me?"

"I should have left you to those wild dogs."

"You think I owe you? I saved you from the LiFT."

Tromp tromp tromp tromp. The beasts are at the door.

"You at least owe me an explanation."

The door flies open.

"I control the tiger farms now, Kora," K2 pronounces, so arrogant smug. "Kai Tak left them to me, on the condition that I dispose of you, our whore of a mother, and that adulterer, your father, Kai Wai. Now that Everest is dead, Kai Tak's invited me to run Jemini with him. That means we can clone as many test subjects as Marcus wants for the LiFT upload. And we control the wine factories. That means we can infect as many desperate flu birds as we want. And Marcus Traskin controls the cure. So we can make those suckers pay and pay and pay some more to save their precious little minds, if not their bodies. We have built a perfect money machine. Together, we will be the richest and greatest men in Saltwater City, as well as on Chang. In time, we will capture Eng too. We will be kings!" His eyes glow beatifically. "I do love you, sister. I wouldn't have done it for anything less."

"You don't love me!" says Kora. "You've run out of both love and sense." Her voice is level, but her emerald eyes are gassing out in rage. "What will you spend your money on if everyone is dead?"

A burly guard yanks Kora's hands behind her back. A slender but unexpectedly strong one grabs Kirilow.

Kirilow horks a great wad of phlegm up from the depths of her lungs and spits in K2's eye. The glob of mucus slides wetly down his cheek, hangs on his chin, then plops to the floor.

"I am the grandchild of Lennox Ko too," Kora whispers, so soft that Kirilow can barely hear. "So part of those dirty factories is mine."

A third guard, one with the round face of a baby, clips handcuffs to her wrists, but her new right hand is too small to stop it from sliding off. A fourth man produces rope, and the baby-faced one binds Kora's arms behind her back at the elbow.

"Charlotte and Wai wanted better things for you," K2 says. "That's why you were sent to the Cordova School. Lennox Ko willed Jemini to his younger son, Kai Tak. Then to Kai Tak's eldest son, Everest. And then to me, in the event of their deaths. Only then to you."

The guard who provided the rope now draws a set of leg shackles from his black bag. He and Babyface bind Kora's legs together.

Kora's dirty scale tendrils wave at the injustice. "Better things? We were slowly starving to death. Why would he will Jemini to his younger son?"

"Because Uncle Wai is a wife-stealer."

"I don't believe you," Kora says, as two booted men grab her, hands hooked in armpits. "Old Lennox willed it to Uncle Wai, didn't he?" They begin to drag her away. "I bet he did. I know he did! And he's my father—" What she's always half known now dawns on her as gut knowledge. The tendril scales wave in righteous indignation. Through her N-lite fog she see a garden of earthen jars. Her vision sharpens as her mind's eye shows her Kai Wai and Charlotte on the rooftop of the old Woodward's Building. She sees the dead goat swinging from the roof of its shed. She sees Charlotte whirl a tattered tiger rug above her head. *Run!* her father-uncle shouts in her head.

Life after life
After life after

"He's still alive," she breathes.

"Not for much longer, beloved sister. Not Kai Wai and not Charlotte. And in the meantime, they can't exactly run the factories, can they? You behave now. If you don't, I'll be forced to kill you too."

NODE: MINOR HEAT
DAY: 3

DEEP IN THE BOWELS OF THE PACIFIC PEARL PARKADE OUR LEGS ARE unbound and we are thrown into a damp cement room that reeks of fish and ammonia. We are supposed to be grateful that the dirty Salty boy K2 Ko has allowed us to live. How did this happen to me? All I wanted was a new starfish for New Grist Village. And to get my mother double back. I didn't ask for Peristrophe Halliana to come back from the dead. Is Old Glorybind alive and well at Quay D'Espoir on Eng with Kora's mother and father? It's more likely she's a captive on Marcus Traskin's Chang. In mind only, without her body. I can hardly bear to think of it. I'd rather think of her as dead. This strange killing and rebirthing is Salty business. We Grist sisters have no faith in such things. If the body is dead, then so is the woman, whatever these occultist Salties think they have copied. Our Mother of fish and roses, I prayed for what I thought I could reasonably have, not for everything I ever wanted. Why do you treat me this way?

Kora sits on the damp floor of the cell and contemplates her new pink hand. It must itch fiercely. She scratches so much that its pinkish-blue hue never fades. The hand glows with newborn liveliness. She clenches it, stretches it, marvels at its flexibility. "Why me?" she says. "What did I ever do to you?"

She wants to do this now? "I saved your life, Kora Ko. No need to gush on about it or anything. We gotta figure out how to get out of here."

"You put an alien hand on me."

"By Our Mother's stinky breath! It's your own hand, growing back, sweet as you please."

"You mutilated me. How would you like it if I did something like this to you?"

"Mine would not grow back," I explain, too patient. "You have the magic. I don't."

"Did you know it would grow back?"

"Well ... no."

"What if I cut off your hand? Or your mama's hand? What if your mama is alive on Chang but really mangled? You Gristies, you were made to be workers and test subjects. What if they test-lifted her but screwed it up? And her Chang body's got three eyes and no arms. And no memory of you. That would be just dessert, for what you did to my hand."

"I saved you, you little ingrate, you Mother-cursèd Salty. I fixed you, I cured you. You'd be dead of gangrene if not for me."

There's a stinking toilet and a sink in the corner. When I turn the tap, the thinnest stream of water dribbles out.

She says, "Is that even true?"

I wash my hands in the thin stream. "You think that without me you'd be living happily ever after at the Cordova School, golden and shining?"

"Maybe ..."

"I think not. And do you know what your healed hand means?"

"I don't know, and I don't care."

"It means you and me, we're gene genies. Sisters in blood and struggle. You're related to me and our original grandmother, Grandma Chan Ling."

"What in Our Mother's damnation are you talking about, dirty Gristie?" says Kora.

"What am I talking about? I'm talking about you. You are one of us. A dirty Gristie, just like me, except in your case there's been some intermarriage with the Salty proles. You really think I put that hand on you?"

Kora nods. "I know you did." She blinks then, and her gaze wavers. She holds her miraculous pink hand up to the light. Stares at it with pure, unmitigated disgust. "I don't know what you did to me, but I'm going to get my mother and uncle—I mean, father—back. Old Lennox Ko must have willed Jemini to Kai Wai, not Kai Tak. Because Kai Wai is the oldest, and the kindest. I'll prove it. Then I really will be Lady of the Flu, just as Myra said. And I will make you pay for what you did to me."

"Why you wanna be the Queen of Death?" I say. "I'll tell you what we're gonna do. First, we escape this hole. Next, I will help you access whatever weird Salty magic you believe holds your mother and father. And then you will come with me to save the sisters of New Grist Village with your clever genetics. The village will grow and thrive and prosper. And you will recognize your ingratitude and atone for it."

"I won't, and I won't."

I gaze at the big steel door that holds us in.

"Even if you're right, you only inherit Jemini through the inheritance rules of men. Our Mother is on the ascendant, and you know it. By her laws, you are a Grist sister, just like me."

"I'm not and never will be!"

"We have a long lonely time together, Lady Kora. A long, long lonely time."

NODE: MINOR HEAT
DAY: 13

WITHOUT THE LIGHT OF CHANG OR ENG, IT'S HARD TO UNDERSTAND the passing of time. We mark the days by the fish dinners that come through the grate, two each per day. I find a loose pebble in one of the room's dark corners. I use it to scratch out lines on the wall to count the passing days, one line for every four fish.

Kora Ko refuses to eat the fish dinners.

"You have to eat," I say, digging in. "You need your strength if you're going to survive this." It's not beets, red mustard, or bok choy, but I eat and don't complain.

For a week, she refuses to eat the fish. She drinks the muddy water they give us and the hard bread. She sleeps a lot because she has no energy. When she thinks I'm not looking, she stares at me.

"The fish isn't bad. Why won't you eat it?"

NODE: MAJOR HEAT
DAY: 5

KORA KO IS NO MARTYR BY ANY STANDARDS, GRISTIE OR SALTY. ON the eighth day, she eats some fish. And promptly gets sick. Our Mother of flesh and fur! Of all the people I could get stuck down here with it has to be a stinky Cordova girl with a weak stomach. At least she has the courtesy to dash to the shared toilet.

On the ninth day, she's a gaunt, grey mess. She drinks more water but won't eat.

On the tenth, she has a bite of fish and again is sick.

On the eleventh, she eats. The fish stays down. Praise be to all the creatures in my long-lost forest. I wouldn't care if she lived or died, except we need her hand-growing talent. All I want is to go home. But I'll take New Grist Village, even if all it means is me, Bombyx Mori, Corydalis Ambigua, and their sister litter. And maybe Calyx Kaki. And Kora? I can't imagine her as part of any Grist sisterhood, new or old.

NODE: MAJOR HEAT
DAY: 10

"STOP STARING AT ME. WHAT IS YOUR PROBLEM?"

"You look kinda like me."

"Yes, I told you. Does this mean you finally see it?"

Her hand, in spite of the fact that she starves herself, has grown. It's not quite full size, and it's still a little pink, but it is most definitely bigger. She's eating the fish now but barely enough to keep spirit and body together.

NODE: MAJOR HEAT
DAY: 12

ON THE FIFTEENTH DAY, SHE EATS TWO FISH. SHE STAYS AWAKE LONGER, and she stares and stares at me when I sleep. I know because whenever I wake up, she's staring at me.

"Dog damn it, do I have to smack you? Don't stare at me."

"I'm sorry, Dr Gristie."

"For the love of all the mothers on this battered earth, please call me Kirilow."

"I'm sorry, Dr Kirilow."

"Okay. That will do."

NODE: AUTUMN BEGINS
DAY: 4

HER SHIT STINKS. WE HAVE A DEAL THAT WE TURN OUR BACKS WHEN the other one has to go. Although I've worked all my life with living innards, sharing the shit ritual with this disgusting Cordova girl is a Mother-cursèd activity. I would very nearly murder an innocent person if it would mean I could get away from having to crap in the same room with this dirty Kora Ko. Even if it meant I were still in jail.

NODE: AUTUMN BEGINS
DAY: 11

"I AM GOING TO KILL YOU IF YOU DON'T STOP STARING AT ME." She turns away. Eats her fish. Not only does the toilet stink, but so does she. Her hair is growing thick and matted between those filthy, infested scales. One of them pops out while she's sleeping. When she wakes I point it out to her, just as a large roach crawls over it. She picks it up and plugs it back in. It's a good thing I have a strong stomach or I'd be sick myself.

NODE: LIMIT OF HEAT
DAY: 4

I'M ASLEEP BUT NOT VERY. THE CONCRETE FLOOR IS COLD AND HARD. I feel her eyes bore into me.

I leap up. I smack her, hard across the face. Our Mother forgive me. Our only starfish.

"Ow!" She comes at me, tries to punch me back, but I'm quick on my feet. She chases me around the room, but I weave and bob, avoid her blows. Dodge left! Skirt right! My feet dance fancy. Finally, she gets tired. Goes back to her corner.

"Why'd you hit me?"

"I told you to stop staring."

We eat our fish in silence.

NODE: LIMIT OF HEAT
DAY: 14

I'M ASLEEP. HER STARE IS LIKE A KNIFE AT MY BACK. I'M PUNCHING her, and I'm not even awake.

"Stop fucking staring at me! It's bad enough being down here with you, and you stink like a dead rat."

I drive my fist at her head. She tries to cover it with her hands and turns left, then right, attempting to avoid my blows. Bam! A score. Whap! A miss. Bam! Whap! Bam! Her ear bleeds. Whuff! She boots me in the gut. Didn't see that coming.

NODE: WHITE DEW
DAY: 12

WE DON'T TALK. WE EAT OUR FISH. WE DO OUR CONSIDERATE TOILET ritual. She stops staring, though, finally.

NODE: AUTUMN EQUINOX
DAY: 2

FIFTY-FOURTH DAY. WHEN THE FISH COME THROUGH THE SLOT, I'M ravenous. I grab mine, crouch in my corner and gulp it down, barely bothering to chew.

She takes hers. Eats it standing, with anxious revulsion.

When I'm done, she says, "I was staring at you because I think I saw them."

"Beg pardon?"

"All Gristies look alike, right? And you lost all your sisters?"

Our Mother save me.

"That night, the night of the revel, when I almost got uploaded—I saw ... some women. Go up as people, come down as fish and roses. They all looked like you. Not exactly, but, I mean, really, really close. Creepy close."

My turn to stare.

Our Mother of fish and roses

Our Mother of flames

Kora watches me, unsure whether to continue.

Did Grandma Chan Ling foresee me here? In this filthy dungeon with this dreadful girl?

"This fish we've been eating—"

I look at the floor.

"I think it might be—"

I don't want to know what she knows. "Please don't—"

She falls silent.

I look up at her. My heart doesn't give permission, but my eyes do.

"—your sisters—"

Now I really do want to be sick. But my body has absorbed its food. I dry retch. I heave until I can't breathe. Then a huge, rasping inhale. "You're lying."

"Why would I lie?"

"Liar, liar, liar!" I scream. I know she's right. With sharp nails, I tear at my own cannibal flesh. I'd pull it from the bones if I could. Dearest ones, now you are many times flesh of my flesh and bone of my bone. Our Mother forgive me, I knew not what I did. I tear, I shudder, I shake. I can't stop. My body convulses as though it's no longer my own.

She's on me then, but not to hurt me. She grips me in a bear hug, surprisingly strong. Holds me until the thrashing finally stops.

"It's fish now," she says. "So it's not them anymore."

She reeks like a stale and putrid ocean with dead things floating in it. It doesn't matter. I lean into her and burst into tears.

LOYALTIES SHIFT

NODE: AUTUMN EQUINOX
DAY: 8

THE BLUE DRESS THAT KAI TAK SENT HER IS TORN AND FILTHY. THERE'S a corner missing too—the corner she used to clean K2's wound the day she rescued him from wild dogs. She loved this dress when she first received it. Now she hates it. To think that Kai Tak and big brother Everest were living high on the hog while she, Charlotte, Kai Wai, and K2 shivered in the damp cold and ate rotten potatoes and pet goat. Her tender heart aches for poor Delphine. She curses this stupid dress. Kai Tak is not even her father! She wishes she had worn the brown bamboo-fibre dress that Uncle—no, Papa—Wai gave her instead. What horrors are he and Charlotte living through now? She shudders.

Kora eats her fish, knowing full well what it is but at last beyond caring. The Gristie doctor lies asleep in the corner. She hears a key in the lock. Miraculously, the heavy iron door creaks open, and there stands another Grist sister, one who looks just like Kirilow, only younger and rounder.

The doctor wakes up. "Calyx Kaki?"

"At your service, Groom Kirilow."

Behind her, there's an armed guard of tiger men uniformed in midnight blue.

"How did you ... You're alive ... and well fed ..."

The doctor stares at the young woman's belly.

"Come, most respected groom," says Calyx. "I know you've been here a long time, but we don't want to upset these helpful men."

The doctor doesn't move. "My bride was a starfish, not a doubler, so forgive me if I'm wrong, but ... are you pregnant?"

"I'm going to pop a puppy." Calyx beams. Her face grows dark then, as though she's remembering something.

Kirilow's eyes rise to Calyx's throat. "You can't be a doubler. You don't have the partho marks."

"Come on, we have to go."

One of the guards says, "Your young friend is now the consort of Godwin Austen 'K2' Ko. And our mistress."

It's the Gristie doctor's turn to go all bug-eyed.

Kora says, "Come on, Dr Kirilow. Let's get out of here."

The men lead Kora and Kirilow up through the levels. The whole parkade reeks of fish, but it is not the wet, dark ruin that it was—far from it. It is lit with a warm yellow light. The floors are tiled in fish and rose vine mosaic. Tapestry tigers cavort on the walls, and a thousand beaming revellers drink from earthen vessels and frolic among intricate tapestry trees. Kora and Kirilow slow their pace involuntarily, so astonished are they by the parkade's transformation. They become aware of a strange cacophony of coughs and laughter, which grows louder and more peculiar as they ascend.

They reach ground level. Daylight pours in through the entrance so bright it burns their eyes. It's been five solar nodes since they've been exposed to sunlight. From the mouth of the entrance sculpture, extends an orderly line of flu-sick men and their families, docile as sheep offering themselves for the tin-can tiger's dining pleasure.

Still up and farther up the spiralling levels they go. Through the open spaces between the levels they can see Saltwater Flats spread out before them, vast, damp, and rampant with flu. At the very top is a door. Calyx knocks.

"Enter," says a deep, rumbling voice.

Guards lead the prisoners into a large room with high ceilings and stained-glass windows. At an oak desk of mammoth proportions, sits a man of even greater proportions, all muscle, hair, and scale. Tendrils wave about him like the cilia of a giant anemone. Kora recognizes Marcus Traskin.

"Thank you, Calyx. Thank you, men. You may go." Above him, rich golden sunlight pours in through a panel that depicts cavorting tigers. "Here she is, Kora Ko of the new world order."

"Please," Kora says in the smallest and softest of voices. "I don't know what you mean."

He laughs, a jolly rumbling laugh tinged with something else, a bit dark, a bit sinister. "Of course you know. Have a seat."

There is a large plush leather couch from the time before facing the desk. And in front of it a heavy coffee table of the same wood as the desk. There's a beautiful rug knotted with birds and flowers beneath it. Kora hesitates.

"Go on, sit. Your friend too."

Kora and Kirilow sit. An attendant brings them each a glass of tiger wine. Kora doesn't touch hers, but Kirilow picks up the glass. Kora casts her a quick glance that says, *Don't!* Kirilow puts the glass down.

Marcus Traskin laughs. "Afraid of your family's best and most famous product, Kora Ko?"

"Not afraid," Kora lies. "Just not thirsty."

"Your loving companion is thirsty."

"She doesn't love me, and she's not thirsty." These words come from bravado, not real strength, but Kora is happy to have what she's got.

"That's better. Find yourself a little pride, girl." The floor shakes with Traskin's laughter. "Don't you know you are the heir to the Jemini fortune? The usurper Kai Tak Ko is dead of the flu."

"I never knew him."

"It doesn't matter. He no longer stands between you and what's yours."

"That's nonsense. My brother K2 is the heir. Besides, I don't want it."

"Wrong," rumbles Traskin. "On all three counts. It's not nonsense. Your brother is not the heir. And you do want it."

He's managed to rile her now. "You can't know what I want!"

"Aha. So you admit it. It doesn't matter if you think you are or not. I have Kai Tak Ko's last will and testament."

Kora glares at him.

"I think you know the truth. You know your brother lied to you. And that Kai Tak wrested Jemini illegally from Kai Wai, who didn't fight back because he was wracked with guilt for taking his brother's wife. You know this, and you have always known it. You just can't face it, because you are the product of Kai Wai's dirty, nasty wife-stealing. The love child of his filthy adultery."

"Don't you dare talk about Kai Wai that way. You know nothing about him. You know nothing about me either. How dare you presume?"

He laughs an even deeper laugh of righteous satisfaction. The floor shakes tectonic. "I knew it. I knew it!" He tries to control his laughter, but a deep, unpleasant chuckle continues to roll out of him. "Are you going to let your little shit of a brother keep you in prison while he owns and runs what's yours?"

Speech leaves her. Her gaze bores right through the flesh of the massive tiger man. She's so furious at his attempt to humiliate her that she's ceased to be intimidated.

"If you don't want it, I'd be happy to take it off your hands."

"If I didn't want it, why would I give it to you and not my brother?"

"Because!" he roars. "Because your brother is so terrified of your usurpation that he wants to kill you."

"He does not. That's why I was in prison. Because he doesn't want to kill me."

"You are a very, very silly girl. Your brother is your enemy. You could get rid of him and rule the whole of Saltwater Flats with me if you had the wits and nerve. And maybe Saltwater City and the quarantine rings beyond it too. Instead, you want to languish in the stinking prison your brother put you in and eat dead Grist sister fish every day? Must be because you're a girl."

Rage and confusion grip her. She launches herself up over the heavy coffee table and straight at the figure behind the oak desk.

Before she can get to him, the doors burst open. An armed guard of tiger men in dark red uniforms rush into the room, all clutching semi-automatic rifles from the time before. And on their heels, taller and more dignified than she remembers, who should enter the room but the young princeling himself, Kora Ko's not-so-long-lost brother Godwin Austen "K2" Ko. Beside him, the pregnant Grist sister Calyx Kaki, looking mightily pleased with herself.

"I see the proposition's been made," says K2.

"What of it?" demands Marcus Traskin.

"Back away, Kora," K2 says.

Sheepishly, Kora climbs down from her undignified post atop the oaken desk.

"She turned me down," Traskin says.

"Kora, is this true?"

"Of course it's true!" Traskin shouts.

Kora's mind races. K2 could kill her if she doesn't support him. Would he? She doesn't recognize this vicious young man. Traskin has confirmed what she suspected, that she is next in line to inherit Jemini. Does she give it to K2 and live? Or does she die and let him take it?

"It's true," she says.

"It better be," says K2. "And you, Marcus Traskin. I've caught you red-handed, trying to take Jemini from me. I suppose I'm my father's son after all." He raises his arm, then lowers it. The tiger men fire.

Marcus Traskin is nothing but a bleeding heap of scale and muscle dripping over a fine oak desk.

Kora screams and can't stop screaming.

"Get out of here," K2 says. "You're my sister, and you did not betray me. So go, and take that Gristie doctor with you, but get out of Saltwater Flats. Don't ever come back. If you do, you're a dead girl, do you get it? In setting you free, I release you from the bonds of family too. If I see you again, I'll treat you as I would any hostile stranger."

Somehow, Kora finds the will to stop screaming. She nods. She makes for the door, and the Gristie doctor follows her.

They flee the Pacific Pearl Parkade.

WHAT A RELIEF IT IS TO BE OUT IN THE SUN AND SMOG AGAIN. THE AIR is dry, though. Monsoon season is clearly over. The lineup of people waiting for the upload to Chang is long when they depart the mouth of the Pacific Pearl Parkade. The people are thin and sick, much more so than the ones Kora saw the night of the revel. The sellers of red bean buns and chicken skewers have vanished, taken by the flu or the upload while Kora and Kirilow wasted away in prison. The woman from the UMK and her disposable clothing are gone. So is the seller of oolichan grease traded down from Haisla territory, the bicycle repairman, and the scale artists. The street is eerily quiet.

Where there were N-lite sellers on the streets, now there are billboards the size of whole houses promising:

Life after life!
After life after!

Silver-bright cans the size of a bed tipped vertical, new since their imprisonment, glide past them stocked with vial after vial of the intoxicating green vapour N-lite.

They hurry along, half-afraid that K2 will change his mind and come after them, and half-horrified by the silence of the streets and the pushiness of the silver cans. From the windows of plague houses, no one peers surreptitiously through torn curtains anymore. A dry wind blows through the streets and seems to extinguish life as it goes.

A group of police gather at the street corner. They wear the same dark red uniforms as the guard attached to K2 Ko. On the next street corner, there's an even larger group of them.

They walk in silence. Kora reaches for Kirilow's hand, afraid the Gristie doctor will disappear. Kirilow must feel trepidation too. She clutches Kora's new pink hand too tightly.

The closer they get to the school, the more brooding Kora's

mood becomes. Will the girls still be there? How have their loyalties shifted in the past eighty-three days? She hasn't been a very good Cordova girl. They'd have plenty of reasons to do her in. She thinks about the vision of Isabelle she saw on that strange LiFT trip. Kora needs to tell her that Marcus is dead. Although Kora didn't kill Marcus with her own hands, he is dead. Is this good enough to keep Charlotte and Kai Wai safe? Kora's liver aches with longing to see them again. She wonders what it would feel like to be uploaded. And more, what it would feel like to be uploaded imperfectly.

The wind eddies in the courtyard, blowing dust and leaves in a circle as they reach the heavy double doors at the rear of the Cordova School.

"I don't like the police we saw at the corner," says Kirilow. "Let's get into the school and then get out quick as we can."

"Where will we go?"

"To New Grist Village of course."

"I need to see Isabelle. To tell her that Marcus Traskin is dead and make sure she's taking care of my mother and father. After that, I'll go with you to New Grist Village. There's nothing for me here anymore."

Kirilow smiles at her. "I'm glad you've finally come around."

Kora glances up at the doctor. It occurs to her for the first time that Kirilow is beautiful.

Kora grasps the brass door handle and presses her new but perfectly functional thumb into the worn latch. They step into the silent rear foyer. Begin to ascend the narrow, creaking stairs to the gathering hall at the top. They are still in the stairwell when they hear the scurrying of feet above. There's the sound of a person stumbling on a loose board, then a quick stomp as whoever it is stutters forward to regain balance.

A split second later, there's Velma, right up in Kora's face.

"Lady Kora! We thought you stole a catcoat, ran away, and died. But you're back. I can't believe it. There's been a lot of changes around here lately, you won't even recognize the place."

"Where is everyone?" says Kora, allowing herself at last to register the quiet.

"I mean *a lot* of changes," Velma says. "Won't you come up and eat some roasted fish, Lady Kora? The doctor is welcome too, of course. Most of the girls have taken the LïFT and gone to the happy after life after. There's only me, Tania, and Myra left now."

Kora feels a pang of nostalgia.

"Is the wheelbarrow still here? We'd like to get going," Kirilow says. "Do you know if the border to the second ring is still closed?"

"I heard that it's open, but only to a lucky few. Lots of people are dying or disappearing on that border. The UMK doesn't want Cosmopolitan Earth to take in too many refugees from Saltwater Flats. They've sent in military police. You should stay here. It's nice. And we have everything."

"My brother has taken over the Pacific Pearl Parkade," Kora explains. "There's more changes coming faster than you think."

"Myra and Tania have the truck," says Velma. "They're out foraging. They'll be back before dark, and we can all have a good talk then. Why don't you relax and eat some fish? Have a drink with me to remember the dead and the uploaded."

"No fish, thank you," says Kirilow. "And there's nothing to talk about. As soon as they're back, we have to leave. I'm going to get my needles and tent and a few other things." She makes a dash for the basement.

Kora goes too, to get her bamboo-fibre dress.

"Is there anything to eat besides fish?" asks Kora when she's back.

"Just fish," says Velma. "I'll get you one."

"No, tha—"

But Velma has already disappeared into the kitchen.

This is Kora's chance to find a way to communicate with Isabelle. While Kirilow and Velma are occupied, she slips out the door and heads in the direction of the harbour.

There's a large group of red-uniformed police at the corner of Cordova and Main. It's as though they're waiting for something. Fear bolts through Kora's gut. She wishes she still had her catcoat. She turns into the alley and heads toward the water.

The little shrine is still there. Before she enters, she instinctively casts a glance south towards the old Woodward's Building. Its neon *W* has gone dark. She ducks into the shrine. Kneels on the old cushion and prays to Our Mother for a communication. Then she rises and examines the sandbox. Could she be this lucky? There is a tendril scale, gas green as N-lite. She sticks it into the slot in her halo vacated by the red one that Tania took.

She's taken by a sense of wonder when the vision of Isabelle appears before her, even though she's been half hoping for it and half expecting it. Isabelle's lovely black hair wafts in the invisible breeze. But today's Isabelle vision is one of fury and vengeance. This time, she's not crying. Her eyes glower. Her whole body is tight with rage.

"And so, this is how you betray me? And to think you were a little charity case my parents rescued from the ruins of Old China out of the goodness of their hearts. How dare you? Do you remember the first time we met, at my parents' house in Shanghai, and how astonished you were that I was a real human being? Well, I am a real human being, with a real heart that can break, just like anyone else's. When my parents adopted you, I thought of you as a real sister. And you? You are nothing but a dirty, traitorous user. Don't think I won't have my revenge. Thank goodness I'm still someone in this town and beyond, someone with resources, someone with people. You'll get hit where you least expect it, I promise you that. Don't imagine you'll get away with everything you did to me, because you won't."

Abruptly as it rose up, the furiously gesticulating figure disappears. The message was not even for her. Why did she imagine it would be? Although it's none of Kora's business, she itches with curiosity to know who Isabelle is talking to. One thing she is sure of, though. This shrine is not a temple to worship Isabelle but to sell her out, to spread gossip. Traskin is dead, but Isabelle's humiliation continues. Although Kora resents Isabelle for kidnapping Charlotte and Wai, she still wishes the great inventor would not demean herself by recording these things.

"Give me back my mother and father," Kora says aloud to the statue of Isabelle on the shrine's altar.

The statue gazes benevolently down on her but says nothing.

NODE: AUTUMN EQUINOX
DAY: 8

WHEN I'VE PACKED ALL MY NEEDLES, MY BEAUTIFUL TENT, AND WHAT remains of my herbs, powders, and insects, I come back upstairs into the late-afternoon light. It will be dark soon, and I really hope Myra and Tania get back before then. Velma has laid out a feast on the school's best china. There are three plates, and atop each one sits a massive roasted fish, head still on, eyes cooked white. Each fish seems to grin, baring a mouthful of sharp, crisp teeth.

"Is this all you've got?" I ask. Although I ate them every day in jail and learned to accept what they were, I cannot ever eat fish again.

The little Cordova girl looks hurt. "Fixed it just for you, Doctor. Best fish, fresh fish. Just arrived today."

She doesn't know what it is, and if it's all she's got, there's no point telling her. "I know. I'm sorry. I would love some chard. Or a scrap of kale?"

"Haven't seen vegetables in weeks, Doctor Gristie. All the best foragers are gone now." Her pale face looks so sad. "How about some tiger wine?" She rushes away to get it before I can say no.

She's back again pretty quick. Plonks the glass bottle on the table. It's the shape of a rampant tiger, hideous grim. She produces a corkscrew from her pocket and, with a surprisingly expert hand, pops the bottle open.

"I don't drink the tiger," I say.

"Don't insult me now," Velma says, now getting really exasperated. "The rules of Our Mother are very strict."

She produces three lovely crystal tumblers salvaged or stolen from who knows where, pours the amber liquor into one and slides across to the next and then the next, without tilting the bottle back even a bit and without spilling a single drop.

"One for Lady Kora," she explains. "And one for you, Doctor Gristie." She pushes one of the glasses in my direction. "Just *try*. It's good for you, very fortifying and so delicious too! Here's to the Cordova Dancing School for Girls as it was, and all the women and girls who lived here!" She lifts her tumbler and draws the wine into her gullet in a single gulp. "Aaahhh! So refreshing."

I feel like a bad guest. I pick up the glass. "To the Cordova School!" I toss it back. The wine is bitter and boozy, not at all pleasant. I try not to make a face. "When will Myra and Tania return?"

"Eat some fish, please, Doctor Gristie. We Cordova girls are proud of our hospitality." She's irritated with me, but I just want to get out of here.

I stare at the fish she's pushed in front of me, and the fish stares back. "I just can't, Velma. I'm sorry."

She grunts, visibly offended.

Myra and Tania come crashing in. "Velma! Any food?" They get to the top of the stairs.

"Doctor Gristie? We thought you died or went back to your village," says Myra.

"Food, great, I'm starving," says Tania and dives into the fish that Velma made for Kora.

Myra sits down and begins eating off Tania's plate. I push mine over to her so she doesn't have to do that.

She says, "We gotta make a plan to get out of here. I mean, within the hour. News on the street is that K2 Ko has taken over the Pacific Pearl and killed Marcus Traskin. He's forcibly uploading everyone who's left in the flats. Wants to rebuild the city with people made by Jemini. Ha ha, kind of like you, Doctor Gristie, only newer and better. And under K2's control."

"I know," I say, though no one listens.

"We're already packed," Velma says. "Just waiting for you to come back with the truck."

"Good," says Tania, revealing the half-chewed fish in her mouth.

"Have some fish, Doctor Kirilow, and let's go," Myra says, pushing the half-eaten creature back at me. Ugh. She pours two shots of tiger wine and nudges one my way. Downs hers.

I don't touch mine.

"We're waiting for Kora," says Velma. "She's packing."

"What does she have to pack?" Myra asks. "She doesn't own anything."

"This is true," Velma says. "She came to us with nothing but a head full of lice-infested scales and two dirty dresses. I'll go look for her."

We hear her running through the building, checking all the offices and smaller rooms, the bathroom, the basement, my clinic, and Madame Dearborn's catcoat lab. We hear her run up the basement steps and out the front door. I get up and look out the window. The streets are swarming with Pacific Pearl police. One of them grabs Velma and corrals her into a cordon where other unfortunate denizens are also trapped.

"Velma!"

The police march the whole cordon slowly in the direction of the parkade.

"They've taken her!"

Myra and Tania come to the window. "That stupid idiot," Myra says. She rushes downstairs to rescue Velma. Tania rushes after her. "Don't, Myra! They'll take you too."

The back door slams. I hear the distinctive sound of Kora's boots clomp down the main floor hall. "What are you doing?"

"Velma ran out into the street. She was looking for you." Myra's voice.

"We have to help her!" cries Kora.

"Don't go out there," Tania says. "They will just take you to the Pacific Pearl, and that will be the end of you. All our other sisters are already lost. Please don't go!"

"Go," says Myra. "And we'll be rid of you at last."

We hear gunshots.

I say, "Come on, Velma's already lost to us. Let's just take the back door and go."

"No," Kora says. Velma was her only real friend in this Mother-forsaken school. "I'll go."

I make for the stairs. I feel heartsick for the little Cordova Dancing girl who tries so hard to be kind. But I can't lose Kora.

A hissing sound. My eyes sting. I turn and see we've left a window open. I close it quick before the hall can fill with tear gas. A ball of fire erupts from the centre of the cordon. Space opens in the ranks of the tiger guard as the ethanol bomb tears through police lines and cops move to dodge it. Their neat columns dissolve. A crowd appears from nowhere to confront them. There's a stutter of machine gun fire, and a whole line of protesters falls, crying for their lovers and mothers. Then a return volley of eth bombs, and flames rip along the ground right in front of the school. One of them tears into the cordon where Velma is held. The screams I hear will never be heard in a world ruled by Our Mother. Blessed are the sheep, and blessed are the roses—I won't be afraid. A searchlight comes on. I duck away from the window. A thin whistling fills the air. I don't wait for the explosion. I tear out of the hall and down the stairs. We need to get out of here now.

"It's your fault," Myra says to Kora as they close and lock the doors of the school for the last time. "We could have Velma, but we're stuck with you. One day you'll pay. I'll make sure of it."

PART IV

CASCADIA YEAR: 127 TAO (TIME AFTER OIL)

UNITED MIDDLE KINGDOM CYCLE 80, YEAR 42 (WOOD SNAKE YEAR)

GREGORIAN YEAR: 2145

NODE: AUTUMN EQUINOX
DAY: 9

"YOU HAVE TO HIDE IN THE BACK," TANIA TELLS KORA AND KIRILOW as they board the Cordova School's precious truck. "We can't cross the border with you openly because both the CEC and the tiger police are culling Grist sisters."

"I'm not a Grist sister," Kora says.

Tania glances down at the new pink hand. "Apparently you are. But don't be afraid. I'm pretty sure we can get you across."

The back of the truck is full of large empty fruit crates from some recent smuggling operation. They're labelled Blue Elk Apples, Moravian Peach Farm, Akal Arnouse Pineapples, Takahashi Mangoes, Kuan Yin Lychees. All farms in the Fourth Quarantine Ring, where Kora has never been. She crawls into an empty walnut box. As the truck rolls along, she feels the texture of the streets she's known all her life, jagged and broken like the city itself. Kora plays with the green tendril scale she took from the Isabelle shrine. If only it went two ways so Kora could talk to that kidnapper and murderer Isabelle, to ensure that Charlotte and Kai Wai, whatever their form, are safe.

They are all kidnappers and murderers, as, she supposes, was the uncle she thought was her father, Kai Tak Ko. What does this mean about her? She pinches her own flesh, thinking of her family history, the horror baked into her body. Myra holds her responsible. Maybe she's right to. Still, of all the people to get stuck with as she flees everything she ever knew. At least Kirilow is back here with her, in her own fruit crate, rolling with her towards a strange and unknown future.

THE WALNUT BOX IS DARK AND REEKS OF ROT. THE SMELL CHOKES her. When she can't stand it anymore, she crawls out.

"Hey, Kora!" Kirilow hiss-whispers. "Get back into your box. The plague rings are dangerous!"

Kora doesn't care. Although she feels a tenderness for the doctor, she hasn't forgiven Kirilow for cutting off her hand. She certainly doesn't trust her. And this may be the last time she ever sees Saltwater Flats, the only home she's ever known.

She watches it flow by through the crack between the folding halves of the back door. Night falls fast. She sees the black shapes of half-collapsed plague houses, the skeletons of office buildings, scale shops, and coconut palms. The truck crosses a neighbourhood where the fighting is live. By the light of a burning cop wagon, Kora sees women run. The truck speeds by. She sees a broken street light topple. It pulls long black wires with it. The wires crackle and shoot sparks that light up ruined houses. Kora mutters an awkward prayer for those who live in them now, if there are any left.

At a check stop, a Pacific Pearl cop on a motorcycle makes Myra get out of the truck. Kora hears him demand papers. Myra fires back some clipped words, impatient, subtly hostile yet still polite. Kora hears Tania get out of the truck. There is grumbling, accusation, a little righteous indignation. The two Cordova girls return to their seats, and the truck begins to move again. It's only when Kora lets her breath out that she realizes she's been holding it.

Kora knows they are at a border when she sees the rows of coiled razor wire on either side of the truck demarcating twelve aisles. There's a long line of denizens, mostly women and children, from Saltwater City proper and Saltwater Flats extending as far as her view through the door crack permits her to see, denizens who have travelled on foot, as well as by every kind of vehicle Kora has ever seen on the streets—bicycles, rickshaws, handcarts, and rusted out shells of cars from the time before, pulled by dogs or mules. Each vehicle is surrounded by small clusters of mostly women and children. The Cordova School truck is the only eth-powered vehicle in sight. Red-uniformed Pacific Pearl cops and yellow-uniformed Cosmopolitan Earth soldiers pull the occasional group to the side.

A large group kneels just to the left of where the Cordova truck is stopped in line. Young children, all with the pale skin and black hair of Lewis Lai, quiver and cry. Only two women take care of the lot of them. Three red-uniformed cops and fifteen or so soldiers in yellow crowd around. The ones in yellow shout and argue. The ones in red raise their guns. In a second there is a spatter of machine gun fire, and the women and children fall to the ground. Kora pulls away from the crack between the doors and scrambles to the corner of the cargo space, guts heaving.

"Hey!" Kirilow whisper-yells from her greengage plum box. "You better hide! You want us to get caught?"

A cold, dry breeze blows through the crack between the doors. Kora begins to shiver and can't stop. She crawls back into her walnut box.

There are voices at the window.

"How many of you?"

"Just two," Myra says.

"Destination?"

"The New Origins Archive in the Third Quarantine Ring."

"Huh. Step out of the vehicle please."

"We've got nothing, and we're in a terrible hurry."

"Please step out of the vehicle."

Kora hears Myra and Tania step out.

"You sure there's no one else?"

Myra speaks with the same steady confidence she used to dominate the dancing girls. "There's no one, ma'am."

"Mind if we take a look?"

No amount of bravado is cover for a thorough truck search. Myra has to unlock the back doors.

I hear Tania's voice. "Could you get Sloane?"

"Sloane?"

"I'm Tania Manuel, General Manuel's niece. Sloane is your commanding officer, I believe. And my cousin."

There's a moment's silence. "I recognize you, Tania Manuel. We have no time here for the ones who run when the going gets tough. Now, I have to do my job. Please open the back doors of your truck."

Tania says, "You know, I could call you and my auntie traitors for handing the reins to the UMK. Where is she? Where is Old Geraldine?"

"She's where you should be. With your mom, trying to bring an end to this refugee nightmare while the UMK rattles its sabres, and Pacific Pearl police kill Saltwater denizens right on our border. Come on, I don't have time for this."

There is a long stretch of silence.

"Don't make me arrest you."

"My cousin Sloane. Please."

There are noises Kora can barely hear. Arrangements of some kind being made. Inside her box, Kora sweats like a pig at slaughter time.

"What's going on here?" Another soldier, perhaps older, intervenes.

"It's Tania Manuel, trying to smuggle god only knows what through council territory."

"Tania."

"Sloane."

"You know how much your mom misses you?"

"I know."

"The city you're departing is generating thousands of refugees."

"It is."

"Know anything about it?"

"There's been a messy regime change."

"What's in the truck?"

Tania sighs. "A couple of Grist sisters. Old gen ones from the time before."

"Weren't you trucking a couple of those last time? They're worth a lot of money on the black market."

"You wanna buy them?"

"Not really. Too stinky," says Cousin Sloane. "These Grist sisters—dangerous ones or just ordinary ones?"

"Pretty ordinary."

"Let me see."

Kora hears Myra fiddle with the keys. The lock clicks. The doors fly open.

"Better come out," Myra says.

Kora and Kirilow crawl out of their boxes and into the light, heads bowed. Kora sweats as her beloved goat must have sweated atop the roof of the Woodward's Building on the day of her sacrifice. *Please don't let me die quick and unknown on this terrible border.*

"Let's see you," says Cousin Sloane. Both Kora and Kirilow raise their heads.

The soldiers are imposing but beautiful, like Tania, with broad faces and brown eyes. They wear their dark hair tied neatly and tucked into their peaked caps. They look at the two sorry travellers, and Kora imagines what they must see—two young, dirty, scrawny girls of no account.

"That one has a lot of scales," says the soldier who is not Cousin Sloane.

"They're all infected. Look," Tania says. She lifts Kora's hair, and they can all see the insects crawling on her scalp and red, angry flesh following the path of her halo. Kora feels ashamed.

"Leave the Gristies and I'll let you go."

Kora opens her mouth to say she's not a Gristie, then thinks better of it.

"No deal," Myra says. "We need the Gristies where we're going."

"And where would that be?"

"New Origins Archive."

Why do the Cordova girls need us? Kora wonders. *Wouldn't they be better off dumping us?* She doesn't know what to want. The sweat pours off her. She begins to shake.

"It's the Gristies or you, Tania. If I brought you home, I think I'd be forgiven for letting them go," Sloane says. "The UMK is pressuring us like heck to shut the border altogether. Your mother and auntie need your skills of strategy and diplomacy."

"Damn mothers and aunties," Tania says.

"Don't be disrespectful," says Sloane. "Come home. It's time."

"Let me talk to my friend."

Tania and Myra whisper together in low voices, so low Kora could not hear if she stood between them.

Finally, they fall silent and move apart.

"I will come home," Tania says. "I'm not averse to coming home, you know. I never was. If the old ladies would just take my advice once in a while."

So Tania is returned to her people, and the truck goes through the checkpoint.

Kirilow climbs into the cab of the truck. Kora goes with her, even though she'd rather not be in such close quarters with Myra.

"Praise be to Our greatest Mother of Chang light and Eng night," Kirilow chants. "Praise to her mountains and rivers. Praise to Our Mother of deliberate actions. Praise to Our Mother of luck. Praise, at least for now."

Kora is exhausted. She closes her eyes and dozes as the truck sails across the Second Quarantine Ring.

She wakes when Kirilow asks Myra, "What did you mean when you said you need us at the New Origins Archive?"

"Nothing. I didn't mean anything. It was just a way of getting out."

Kirilow casts Kora a worried glance. Kora gazes back with eyes that say, *Watch out.*

The road continues alongside a mountain that grows ever steeper as late afternoon becomes early evening.

As the land flattens out, the misshapen heap of the New Origins Archive looms on the horizon. It's very dry now, and the air is full of smoke from the forest fires that burn up north. The NOA sits atop the sagebrush-and-sand-dotted earth like a giant pile of snakes. Or naked ladies' legs.

I know what it looks like, thinks Kora, remembering the first scale Wai ever gave her, on the subject of reefs and corals. It looks like a brain coral, a really enormous one. This one's all curves and convolutions, pale violet flecked with green. Off its surface, fine, translucent tendrils wave, so fine she doesn't see them at first. They are a million times finer than her own tendril scales and infinitely longer. When she first registers them, she thinks they're made of pale blue light, beaming down from Eng, who hangs high, small, and round above the archive as they arrive. The tendrils don't touch the distant satellite but only wave gracefully at it, like the finest seaweed swaying with a gentle tide. As they get closer, Kora's horrified to see a tendril snatch a little sparrow out of the sky and yank it down into the hungry folds of the archive's pulsing surface.

The New Origins Archive has been built into the side of a copper quarry with a lake at the bottom. Its structure looks like a stack of vertebrae for some prehistoric gargantua, spine diving deep into the ground. The visible part of the spine leans into the wall of the quarry and seems to merge with it, as though the stone and earth of the wall are all that remains of that gargantua's flesh, older by far than the Caspian tiger brought back from extinction to make tiger-bone wine. The earth of the wall glimmers a rusty green. Down one side, a steep, narrow waterfall tumbles, feeding the artificial lake below.

MI CASA ES SU CASA 38

NODE: AUTUMN EQUINOX
DAY: 9

THE LAST TIME I CAME TO THE NEW ORIGINS ARCHIVE WAS AFTER THE HöST destruction of Grist Village, after the death of old Auntie Radix Bupleuri and my beloved Peristrophe Halliana, under a fog of my own forget-me-do. And it was only a year and a half ago that I came to the New Origins Archive with my mother double, Glorybind Groundsel, for my rite of spring. It feels like a lifetime. I ache for the old Grist Village that I will never see again. Let this be the briefest of stopovers, a place to rest and refuel, quick so quick. I want to find the place where I killed that elk last summer, the place where Bombyx Mori, Corydalis Ambigua, and their fresh litter of puppies wait for me and Kora to come and start a new sister village.

When I see Elzbieta's face, I want to weep, but I know I can't show any such weakness. We are safe from the clutches of the new tiger police, but that does not mean safe generally.

"Our Mother has blessed us, Kirilow Groundsel. I feared I might never see you again." Elzbieta's small teeth are too white, too sharp.

I beam at her, bright as I know how. "My hands have been a little full." I nod in the direction of my dwindling entourage. "There were many more, but our luck has not been the best."

"Myra Mao of course I know. Welcome back," says Elzbieta.

Kora casts Myra a resentful glance.

"That's not Peristrophe Halliana is it?" She nods at Kora. "She looks young. And if you don't mind my saying, she needs to wash her face."

"I lost my beloved Peristrophe to the flu, remember? That's my sister, Glorybind Groundsel's last daughter double." A white lie to keep Kora safe.

"My good friend, I'm so sorry about Peristrophe. I had forgotten. This Wood Snake year has been one of many changes." Elzbieta's look of sympathy might be genuine, but there is something beneath it that unsettles me.

"I had hoped to come back sooner, with your money."

"Never mind that. Come in, come in. *Mi casa es su casa,* let's have a good catch-up and talk about business later." She hasn't forgotten either.

I beam brighter to hide the squirming in my belly.

She beckons us in through the navel of the archive, this gorgeous conservatory of seeds, spores, and cells from which new life could spring and make the world anew.

Lights from the time before made of sparkly teardrops hang from holy high ceilings, over a glorious, wide hall all grey stone and cedar beam. Those teardrops catch light from sky-high windows, cast sparkles and shadows over red leather armchairs and sofas, tiger-skin rugs, and elk-wool wall weavings.

"Please, sit wherever you like," says Elzbieta. "Make yourselves at home."

Myra flops down in one of the comfortable armchairs. I wonder how long she's been trading with the NOA. Her relaxed posture says it's been years. In a moment, a trio of lovely women—one very young dressed in yellow satin, one perhaps my own age in green linen, and one quite elderly in vibrant pink silk—file into the room bearing flasks of tea and baskets of steaming food. Elzbieta introduces them as Buttercup, Vera, and Rose. I remember Vera from that long-ago night of the bonfire at Mourning Rock.

Kora eats six dumplings and has a few sips of tea. While the rest of us chat, she nods in her comfortable armchair, unable to stay awake. The shame of it! My mother double would have rapped me across the knuckles with her arbutus wood cane or popped me on the skull with the back of her pipe. *Wake up, girl! Did that old Cordova Madame teach you nothing of Our Mother's simplest etiquette?* Kora actually begins to snore, though softly. I'm mortified.

The pink and green clad attendants appear as if from nowhere. One of them casts me a discreet glance, as though asking permission. What to do? I nod. They wake her gently and guide her to the back of the archive, where the guest sleeping quarters are.

"Where did you find her, Groom Kirilow?" Elzbieta asks, as soon as the girl and the two attendants are out of earshot. "She's the spitting image of your elegant Peristrophe Halliana, or she would be, if she were cleaner. But she's not really your sister, is she?"

Myra takes six dumplings at once, leans back, and slurps them down. Leans forward again and takes six more. She doesn't belong to me the way Kora does. I don't have to feel shame for her.

"Of course she is. Who else would she be?"

"I think you found her in Saltwater City. I think she's a descendant of the Jemini escapee and Grist queen Chan Ling but from the left-hand line of tiger wine factory workers, the ones who were hidden and so not expelled in the Great Grist Purge. Am I right, or am I right? But she's a mongrel. There's some non-Grist blood in her too. Don't deny it." Her eyes follow mine until I'm forced to look at her. She holds my gaze and won't let go.

"What do you want?" I ask.

"You're fond of her, aren't you? Planning to adopt her?"

"It's not like that."

"A lover? Aren't you the precious pair ..." She beams, but there's something dark and troubling beneath her teasing.

"Don't be rude." I wish she would stop, and I know she won't. "She's nothing, just a girl I found ..."

"I thought so. In Saltwater City."

"By Our Mother's teeth, she's travelling with me, and it doesn't concern you."

"And yet you eat my food and drink my tea."

"I thought we were friends. I thought you might help."

"Of course we're friends, Groom Kirilow. Aren't I helping you?"

"I'll find the renminbi I owe you and pay you back on the next visit, I promise I will."

"Kirilow Groundsel, you wouldn't lie to me, would you? When I'm such a good friend to you? I know Grist Village was burned to the ground. I know there are survivors who have moved it elsewhere. You're going to New Grist Village, and you are not coming back." She claps her hands twice, and yet another lovely attendant darts out from behind a cedar post.

"Bring us some wine. *Gan bei, gan bei!*"

Her civility is the thinnest of veneers. She knows the world has radically changed since I was here with my mother double. If she were offered a womb bomb filled with Grist sisters for a good price, she would buy it and not bat an eyelash. I stop arguing.

Elzbieta orders dish after opulent dish, and wines and spirits made from all the herbs, fruits, and grains grown in the massive green domes of the New Origins Archive. Myra piles her plate and eats like she hasn't seen food in a week. I am in no mood to eat or drink, not even when the beets and red mustards appear. Like a child, I play with my food, and excuse myself as soon as it is honourable to do so.

"You'll stay long enough to celebrate Mid-Autumn with us, won't you?" says Elzbieta before she'll let me go.

"I hope to be on my way sooner than that."

"Nonsense. Of course you'll stay."

NODE: AUTUMN EQUINOX
DAY: 9

KORA DREAMS SHE'S FORAGING AS THE CORDOVA GIRLS HAVE TAUGHT
her. She's digging through earth so radioactive it glows. She uncovers
the tar and stucco roof of some ancient supermarket, bashes at it
with her shovel. It gives more easily than any roof she's ever known
in real life. She descends through the hole on coarse hemp rope,
pulls out her jar of fireflies. Rows and rows of tuna cans, covered in
the dust of ages but otherwise intact, reveal themselves in the pale
light. She hears footsteps in another aisle. She should be afraid, she
thinks. But she's not. The footsteps are uneven in a familiar way.
Papa Wai? Is that you?

Then a gentle knocking, knuckles on wood. There's no wood
among these ancient cans. *Where am I?* A jolt of fear bolts through
her. Police? No, Kora, you've left Saltwater City. You are safe. Oh,
the door. She gets up.

The knock at the door keeps coming. Kora attempts to put on
the robe that's been laid out for her, but its tie gets tangled in the
intricate latticework of the chair on which it lies. By the time she
untangles it and gets to the door, the person is gone. She hears their
footsteps turn a corner. Rushes after them just in time to catch a

glimpse of a familiar figure. Charlotte? She hears a familiar bleat. It cannot be ... But this goat is alive and whole. "Ma-aaa-aaa-aaa." Just like old times.

She hurries around the corner, chasing the sound of Charlotte's footsteps and the bleating of the goat. Halfway down the hall, a blue door stands open. The goat's bleat echoes as though it has entered a cavernous space. The footsteps that can't be any but her mother's echo strangely too. As Kora approaches the blue door, her feet begin to weigh heavy. She stands at the open entrance and stares down into the dark. That baleful bleat again. Kora knows it can't be her own goat, but the tone of its bleat is exactly what she remembers. "Maaaaaa-aaaaaa-aaaaaaa."

Kora puts her foot on the top step, and nearly trips over a single red beet lying there as a chemical candy smell engulfs her. N-lite. She could turn back now, before it's too late. She pauses for a second, then stoops to pick up the beet. What does this mean?

"Ma-aaa-aaa-aaa."

"I'm coming, Delphine!" She puts the beet in her pocket and steps onto the second step.

A rumbling dread fills her, a quiet, earthly dread, warm and dense. Her head fills with strange language, a chant she half recognizes:

eng low soul bowl
fool pool true who
low load new you
right brain crime scene

Her limbs weigh as though pulled by the gravity of a much larger planet. Madame taught her how to slide into dread when necessity calls. She settles into the rumbling darkness and prepares for whatever comes. Catches a whiff of something green and bitter. Charlotte's footsteps echo in the hollow stairwell. It is truly dark now, a darker dark than Kora has ever known. Dark that smells of stone and damp and the low hum of the elemental force that sustains the earth itself.

She hears Myra's voice in her inner ear, competing with the chant: *Don't you know you are the source of the tiger flu? If not for you, all our brothers, sons, fathers, and uncles would still be alive. If not for you, the ice caps would not have melted, there would be no disease, no war, no death. We would live in fields of abundance, with all the apples and rice, pork and fish we could possibly want. We would live in houses of glory on streets paved in renminbi. We would drive hummers so fast that departure and arrival would be the same moment. We would be happy, perfect, loving, magnanimous. Stories of our beauty and wealth would spread all over the world, and people would come from distant lands to pay tribute. If not for you, if not for you ...*

But beyond Myra's voice—Charlotte's footsteps and the goat's gentle bleat.

The voices of the other Cordova sisters join Myra's. The deep hum of the chant *brain frame face drain* clamours in Kora's inner ear in dissonance with *if not for you if not for you* until she thinks she will go deaf. She feels them on her skin. They pinch her arms, her legs, her back, her face. And where they pinch, she feels infection stir. Now the pinchers are gone, but where they have dug their sharp nails into her flesh, great lesions bloom and fill with pus. They burst and a hot, noxious filth from inside her body gushes out. The pus oozes over the surface of her skin. What if she catches the flu down here, and dies of it, and no one ever finds her? It's not too late to turn around and go back up the stairs. She glances over her shoulder at the light coming from the hallway above. She looks down into the velvet dark.

Don't cry, don't cry, spoiled girl, plague source, foul and revolting. If you cry, it's all over. If you cry, it proves you did it, say the voices.

She bites her lip and listens for Charlotte's distant footsteps. Her body weighs like a sack of rotten potatoes.

If only you would give us everything you are withholding. If only you were not so stingy, so selfish, so mean and uncaring. If only you had never been born, and your mother and father had never been born. If only your grandfathers and grandmothers had never been born. If only this world had never made the conditions to bring you into being. The tiger would not be free from its rug. The wine would not be free from its bones. The flu would not be free from the wine, and we, who are good, holy, and blessed by Our Mother, would be healthy, wealthy, and well.

The goat bleats loudly and so distinctly that Kora knows it can't be any other than her own Delphine. *Rain same main game.*

She feels something sharp against her chest. In the next moment, a blade tears through her, sinks into her beating heart. In another moment, there's a knife in her eye. Her skull opens, and the coils of her brain snake out and down her face, spongy, wet, and soft. She shrieks. A knife goes into her belly, slits her open from zip to zatch. Someone's pulling, tugging at her organs. She feels them, coiling her intestines out, loop by loop. She screams and can't stop screaming. She becomes the scream, the howl of a lost dog in the night, the scream of a decade past and the decade prior to that, the trail of tiger flu in reverse. She screams the emergence of the quarantine rings, the first epidemic, the tiger wine craze, the end of oil, the launch of Chang and Eng, the expulsion of the Grist sisters, their legalization for labour on Pacific Gyre Island, the discovery of Chan

Ling's genetic mutation, Chan Ling's immigration from the United Middle Kingdom to Cascadia, the consolidation of the United Middle Kingdom from China and all the little Asian countries that surround it, the Japanese occupation of Hong Kong, the birth of Chan Ling's great-grandmother to a young Hakka woman in the village of Happy Valley in the early days of the British colonial administration, the Opium War, the fall of the Ming dynasty ... She screams and screams and screams, and in her mind's eye sees a sideways figure eight, the loop of infinity screaming the scream of her long history. The howl of the O of ooooooooooooooooooooooooo green dark and the earth and the blue dark beneath it. She howls the woooooooooooooooooooo of the blue dark turning purple and groans the groan of the heavy wet earth, the hum and rumble of its darkest core, a sleeping tiger moaning nightmares to the world, burning burning the infrared flame of immortal forest everything it longs to release but holds within only by the grace of Our Mother.

When Kora is sure that she is pure pain without a body, she feels an unexpected warmth in her new right hand, the only part of her that is real.

Charlotte.

"It's all right, child. It's okay. You made it."

Her mother's hand is the temperature of her own blood. The skin is soft and wrinkled.

"You're alive." Relief floods through her, followed by unbidden tears. As fast as it came on, the searing pain dissipates. "Oh, Charlotte. Oh, Mom."

"Praise Isabelle, I am alive, though changed."

"Changed how?"

"I'm an attendant of the great satellite Eng."

Kora raises an eyebrow in the dark.

"Don't be afraid. We will visit the underground sisters. We will visit the Dark Baths. You will have a dream that will show us how to proceed. You've found us now."

The goat gently butts Kora's left hand with its hard, rough head. She strokes it between the eyes. "Who are the underground sisters?"

"My subjects," Charlotte says. "Some have been here since the last ice age. Some come from the end of oil. One is a Grist sister, like you and me."

"We're not ... You never said ..."

"Since my arrival I've wanted to meet them, but they will not speak to me. If they speak to you, it's a sign you are meant to stay here with me, inherit the archive and everything in it."

"I can't ... There's not ..."

"No reluctance," Charlotte says. "You take the fate you are given. It's the law of Our Mother. This archive is a good place, a place of memory. It holds the blueprints for everything animal, vegetable, and mineral that lived in the time before. If it is given to you, it is a gift you must accept with grace."

The chant in Kora's head grows low and slow as the darkness deepens:

face place grin fine
small game goon tool
soon rule soul bowl
kow tow know how

"I wasn't sure if the you I saw that day at the Pacific Pearl was real."

"I'm real now ..."

Kora begins to shiver. "Cold ..."

auld syne small game
main frame brain drain
old sign self same
true fool goon you

Charlotte pulls something out from the folds of what sounds, in the dark, like a heavy cloak, though Kora can see nothing. The something mewls, high and thin.

"Catcoat?" Joy wells up in the pit of her belly. She feels her belly. It is small but whole. She touches her head. It too is intact. She takes the catcoat and steps gratefully into it. Its contented warmth flows deliciously through her.

"We start at zero," says Charlotte.

And even further down they go on the cold stone steps. As they descend, Kora begins to see again. A thin light glows from the deep earth itself. *Phosphorescence,* her geology memory scale tells her. Kora is tempted to look at Charlotte's face but is afraid to.

At minus three they are met by a pale young woman with white hair and eyes. Her skin is so translucent the veins glow with blue-grey blood running beneath them. She speaks the same Salt Inglish as Kora and Charlotte but with a slightly earthy accent.

"At last you've brought the one who will care for us. We eat well here but require more root vegetables, especially more beets and purple carrots. There are seven of us who are willing to come to the surface in the daylight hours to work the root gardens, as long as we can return to our home at night. We sleep well, though we hear the archive's construction noises sometimes, in the early morning."

Kora stares at the young woman in pure astonishment. "Who ..."

But Charlotte puts her index finger to her lips, gives the pale woman a polite nod. "Seen and heard, sister," she says.

"Who are these women, and where are we?" Kora blurts before Charlotte can stop her. "Why did you agree to go take part in Marcus and K2's terrible experiments? I hope it wasn't to fund my education at the Cordova School. How did you end up with Isabelle?"

Charlotte gazes at her sorrowfully, as though she wants to say something. She opens her mouth, but no words come out. Again, she puts her finger to her lips.

Below minus six, the phosphorescence diminishes and the dark grows thick again. At minus nine, Kora senses a short stocky body moving in the dark. She hears the person sit down. Charlotte sits too and pulls Kora down beside her. Kora can receive only fragments of this earth sister's croak.

" ... neglected and ... so alien so ... your language ... misunderstand ... distraction from the truth ..."

Charlotte explains as they descend farther into the dark. "I couldn't get them to talk, but I can translate now that they are speaking. The sisters at minus nine want us to come down here more, to sit and be with them. They carry the history of the time before. That sister remembers the collapse of the dollar, the riots, the lootings, the genocides, and the Six Quakes—did your dancing teachers teach you about those? Most surface people cannot remember. The sisters at minus nine hold the horror for us. It is an important service. They eat mushrooms and earth fish. They want nothing from us but our time."

Kora nods gravely, but she feels like she is going to burst. "Charlotte, I should never have left you. I'm sorry, Mom."

That look again, but no words.

The sister who meets them at minus twelve does not attempt surface language at all. Charlotte hails and praises her, but she grunts dismissively, then groans as though in terrible agony. Kora thinks she sees eyes glitter in the darkness of the stairwell, but there is no light here. Her own eyes must be playing tricks. The groaning sister accompanies them to minus fifteen.

At minus fifteen, the sister who meets them towers over them in the dark. She is so tall, Kora can hear her head brushing against the ceiling. She takes Kora's small mittened hand in her own earthy enormous one and leads them farther down into the dark.

The sister who meets them at minus eighteen is so silent they cannot even hear her feet on the stone steps. Her silence echoes the silence of the earth. Down and farther down they go, until, at minus thirty-six, the earth itself leaves them at the door of the Dark Baths. The warm, moist air reeks of sulphur. Kora feels as though she has acquired another language, one with much wisdom but no words. She wants words more than anything. Presses Charlotte one more time, but her mother will not respond to her questions. Instead, Charlotte guides her to the chamber that houses the Dark Baths and hands her a towel.

Kora sighs. "I'm sorry, Mom. I should have been a better daughter. I was a terrible daughter, wasn't I?"

Charlotte gives her a sad little smile and pushes her towards the water.

Kora resists. The water's darkness makes it look deep. What if there are living things in it?

"Go on, daughter. While the water is open to you."

She takes a step forward. The damp air grows damper still, as though the pool were pulling her.

Kora surrenders. She slips out of her catcoat and into the water.

She arcs up onto her back and floats. No need to close her eyes. It is so dark that inside and outside have become one and the same. She hears voices. She closes her eyes and thinks she perceives brief flashes of light through her eyelids. She opens her eyes, and it is dark as ever. Something like sleep descends, and she surrenders to it. She sees a city of towers. The outside of every tower is lined with elevators going up and down, up and down, as day turns into night and night turns into day. Squid things from another dream, long ago, sit atop the towers, growing fatter and fatter as the elevators go up and down. All along, the voices of the Cordova girls echo in her head: *If not for you, if not for you.*

She wakes. *You've arrived at Quay D'Espoir, the very first settlement Isabelle built for the travellers to Eng,* says a new voice in her head.

The water of the Dark Baths feels cold and smells unpleasantly of stale urine.

What are the Dark Baths? she thinks to the new voice.

brain frame face drain
rain same main game
pin time dream wine
crane brine sync line

Upload interface? Kora mouths.
Download.

SHE KICKS GENTLY TO PROPEL HERSELF TO THE STONE STEPS AND climbs out of the baths. Where she left the catcoat, someone has left a towel on the rail. She dries herself and dresses. A damp chill wafts off the surface of the water. A different, stonier chill emanates from the walls and with it a faint light that renders the shapes around her in shades of grey. It is strange to be awake down here, stranger, almost, than to be asleep and dreaming. Yet she can't drum up the intention to leave. Where are Charlotte and the goat? Have they abandoned her?

"Delphine!" she wails, or tries to. No sounds comes out of her N-lite stoned throat.

She wanders back towards the hall. Instead of stairs, there is an elevator door. She presses the button and waits.

Presently, the elevator arrives, lit pink from within and full of root vegetables—beets, yams, sweet potatoes, lo bak, carrots, onions, garlic, ginger, and radishes—so many that, as the doors slide open, half of them tumble out, nearly crushing her. As though still in a dream, she begins to empty the elevator. To her surprise, a clutch of burly sisters with round, fleshy faces clomps in from one of the hallways behind her. They have wheelbarrows in which to put the vegetables. Within a matter of minutes, the elevator is empty. Kora takes a step forward to enter, but one of the sisters takes her hand.

"What did you do with Charlotte and the goat?" says Kora.

In the rosy dark, the sister shakes her head. She touches Kora's mouth, and then her belly.

"Eat?" Kora says.

The sister pulls her hand.

She could become one of my people, if I become high priestess here. I have a responsibility. Where did that come from?

She allows herself to be led.

Deeper than the Dark Baths lies a Dark Kitchen. The sister now helps her sit in a pile of soft cushions that smell of rooty and rhizomey spices—ginger, turmeric, licorice. The dark is at its full velvety thickness again. Kora hears knives chop and grinders whirl.

Liquids splash from bottles to bowls. Bowls and chopsticks clack against one another. There is a brief flash of light as a stove is lit, and for an instant, a dozen broad faces catch the light and wince. The cook covers the stove, and then it is dark again, though not quite as dark as it had been. There is just enough light coming from the cracks in the stove for Kora to see the dark shapes of the kitchen sisters moving around the cavernous room.

Soon, steaming dishes are placed on the long communal table, and Kora is invited to eat. The food smells strange, and she has no appetite. One of the sisters loads her plate and places it in front of her. There is no way around it. She eats.

Kora recognizes some of the flavours. There are vegetables from the elevator. There are also mushrooms that she doesn't know and wet, sour fruits that have been cooked into a grainy, meaty pudding. Not pleasant to her taste buds, but she doesn't want to offend these silent, benevolent sisters.

As she eats, she feels a presence to her right? "Mom?" she whispers. The presence pats her leg. She feels a presence to her left. The goat nudges her old left hand.

The sisters help Kora back to the cushions on the floor. They lie down beside her, and collectively all life in the Dark Kitchen falls into a deep slumber. Kora dreams again, stranger things than she dreamt in the Dark Baths, things without words or images.

ENG'S FIGMENTS 40

NODE: AUTUMN EQUINOX
DAY: 9

I'M AWAKENED BY A DULL THUD, AS THOUGH SOMETHING HEAVY HAS landed atop the roof of the New Origins Archive. Our Mother of blood and bacon, it's a fleshy thing that weighs down both the building and my spirit. I'm overcome with journey weariness.

There's a knock at my door. I open my eyes. Haul my leaden body upright. I light a candle, yank my tunic over my head, and drag my feet across the lush if worn carpet. Place my hand on the knob. I shiver.

Blink my eyes open. I'm still in bed and someone knocks insistently. Had I dreamt I was by the door? Go away, go away, who needs you? The knocking becomes thumping, bang bang bang. I haul my carcass out of bed for real this time, light my candle, put on my tunic, and go to open it. Myra stands there in a yellow nightgown, looking ridiculously unlike herself.

"Let me in. Quick!" She pushes past me and shuts the door.

"Someone has taken Kora Ko. What should we do, Doctor Kirilow?" Her eye twitches oddly.

"What do you mean 'taken'?"

"I mean kidnapped. I mean imprisoned. She's not in her room. Go see for yourself if you don't believe me."

She grabs my hand and pulls, barely giving me time to snatch up my robe. We tiptoe down the brightly lit hallway. If anyone comes, there's nowhere to hide.

I hear footsteps behind me. Our Mother who art artful. I pull Myra quickly around the corner.

"We've been seen," I whisper. "We should go back."

"Not possible," says the feisty Cordova girl. A scale beetle scuttles over the crown of her head. "Come on."

We turn another corner. Here's the room they gave Kora. Myra pulls a bump key from beneath her nightgown. She inserts it in the lock. The key promptly snaps.

"Our Mother's guts," I curse.

"This kind of lock is so obsolete."

"Everything old is new again," I say.

Myra's got small fingers, ones used to picking locks. But they are no use in this ancient building. I push her away and, with my large but practised surgeon's hand, manage to fish the broken key out of the lock. I pull a needle from my tunic pocket and try again as the footsteps echo closer and closer. The lock clicks and we push in, just as I catch a glimpse of an animal at the corner of the hall. My mind must be playing tricks.

The bedclothes sprawl in disarray. No Kora Ko.

"Of all the dishonourable, sneaky, Mother-cursèd things," I hiss.

"I told you. What should we do?"

"Elzbieta thinks I'm no good for my debt."

"Or she wants my delinquent Cordova sister more than renminbi."

"I found that girl," I say. "That little Susie belongs to me."

"Someone really doesn't think so," says Myra.

It feels wrong to go through her things, but we do it anyway.

I find Kora's torn and muddy blue dress, a small bag with three pieces of hard tack in it and a tube of that nasty eyeliner that all the Cordova girls wear. In the luxe private bathroom, the tap's been run and the hairbrush used. A bit of metallic scale casing sticks to it.

When I return to the bedroom, Myra is gone. "Hey, Cordy!" I call. "Where are you?"

I go back out into the hall. No sign of the Cordova Dancing School's best thief. What I do notice is a bit of animal fur caught in the textured coral plaster of the hallway wall. I pull it off and sniff it. It smells like elk.

I pull Kora's bedroom door quietly shut and follow the trail. It leads farther down the hallway, drawing me deeper into the archive. I round another corner. Halfway down the hall, there's a small blue door that gapes wide open.

Apprehensively, I go to it. It opens onto an abysmal darkness. I stare down the dark passage, and as I do, the weight of my travel-weary body returns as an ache in my bones. I catch a whiff of something unpleasantly familiar. N-lite. I try to call for Myra, but only a hoarse rasp emerges from my throat. "My ... ra ... Cor ... dy ..."

The darkness thickens like mist. The drug enters my lungs and a green film descends over my eyes.

"My ... ra ..." I groan.

There is no answer. I put a foot into the darkness and step onto something round and smooth. It rolls down the stone steps with a fleshy bump and thump.

"Myra?" This time a hiss-whisper I can't control.

In the darkness, a hand reaches out and grabs my arm. A yelp escapes my mouth.

"Sh!" says a familiar voice. Not Myra's. So familiar and so homey I can almost smell bitter greens steaming.

I fling my arms around the dark figure. "Mother double! Glorybind."

"Quiet, daughter," she says. "You've entered a precinct of Our Mother, a holy hallway of Eng."

I pull away. "Mother Glory? Is that really you?"

"Of course, my daughter double. I've been waiting so long."

It feels like her. But a little worm in my brain cries, *Careful, careful.* "I don't understand."

"Come with me," she says. "I will take you to the starfish. She may not seem herself. She has eaten the five forbidden roots and the shed flesh of the emigrants to Chang."

"Our Mother's hooves and feathers," I say, myself for a moment. "I have eaten that flesh too."

Old Glorybind claps her hand over my mouth. "Do you not understand where you are, child?"

I shake my head, and she releases her hand.

"These are the blessed convolutions of Our Mother, the holy hallway to eternal life on Eng. You must not take her name in vain. You must feel the remorse," she says, touching my head. Where she touches, remorse floods through me.

"Praise be to Our Mother of flow," I say.

"I raised you well after all," says Old Glorybind.

But she can't stop the questions that pour out of me. "Is it really you?" I gush. "Have you been here all this time? Why didn't you leave? And come look for me? Are our sisters here with you? Why did Isabelle Chow launch that batterkite against us? Mama?"

She gazes at me as though she knows the answers to all these questions, but she says not a word.

"Mama Glory, come on!"

She smiles sadly.

"If you love me at all, answer me. I'm your only living daughter double."

She gazes at me long and hard. Her eyes brim with tears. They spill over and splash on the cold stone steps.

She takes my hand and tries to pull me farther into the darkness.

"Why are you crying? If you can't answer me, Mama, I can't follow you."

Still she doesn't speak. She pulls my hand harder, as though to say, *Follow me and I'll show you the things I can't speak about.*

"I'm looking for a girl called Kora Ko. She has starfish abilities, Mama. Like my own lost beloved Peristrophe Halliana. Do you understand? I found another starfish, just like you asked. Is she down here?"

She grips my hand tighter and pulls harder.

"I'm looking for Myra Mao too, a thief from Saltwater City who was travelling with us. She was ahead of me just a moment ago."

She pulls my hand even harder.

"Why won't you speak to me?"

She pulls so hard, I stumble down several steps and nearly fall. "What terrible trick of Our Mother is this?"

I burn with suspicion, but I so want this to be real. Her hand in mine feels the same as it always did.

The green haze of N-lite surrounds me, dissolves my will. I allow myself to be pulled and step farther into the darkness. We enter a small cavern. I feel the space expand around me before I realize there is light. Phosphorescence glows softly off the stone walls, and I can see. There's a face the size of a frying pan up in mine before I even know where it's come from. I shriek. The breath is foul.

"No, Sister Caulis," says my mother double. "Groom Kirilow

has not yet decided to join us. She has nothing to offer and nothing to say."

The large face pulls back, disappointed. Attached to it is the body of a very old woman with stringy grey hair, drooping breasts, and a sagging belly, naked as the day she was born. Her eyes are large and deep. She gazes at me balefully.

I remember a Caulis Entadae at Grist Village. She was a quiet sister, older than me but younger than my mother double, who used to live at the edge of town with her sister double and two house cats. But she looked like the rest of us—dark hair, round face, short legs.

"Mama, is this Sister Caulis of the blackberry pie?" I ask.

That look again, of helpless sorrow. Why is it that she can speak but not answer my questions?

Her gaze is so grim and hopeless, I wither beneath it.

Finally, she opens her mouth. "Don't mind Sister Caulis," says Old Glorybind. "One day we will find a way to help her. Praise be to the great inventor Isabelle Chow—she is trying."

I brush my fingers along the phosphorescent wall, feel the damp earth crumble away at my touch. My fingers contact something smooth. Metal? I glance at it. The point of a triangle touches a circle. I brush away more dirt and can read part of a name. "Von Brau ..."

Her footsteps are getting away from me, echoing in the deep. I hurry after her.

Hundreds of sisters emerge expectantly as we descend towards the planet's tugging core. For a minute, I think one of them is Kora. "Hey, jailbird!" I yell. But she recedes into the earth of the wall and becomes part of it. What is this place?

At last, deep down at the very bottom of this ancient copper quarry, we reach a pool of water, deep, warm, and strangely alive.

"The mouth of Eng," says Old Glorybind. "You must get in, daughter, to prove you are not afraid."

I feel fear. But also a strange attraction.

"Go on," says my mother double.

I shudder.

There's a faint hissing sound then. The scent of N-lite intensifies, and the air grows subtly thicker with green gas.

I feel my brain become spongy soft.

"The opening won't last forever," Mother Glory says.

I shed my clothes and step into the water.

Its heat is soothing, and I half close my eyes. I wade in up to my waist. I float up onto my back and close my eyes. I see Peristrophe Halliana, or at least, her body, lying beside the body of Auntie Radix on a cedar pyre the height of a house from the time before. I see the descent of the batterkites that sit, squid-like, atop the old skyscrapers of Saltwater city, sucking up the biological remains of the flu-sick men who journey in mind only to Chang. I see HöST Security men round up terrified Grist sisters. I see nets of writhing sisters swing below batterkites lifting from the ground, up and away to Our Mother knows where. I strain to stay with the kites as they sail towards mountains, as wakefulness pushes me to feel the cooling water in which I float.

My eyes blink open. There beside me, up to her ribs in dream water, stands not my mother double but my own dearest beloved, Peristrophe Halliana herself. Somewhere in the soggy sack of my brain, I'm aware that I'm supposed to be looking for Kora, not Peristrophe. Peristrophe is an impossibility.

But I pull her into my arms and kiss her deeply. "Peristrophe! Alive after all? How can it be? I felt your stopped pulse. I laid your body on the pyre and brought a flame from our own hearth to light it."

She gazes at me from her full brown eyes with such grief.

"Look how well your eyes have grown back! But who's been taking care of you?" My eyes search the darkness for another groom, a rival, but I see none.

I pick her up and cradle her in my arms, assisted by the buoyancy water gives. She weighs in my arms exactly as she should. "Come on, you'll catch cold. Our Mother of hearts and roses, here you are, never mind how."

Something is not right, but I don't care. She is here with me.

Her hair streams with dream water, and bright new eyes shine from her head. She smiles sadly at me but says not a word.

I take her warm, soft hand in my own rough, scabby one. "Can you talk? You have no idea how I've missed your voice, our conversation. I've seen so many things since you—left us. I went to Saltwater City and lived with a whole convent of lady Salties. I met the men who live with the tiger flu. They have a technology for saving minds if not bodies. They threw me in prison, but I escaped. And then a new police force took over the city … Peristrophe, can you hear me?"

She radiates love. I close my eyes, relax for the first time since I saw that dirty Salty below the bluff near my cave. I help her stretch long and then float beside her.

"What's happened to you since I last saw you?"

She doesn't reply.

"Are you still there?" I blink my eyes open to make sure. She smiles.

"Will you wash my hair?" she asks.

She does speak! Delight surges through me.

"Of course, my love." I drop back down to my feet. The pebbly bottom is pleasant against my toes. She continues to float, relaxed and lovely. I have no soap, but I massage her scalp, and run my fingers through her long hair so that it fans above her head in shifting, undulating strands.

"I don't want to give Auntie Radix my heart."

"Then you won't give it to her, dearest. You are worth a thousand Auntie Radixes to me."

"Your mother double says I have to, and I have to do it now, or Auntie Radix will die."

Auntie Radix is dead. You are dead, says my head. But my mouth says, "I've never disobeyed my mother double."

"Would you disobey her to save me? Do you love me that much?"

Yes.

Glorybind appears above us then. "It's time, my daughter double. Auntie Radix needs Peristrophe Halliana's heart now. It's now or never, dearest one." Her face looks sad, so sad, but her words are firm and unwavering.

I lift Peristrophe Halliana out of the water and up the underwater stone steps. She is so light!

My mother double wraps us each in a towel. "Cutting table now. There's no time."

In spite of my promise, I carry Peristrophe in the direction my mother double takes us. There's an open door in the wall. Glorybind goes through it, and I follow. I'm in my operating room back at Old Grist Village. I'm wearing my worn operating smock. How can this be? All my favourite scalpels are laid out on a tray for me. There's a pot of forget-me-do, and a small dose of precious poppy too.

"Please," Peristrophe begs. "Don't cut me, Kirilow."

"It will be all right, my love," I say. But my own heart is thumping in my meaty chest, loud as monsoon thunder.

I give her the precious poppy.

"Kiri, I'm afraid. I don't want to."

I give her a cup of forget-me-do. Obediently, she gulps it down, but she is crying. "Please, please, dearest groom."

"The sisterhood won't survive without us. We are the last line of defence against our own extinction. I have to cut, my darling."

No, no, no. Don't make me do this!

"Please don't. I will die. I have the flu. I'm not strong enough to root a new heart." She's sobbing now. I pull her up into my arms and cradle her until, under the influence of precious poppy, she falls asleep.

I don't want to cut her. Please don't make me, Mama Glory. My hand picks up the scalpel and I begin to cut.

She is so thin it is difficult to cut without damaging major arteries. I have to cut a rib. It pops unpleasantly. Not enough. Another. Pop! Still, I don't have the space I need. One more. Pop! When I finally get inside the body cavity to the most secret of chambers, I see her heart for the first time. It is small, much smaller than in my imagination, like the heart of a young deer. I harvest it with the gentlest incision. Although she remains asleep, she releases a thin, sad whine.

I carry her live heart, pumping and thumping in the bowl of my hands. Outside the room, Auntie Radix's young groom, Bombyx Mori, is waiting. I place my beloved's heart in Bombyx Mori's waiting hands. I turn to go back to Peristrophe Halliana, to check the new heart that should be rooting now in place of the old one. The door to the operating room is gone.

I'm awash in horror and grief. I cannot bear it. The blue pool is still there. I shed my clothes and step into it. *Cleanse me, Blue Mother, wash me clean.*

I fall into a sick sleep.

I OPEN MY EYES. GLORYBIND GROUNDSEL SITS BESIDE THE POOL WITH A towel. "What was that, Mama? Was that real?"

"In a manner of speaking."

"But she died in my arms, you remember, back at Grist Village."

"There is real, and there is real."

"Mama Glory, I don't understand."

"We're riding the dark frame Eng."

"I don't know what that means."

"The Dark Baths are a place of interface. Eventually, the pool drains your being and transfers it to Eng. But not always whole. Isabelle is working on the path to Eng as an experiment in sensation. She calls it the deep download. It's designed to make us more real than we were before."

"But Peristrophe Halliana died, Mama, in my arms, at home ..."

"Eng accepts downloads, but Isabelle also makes retakes of her own with a scrap of DNA, a bit of code, and the essence of pure emotion concocted from our very own forget-me-do combined with distillates from other plants, animals, and minerals. Their being expands through the feelings of those who love them."

"So this Peristrophe Halliana was a fake?" I begin to blubber like the little child I promised her I would cease to be. "I'm sorry, I ..."

"There, there, my dearest little one ..."

"What about you? Are you a fake too? Or are you dead? How could I cut out Peristrophe's heart if this is already a place of the dead? Am I dead too?"

"I'm not dead, but I'm done."

"Downloaded to Eng."

"Yes. Alive of mind but heavy in the body."

"It feels so real down here ..." I pull into the softness of the towel to confirm this.

"Isabelle Chow is working hard on verisimilitude."

"And Peristrophe?"

"Real and whole and true as you, my dearest one."

"So I cut out her heart for true and real. I killed her."

"Did you see her dead?"

"We Grist sisters believe that body and mind exist together in harmonious balance. When one dies the person no longer exists." I take my left arm in my right and pinch hard, afraid I might no longer be real. I've never been so relieved to feel pain. I'm cold too. I shiver.

"We Grist sisters may have to get with Our Mother's times," says Glorybind.

"No," I say. "That's not what you taught me. Who are you?"

"I'm your mother double, Glorybind Groundsel. Just changed, ever so slightly." Her voice wavers. Inside me, a door slams shut.

"I have to find Kora Ko. And that troublemaker Myra Mao. I'm sure she came down here." I find my old tunic, the one I took off in what seems like another lifetime, still hanging on the rail. I take it now and pull it on.

My strange mother double follows me as I roam the barely lit halls of the Dark Baths looking for Kora. There are no rooms branching from the room with the pool, as I am sure there were when I arrived. Its walls are now smooth and closed as an unbroken egg. I need to get out of there. This is not a good place, not a good place at all.

My dreaminess has fully left me, except for the memory of Peristrophe's hot heart, pulsing in my hands. I shudder. I look at the ghost of Glorybind Groundsel. "Stairs," I say.

"No, Kirilow," she says. "Don't leave. Now that we are finally together again."

"Stairs."

The stairs reappear at the far end of the room. As they do, my legs grow heavy, and I hear a faint hiss. The air grows subtly green. I heave towards the escape like a dying mammoth. Dark shapes amass behind me, moan and whisper as they lumber through the moist dark.

My legs weigh as I ascend. It takes every ounce of effort I've got to move them. I move like a rock returning from the dead. It takes hours to climb the hundred or so steps to the top. Above me, a familiar figure scrambles, lithe and light. Myra? She should be down here with me. There's a flash of light as the blue door swings open for a second and a slam as it closes. I plod, groaning heavy, towards where I saw the flash.

"I can't come up into the light with you," says the Eng version of my mother double. She grabs my hand, and it feels so much like her hand I think I will faint.

I don't want to feel this longing. I try to pull away. Although the sensation of her grip remains gentle and light, somehow, I can't extract my hand.

"Will you say goodbye?"

I don't look at her.

"Child, I'm as real as I ever was."

"Please let go of my hand," I say.

With such reluctance, such grief, she lets go. Peristrophe Halliana appears beside her in the grey darkness, pale as a birch tree and bleeding from her open chest. Her eyes stream silently. The thin sheet of light that comes through the crack between the door and its frame above catches on a tear, and the tear glistens. Its light bounces off the passage wall into my eye and nearly blinds me.

"Kirilow—"

"Peri—"

"Your best beloved ..." says Glorybind.

"I killed her. I cut out her heart. She wasn't strong enough to root a new one. She is dead."

"My only groom, please don't leave me," the fake Peristrophe Halliana says.

Deep inside my chest, I feel my own heart split right in two.

"Kirilow ..." she wails.

"Dearest Peristrophe," I whisper, so hoarsely it comes out a croak. "Look at me—"

"I can't. You know I can't."

"My best and only groom ... Kiri ..."

A frail cry escapes my throat.

"Please, Kirilow, don't leave me here."

I begin to turn my head, but then I think I hear Kora's voice on the other side of the door. "Hurry up, come on. Don't listen. Don't let them take you."

Before my split heart can speak again, I turn the handle on the blue door. It won't budge. From the other side come voices: "The handle moved! She's back there."

"She's gone over to Isabelle. The high priestess will be furious. Don't let her out."

"She doesn't know. She's just a stupid Gristie. She won't understand a thing she's seen."

"She's a doctor. She is smart ..."

"Let her through. Elzbieta wants everyone at the feast."

The door opens suddenly, and I tumble out into the light.

SACRIFICIAL GOAT 41

NODE: AUTUMN EQUINOX
DAY: 10 (MID-AUTUMN FESTIVAL)

KORA WAKES WITH A CHILL IN HER BONES. SHE'S LYING ON A HEAP OF soft but musty cushions. Someone has laid a tattered blanket over her and tucked it lovingly around her face. The Dark Kitchen is empty. She strokes her arm, and the catcoat hugs her tight, purring. She throws off the blanket and wanders out of the kitchen and down the faintly lit hallway.

"Charlotte!" she calls. "Delphine!"

The cocooning earth of the hallway warms her gently. But neither her mother nor her beloved goat are anywhere to be found. They felt so real. The heat radiating off the humusy hallway walls intensifies. She feels comfort. But beneath that comfort, anxiety, and a desire to see Kirilow. She's got to find Kirilow.

Here's the elevator. She presses the button, and the doors open. Clumps of earth that must have fallen off last night's root vegetables litter the elevator floor. As she steps in, the catcoat mewls. Kora presses the button marked *0*. As she does, the cheap candy smell of N-lite makes her nose twitch. The elevator ascends. The catcoat embraces her more and more tightly, and the N-light smell intensifies. The elevator doors open, not far from her bedroom door on the main floor of the New Origins Archive. The catcoat squeezes and vibrates so intensely it gives her a headache. The green gas wafts about her thickly. Between the two, she can hardly breathe. She steps out into the hallway, and the catcoat lets go. She gasps for air. The catcoat is gone, and she's standing there in her robe and nightie, blinking in the glaring lights.

Crowds of New Origins sisters rush down the hallway. A dense pack of them come so fast and thick Kora is rushed along with them. The lights sting her eyes. She throws her pink right hand up to protect them.

A young acolyte pushing a cart that overflows with pungent-smelling herbs nearly bumps right into her, only swerving at the last minute. "Watch where you're going, damn ignorant Gristie!"

"Not a Gristie ..." Kora rasps. She turns, too N-lite slow to follow the whirl of the impatient acolyte. She finds herself instead face to face with a different New Origins sister pushing a cart full of roots.

"Elzbieta thinks you Gristies are the future. Can you imagine anything more absurd? What is the world coming to?"

"Not a Gristie," blurts Kora, more clearly this time. She has got to find Kirilow. And they've got to get out of here.

"Better get cleaned up," says a kindly older nun, coming from the opposite direction carrying a bottle full of amber liquid. "You don't want the high priestess to think you don't care."

"Just an hour to go," says a helpful acolyte she meets at the crossroad of two hallways.

A non-goat, very human hand grabs her wrist. "Lost, Lady Kora? You have an appointment with the high priestess. Don't you know? And you're late. You better get going—you don't want to get in trouble." It's the middle attendant from the night before, Vera, dressed in emerald green.

"I have to find the Gristie doctor."

"Never mind. You can catch up with her later."

Kora's mind is crawls through N-lite fog. Her eyes are full of mucus she can't blink away. She would like to get out of this Mother-forsaken place, but she needs Kirilow to lead the way to New Grist Village. She allows herself to be pulled into one of the great biodomes, inside the convolutions of the NOA's massive coral brain. The attendant pulls her into a bamboo thicket. Her feet don't quite seem to reach the ground, and she walks as though flying, as though she could fall from the air at any moment. The attendant in green rushes through the lush foliage and supple, swaying limbs of bamboo so quickly that Kora finds herself chasing nothing but the violent shivering of leaves.

At last, she finds herself in the courtyard of a small temple carved out of copper porphyry, deep in the grove.

"It's the first entrance to the mine that used to operate here," Vera explains. "Way back in the time before. Come inside."

Light from the many gaps in the temple's roof filters in and casts a flickering pattern of brightness and shadow on the gravel floor. There's a statue embedded in the alcove at the end, a figure of Our Mother of a Thousand Hands. Each hand holds an object of ritual significance—a scale, a shoe, a rocket, a peach ...

The statue moves.

Instinctively, Kora leaps into empty cat stance. N-lite doesn't own her yet.

The statue laughs and steps into the light. The arms were the backdrop of the altar, but the statue is a woman of flesh, with two arms. She is abnormally beautiful. With pale hair piled in an intricate knot atop her head, she is as lovely as Our Mother in her manifestation as the moon goddess Heng'e. Why does Kora think such things? Knowledge of Our Mother, if not fervency for her worship, must be rubbing off on her from spending so much time with Kirilow.

Kora draws herself upright and brushes the waving tendril scales from her face.

"Your Majesty," she blurts cluelessly.

She recognizes Elzbieta from the hour of their arrival, but this strange place accentuates their host's aspect as high priestess of the New Origins Archive. She looms, imposing and holy. But her laugh tinkles and twinkles like a rope of silver bells.

"Sister Elzbieta is fine," she says. "Did you lose your companions?"

Kora nods. "A while ago. Where are they?"

"They've gone to the Speaking Waterfall, in all likelihood," says Elzbieta.

"In this biodome?"

"Yes. Buttercup and Rose take all our guests there. If you throw a pebble in, Our Mother will disclose the future to you."

"I'm not a follower of Our Mother," Kora says. "So I don't believe in such things."

Elzbieta laughs her tinkling laugh again. "What do you believe in, Kora Ko?"

Considering the beauty and abundance this place provides, Kora could be more gracious. But Kora's head is still full of her strange experience in the Dark Baths. "I don't know anymore. I saw my mother and my goat. Were they real?"

"Did you now?" says Elzbieta. Her smile remains as benevolent as ever, but her eyes have grown dark.

"Did I say something wrong?"

"Not at all, child, not at all." Elzbieta's displeasure is palpable.

A bolt of fear zaps Kora's gut. She's betrayed someone without knowing who or what. Worse, she's put herself in some unknown danger.

The high priestess sees her fear, and her eyes light up again. "Perhaps you'll sit with me at the Feast of Abundance tonight."

Kora hesitates. The N-lite fog is lifting. "I don't know ..."

"And one day, maybe, you'll inherit the New Origins Archive in all its bounty. Wouldn't that be better than going to New Grist Village with that dirty Gristie Kirilow Groundsel?" Her voice again silver sweet.

"Well ..."

"Don't play coy with me, tiger flu girl," says Elzbieta. The silvery tinkle leaves her voice, and a hiss enters it. "I know that Isabelle has tempted you."

Kora takes a step back.

"Are you already loyal to her? Hmm? Are you?"

"I don't know what you're talking about."

"You've discovered the portal to Eng. You all but told me so yourself. It's too late to play ignorant." Her eyes blaze with rage.

"Please," Kora says, "I really don't understand."

"So young and yet so sly. This is a war, Kora. A war."

"I don't care about your shitty war."

"Do you care about your father?"

Kora takes a great, croaking breath. She blinks hard, but the tears come anyway.

Elzbieta smiles.

"Oh," she says. "Oh, there now. You miss your father. Of course. Of course you do. Would you like to see him again?

Kora backs away, but Elzbieta steps forward. "You haven't

seen your father yet, have you? Because Isabelle doesn't have him. What's his name? Kai Wai ..."

"I saw him at the Pacific Pearl LiFT."

"That was just a tiny taster before they were fully transferred."

The attendant in green moves in and kindly takes Kora's hand. "He didn't make the transfer to Eng. But the upload to Chang is better anyway."

Elzbieta says, "More verisimilitude."

The attendant in green says, "That means more real, Priestess Kora."

Elzbieta beams too bright. "Come with me and I'll show you."

Kora aches for her father. She would give anything to tell him she knows. And to ask him why he and Charlotte kept the secrets of her paternity and inheritance from her all these years. Her foggy brain is a cloud of emotions—rage at him for lying to her and for sacrificing himself without asking her if she wanted him to, but deeper than that a love and a longing that she'll never be able to tell him about. She drags her pink right hand across her eyes, making a great smear of kohl and tears across her small unhealthy face. Vera takes her hand and squeezes it.

"Come along, Priestess Kora!" Elzbieta calls. "If you want to see your father on Chang, you've got to be quick." She walks out into the courtyard and then deeper into the thicket. In the distance, Kora hears the sound of rushing water.

"Yes, hurry!" It cannot be. Kai Wai's warm, embracing voice.

She follows the high priestess and the attendant in green back through the Blossoming Baths. All round Kora and Elzbieta, sisters gather last-minute crops for the coming Mid-Autumn feast. Among them are nuns, acolytes, lay practitioners, and guests from the

Third and Fourth Quarantine Rings. They heap carrots, parsley, mint, forget-me-do, and kabocha squash into large rattan baskets.

"This way, this way," says the high priestess.

"Going to Mid-Autumn supper, Lady Kora?" An acolyte smiles brightly, but as soon as Kora passes, she hears her titter.

"The sacrificial goat," she hears another say.

"Saltwater meat ..."

Something is very wrong.

"Maybe I should wait until after the feast," she says, as Elzbieta pulls her insistently forward. "A body can't come down from Chang, right? I'd like to see Myra and Kirilow one last time ..."

"Kora!" calls her father from somewhere in the foliage of the Blossoming Baths.

"You can message them from Chang," says the high priestess. "The technology is almost there. But right now, we have to hurry." She's pulling so hard, Kora fears her arm might come right off. "It's now or never, Lady Kora. After the feast, the lineups for the LiFT will be long, and Chang is running out of space. You don't want to lose your chance, do you? Your father is waiting for you. Don't you want to see him?"

"Of course I do. I just ..." Fear and longing knot together to form a massive lump in her throat.

Three young acolytes huddle together at the next bend. They glance up at Kora and fall into a fit of giggles.

"No time to waste," says Elzbieta.

At the back of the complex, they enter the LiFT sanctuary.

"Are you sure he's there?" Kora asks.

"Of course. Come along now."

"It's dark back here."

"It is the only way if you want to see him. You want to, don't you?"

"Yes. I want to see my father more than anything."

"Well, keep moving then. We don't have—"

Before Elzbieta can complete her sentence, a fine, sticky net falls over each of them. Kora shrieks. The net's a sack with a strong drawstring. Someone yanks the string and Kora jackknifes into fetal position. "What the hell!"

She can hear Elzbieta yelling too. "How dare you, demons, cursed for all eternity by the Great Mother of us all—"

The candy stink of N-lite fills Kora's nostrils, stronger than she's ever smelled it. She blacks out.

CHANGE ENGINEERS

42

NODE: AUTUMN EQUINOX
DAY: 10 (MID-AUTUMN FESTIVAL)

THE HALLWAY LIGHT IS SO BRIGHT IT STINGS MY EYES. MY HEAD'S A balloon full of N-lite fog.

Two women appear at my side, one in pink, the other in yellow—Rose and Buttercup, our attendants from last night. "There you are! Come on, let's go."

"Where's Kora?" My voice sounds strange in the bright hallway.

"She was just here a moment ago. I think she went to the Blossoming Baths," says Rose. "Come on." They rush me into a biodome, overgrown with lush green plants and flowers the size of my face.

I need to find Kora. I need to find Myra. And the three of us need to get out of this writhing brain dome.

A waterfall flows down from the wall of the long-abandoned open-pit copper mine. It originates outside the glass bubble and flows into the Blossoming Baths through a chute in the roof just wide enough that the water gushes in but no toxic air can enter. Excess water splashes over the glass roof and tumbles down the outside. We're so close that its mist envelops my entire being.

"Very beautiful," I say to Rose. "But why are we here? What have you done with my friends?"

"They'll show up," says Rose.

"Any minute now," says Buttercup.

"Don't worry about it," says Rose.

"She's here, the great inventor herself!" Buttercup cries then.

"I don't want the great inventor. I want Kora. Will you please stop messing with me?" My head aches with the brightness of this dome, it's moist green smell, conflicting with the candy fog of the N-lite gas I inhaled in that strange underground place.

"You do want the great inventor," Rose says.

Buttercup offers, "Don't worry about those two funny Cordova girls, with their heads full of infection sticks. They must be around. I'll go find them." She tears off back the way we came, just as the most graceful and elegant of women appears behind the curtain of the waterfall, a dark-haired fairy lady from another world.

Light as air, the woman steps across the stones that bridge the rushing stream. "Kirilow Groundsel, the famous groom of Old Grist Village. At last."

Our Mother bless and preserve me! It is the great inventor Isabelle Chow. I recognize her from projections I saw the night of the revel at the Pacific Pearl Parkade. I'm hit by a swirl of contradictory emotions—awe and wonder but also rage, pain, and resentment. She's tall and otherworldly. Her shiny black hair gleams in the refracted light that comes through the glass dome roof of the Blossoming Baths. But there are strands of white in her hair and wrinkles around her sharp, bright eyes. Do I detect a sadness? It's hard to tell with wealthy city folk. She wears the flowing white robes of the Goddess of Hope—a costume hiding something both sinister and sad. I need to get out of here. As though sensing I might bolt, Rose grabs my arm. She's unnaturally strong. And in the leaves, I hear half a dozen rifles cock.

"What do you want from me?" I ask. My head is still cloudy with the candy gas of the caves, but I'm lucid enough to know I'm in a bad situation.

"Such extraordinary impertinence," says Isabelle Chow. "What's become of the Grist sisters' reputation for diplomacy?"

"It died when your police force invaded our village, then abducted and killed my people."

"Such bitterness, when you don't understand a thing, Dr Groundsel."

I arch an eyebrow.

"My HöST men *saved* your people. Didn't you see your mother double alive and well behind the blue door?"

"An illusion. What kind of fool do you take me for?" I demand. Rage rises in me, sharp enough to dispel the N-lite fog.

"No, my good groom. Not an illusion. Truer than true. Realer than real. Didn't you feel her presence?"

"Our Mother curse you," I say. She has no right to talk about my feelings.

"You know you did, Dr Groundsel. You know what you felt. They are all there, downloaded to Eng, safe as houses from the tiger flu and, more importantly, safe from the thieving predations of that dead man Marcus Traskin, his usurpers, and the faulty memory banks of doddering Chang."

My mind reels. "Whatever I saw, they were spooky and mutated. And how can you put down Chang? You invented the LiFT to Chang yourself. All over Saltwater City, the sick and the fearful well are uploaded to the model village you established there. What do you call it ... Quay Sera?"

"It's a faulty village, an experimental village that I built, good enough to save the flu-sick men who were going to die anyway. Now that those traitors have taken the LïFT from me, I will never fix it, never build more or better settlements on Chang, never migrate those men or their loved ones to improved villages. All those people will degrade, deteriorate, and vanish. But it's in your hands to prevent this from happening to others. And there is benefit to you too. Didn't I show you your beloved Peristrophe Halliana behind the blue door, safely downloaded to Eng?"

Our Mother, merciful and benevolent, it's more than I can bear. "I saw her, but something was wrong."

"But it was her, was it not? I know you wanted to stay."

"I saw her die at Grist Village," I say.

"But tell me what you felt. Was it or was it not her?"

"It felt like her."

"I still control Eng. I can make it better, but I need your help."

"What kind of help?"

"I need the Grist sisters."

It takes a minute for me to register what she means.

"I need healthy volunteers to go to Eng."

The drum of rage building inside me bursts. "Never," I say. "Not as long as I live and breathe." If the Mother-cursèd developers of the LïFT can use clones to test their technology, or disposable denizens of Saltwater Flats, then they don't need Grist sisters. But if Isabelle can't get either, a colony of Grist sisters who won't fight back could be a very useful thing.

May Our Mother arrange many blades and burns at her death.

"The Grist sisters need me too," says Isabelle. "You know it. They are dying, and you have no starfish to give them fresh organs. I could help you breed new ones. I have a source."

"I don't need you. I have a new starfish," I say. *Don't tell her! Stupid Kirilow, stupid Gristie.* I curse myself. But it's too late.

"Do you? And where is she, pray tell?"

I hesitate. I haven't seen her since Elzbieta's attendants took her to her room for the night.

My head reels. I stare at Isabelle Chow like a complete and utter idiot.

"I can help you get her back, but you must promise to work with me."

"I don't see how going to the feast will bring Kora back. Will she be there?" I ask the great inventor. "Otherwise, we should be searching the archive."

The light coming through the roof of the dome dims gradually. Evening is coming.

"She will be there," says Isabelle smiling.

"I think I'll just have a little look around," I say, and move to break away.

Rose sidles in close. Buttercup comes behind me. Although their calm and elegant demeanor hasn't left them, there's intimidation in the proximity of their bodies to mine.

What by Our Mother's feet is Isabelle up to? I could make a scene, push Rose and Buttercup away. But I know there are guns in the dome. I need to keep cool. I need to find Kora. I follow but keep my eyes whetstone sharp.

We leave the Blossoming Baths and enter the coral convolutions of the main building. The New Origins Archive has two large generators—one wind powered and one solar. Today, they've been turned off, out of respect for Our Mother at Mid-Autumn. As we approach the main hall, firefly lamps light the way. The closer we get, the more sisters surround us, and the more slowly we move.

The sisters are dressed in their finest clothes, though this seems to mean something different for each of them. One wears blue silk, another undyed linen, another a coat of appliqué with buttons, another some shiny fabric I've never seen before, and still another beaded leather.

"The sisters you see come from all over the archive and all over the world," says Isabelle. "We have visitors tonight too, from the surrounding quarantine rings. Maybe you'll see a neighbour."

"Where is Elzbieta?" I ask her, point blank.

"She'll join us soon, don't worry," Isabelle says.

I don't believe her.

To be so close to so many different kinds of people in such a tight space discomfits me further—I feel nervous and restless. At the gateway to Chang Hall, they press in, giving wide berth to guards with rifles at the door. There's no pretending now that I'm anything but a captive.

"It's called Chang Hall because of the skylight that follows the arc of Chang as he journeys across the sky," Isabelle explains. "I designed it myself when the NOA was my primary residence."

The hall opens cavernous and grand. The domed ceiling with skylight looms high. When we enter, Chang is just beginning his climb on the western side.

"What do you think?" Isabelle asks.

I can't deny its beauty. Painted with stars as they appeared in the time before, the domed ceiling sets off Chang's climb gorgeously. His bearing is holy as the moon's. His massive body fills the skylight, flooding the hall with golden-orange light. He orbits nearer than usual tonight, and I think I can feel his gravitational pull.

Round feast day tables covered in orange cloth and decked with lazy Susans, flowers, and polished crystal from the ruins of some buried town fill the room. Sisters bring platters, bowls, and cauldrons of delicious-smelling food from kitchens all over the archive, representing the many traditions of the many peoples who now make up the sisterhood at the NOA.

Isabelle leads me to the head table, overseen by the same three attendants who looked after us last night.

"I don't understand," I say. "Why up front? I'm a chance visitor."

"On the contrary," says the great inventor. "You are a guest of honour. Ever had a scale implant?"

She presents me with a fine filament in a glass vial.

"Oh no," I say. "No, no, no. My people don't do that. We don't go there. That's a backward and disgusting practice for Cordova Dancing Girls and Saltwater denizens. You don't also ...?"

"Inhale this first then," Isabelle says. She hands me a second vial with a greenish-grey vapour swirling inside.

"N-lite? I don't—Great Inventor, my people live clean."

"Spider Dream," Isabelle says. "Made with herbs from the Blossoming Baths and minerals from the earth itself. Clean as the day you were born."

"We weren't born clean. That's why—"

"Then what do you have to worry about? Don't be a bad guest now. Haven't the high priestess and I taken you in, given you food and shelter?"

"Bless and water Our Mother, who always provides," I say, intentionally formal. My mother double, Glorybind Groundsel, raised me too well. A sense of obligation fills my gut. Still, I wave the great inventor off with a nod and a smile that says, *No offence.*

"You will not survive the night without it," she says, pushing the vial into my palm.

I take it and lay it on the table.

She sighs. Picks it up, pops the cork, and before I know what's hit me, she grabs me and presses the open vial to my nostril. Rose steps forward and places her hand over my mouth. Our Mother spit on them! I'm forced to inhale.

"Now this," Isabelle says, popping the cork on the first vial she offered, "goes here, where the whorl of your ear ends. She taps the soft flesh, an inch above her earlobe. We Grist sisters all have a fistula there—a small hole that tunnels into the head. It's one of the defects. I don't like putting things near it as a rule."

"No way." I try to push her off me, but Rose and Buttercup hold me down.

She places the fine end of the tendril there. I expect it to sit in the tiny hole and wave about, as Kora's scales do. But as soon as she touches the tip to my flesh, the filament springs to life, wriggles, then burrows sharp and deep into my brain. I try to scream, but the Spider Dream won't let me. My mind grows suddenly sharp yet strangely not my own.

"All the sisters here are committed to Our Mother's ways of knowing," Isabelle says. "Now you are ready for the Mid-Autumn collective projection. Mid-Autumn Festival is a day of forgiveness too. We can't act retributively on the things we see. So it's a wonderful show, free of cost or consequence. Sit down, Groom Groundsel. Don't make a scene."

"I want to see Kora and Myra," I say, fighting the tidal pull of the drug. I sit.

"I thought you might miss some of your other friends," says Isabelle.

Two young women are led to our table then, to sit on the other side of Isabelle Chow. It can't be. By Our Mother's hooves, it is. Bombyx Mori and Corydalis Ambigua, here in the flesh. Has

Isabelle captured them too? Or have they come as visitors for the Mid-Autumn feast, knowing nothing of the deadly internal battles that ripple out to affect us all? Since they are both here, I fear that their litter of baby sisters is dead.

The NOA sisters begin a familiar chant that marks them as my kin after all:

> *Our Mother of dust and destruction*
> *Our Mother of earth*
> *Or Mother of mind and matter*
> *Our Mother of sound*
> *Only you know the paths of renewal*
> *The signs of succor*
> *The house of help*
> *Light the way for us gently*
> *Not with the sun but with the moon*
> *Make our humanity whole again*
> *You who have split it*
> *Open as our hearts*

This Spider Dream is a strong drug. It pulls me into the experience of all the others in the room, but there's no fog. I'm lucid sharp yet not quite myself. Projections flicker on the walls, the floors, the high-domed ceiling, even across the face of Chang himself as he lumbers upwards to the apex of the dome. They ripple over the tables, spin on the lazy Susans, ruffle the many festive outfits of the NOA sisters. Bits of an old movie about a man with a creased hat flash over a standing firefly lamp in the corner. Someone replays the murder of her parents at Houston North. Another plays audio from a lovers' argument two decades ago in the United Middle

Kingdom. Projections shimmer and flicker quick as winter rabbits over every available surface.

With all the will I've got in me, I try to hold back the night of the HöST invasion of Old Grist Village. But the Spider Dream is too strong. Its visions spill from my eyes in three dimensions onto the head table for anyone to see. Our Heavenly Mother of guesses and groans, please make this stop! I attempt to get up. I've got to find Kora. I've got to find Myra. My legs wobble like they're made of water. My eyes gush out the pyre that burns Auntie Radix and Peristrophe Halliana. It sends flames almost as high as Chang himself. HöST batterkites descend from the dome of the ceiling. Uniformed HöST police rampage through my home village, wielding automatic rifles from the time before. Screaming Grist sisters are kettled against outer cave walls and captured in nets that lift them high above the village, crying and weeping for mothers and sisters and daughter doubles.

Into the mass of this unbearable fray, in the meet-and-greet world of Chang Hall, dishes are placed before us: roasted fish, stewed fowl, stuffed squash, and fragrant garlic-fried greens. Bottles of tiger wine dressed with herbs appear, and sisters begin to drink. Clusters of erhu players and sound singers make music that dances and improvises with the interlocking and overlapping projections of a thousand NOA sisters reliving dreams, anxieties, and nightmares. Some sisters get up to dance.

The last thing I want to do is eat, but Isabelle heaps my plate. "Don't insult me now. The NOA sisters have been preparing this feast for weeks. You have to eat."

I don't want to eat. I want to go. I try again to get up. The attendants in pink and yellow step forward again, ready restrain me, but they don't need to. Spider Dream has made me a floppy sock.

My eyes spit out visions tinted bruise purple with rage, of K2 Ko's tiger police corralling the denizens of Saltwater Flats. No more pretenses of courtesy. The music that accompanies my visions whirls and screams. My hatred is out in the open now.

"Eat," says Rose.

"An offence against Isabelle is an offence against Our Mother," says Buttercup.

I don't want to eat. Rose hovers over me, beady eyed and insistent.

"I'm not hungry," I tell her.

She reaches into the folds of her dress for what can only be a weapon.

I eat. I have some roasted char, a bit of stewed ptarmigan, some roasted potato. I sip the herbed wine. "There, I've eaten. Now tell me what you've done with Kora."

"Have some stuffed squash," says Isabelle.

I don't want to.

She scoops some onto my plate.

Rose steps forward again.

I sigh. I take a bite.

"And what about High Priestess Elzbieta Kruk?" Bombyx asks.

"Soon, soon. They will both join us soon," says Isabelle, her eyes bright with pleasure.

"Our Mother praise the high priestess!" shouts a sister from the crowd.

"Surely, she is delicious!" shouts another, raising one of the stuffed squashes high.

"The high priestess is dead! The high priestess lives within us! Long live the high priestess!"

"Long live Isabelle Chow!"

Isabelle beams even more brightly. Crams a great mouthful of squash stuffing into her mouth. Through my Spider fog, I stare at her.

"You haven't just ..." I can't say it, so Bombyx does.

"Murderer. You've killed your best friend."

Isabelle beams brightly. "All hail the life and death of Elzbieta Kruk!"

"We've got to go. We've got to find Kora," I say to Bombyx and Corydalis, not caring if Isabelle hears.

While a thousand sisters applaud, whistle, and stamp their feet, Bombyx, Corydalis, and I attempt to rise.

"Not yet, sillies," Isabelle hisses. With the help of the pretty attendants, she yanks us back down to sit on either side of her.

A sudden rumble, low and deep.

What in Our Mother's thousand names is that?

The rumble deepens, and the earth trembles.

Plaster begins to crumble off the northern wall. The roar is deafening. The floor cracks, and a whole sheet of plaster crumbles at once from the wall. Shiny, sleek, and spitting fire from its tail, a projectile arcs across the skylight. I can see the symbols on its side:

C E C

VON BRAUN

My wriggling scale tells me what it is. A rocket from the time before, with a special kind of bomb inside, one that splits atoms wide. My jaw drops and my eyes bug. Anxious minutes pass as the rocket ascends higher and higher. Smashes squarely into the lumbering body of Chang. There is a brilliant flash of light. I cover my eyes. Light sears the backs of my hands. When I look again, I see Chang fall backwards into the night—a massive, fiery beast sinking in the depths of the dark galaxy. A gargantuan mushroom of dust spills from the vast empty space where he was, fills the skylight, engulfs the archive.

Isabelle leans back in her chair, laughing the giddy, uncontrolled laugh of someone who's lost her senses.

"There you go, lover! There you go, best and most adored sister! You can't say I struck you first."

The north wall of Chang Hall collapses, showering projections and dust and insulation over the Spider Dreaming NOA sisters.

Isabelle laughs and laughs and laughs. She holds her stomach and tears stream down her face. With no wall to hold it up, a massive cedar beam falls from right above our heads. I leap out of the way. Isabelle leaps too, but not quick enough. It thumps her head hard before rolling away. She collapses. Rose and Buttercup rush to her aid.

"Time to go, friends!" Bombyx shouts.

It's now or never. We scurry out through the east door and run as fast as our Spider-heavy legs will carry us.

The NOA collapses around us as we run. Cedar beams, hunks of plaster, chunks of coral cement smash to the ground. The east wall looks none too stable. We are yards from it as it begins to fold. I grab Bombyx's left hand with my right and Corydalis's right hand with my left. We dive. Plaster and coral dust sprinkle our toes as we land face down on the other side of the wall that was. Just as I'm getting up a large jagged chunk of coral crashes down on the back of my calf. Cuts a deep gash. But I can still move.

We pause at the central atrium, from which hallways branch out in many directions.

"We have to find Kora," I say.

"What does she look like?" Bombyx asks.

"Like you and me, only a bit paler."

We hurry in the direction of the Blossoming Baths, even though it's more than likely she died when the rocket went up. But New Grist Village will be nothing without her. I have to try.

We run along the east corridor. A massive hole in the earth looms deep and wide. The rocket has blown out the Dark Baths, the Blossoming Baths, and anyone and anything those biomes contained.

"It's too late," Corydalis says. "We've lost her."

"Don't be ridiculous," Bombyx Mori says. "We'll find her."

I'm already skirting the burning hole, peering down into its smoking, steaming depths. We hurry back up to the atrium. The western hallway leading to Chang Hall is now a crumbled heap of debris. Bombyx takes the north hallway, Corydalis takes the northwest, and I go south.

I run, casting my eyes left, then right, then up, then down. If she's hiding somewhere, I want to see her.

The hall is long, and other denizens of the archive push past me, also looking for loved ones, or just trying to escape. All around us, the building rumbles. To my left, a whole wall collapses.

In the distance, Bombyx calls me. "Groom Kirilow, I see her!"

I turn and run.

Bombyx continues to call me. "Hurry!"

I scramble down the hall fast as my aching leg will allow.

"Here!" Bombyx's voice in the north corridor. My cut calf screams, but I ignore it and keep running. Against all odds, Kora runs towards us down the rapidly collapsing hallway. A true gift from Our Mother at last.

A beam falls behind me and whacks me in my already injured leg. I bite my lip and run run run. The distance closes between us. Almost there. A cedar beam collapses right in front of me, barely missing my Spider-fogged head.

Behind me, Bombyx gives a belated yelp of warning. "We can go under it," she yells.

I test it first, to make sure it won't fall on us as we're crawling. And then there is another great crash.

We wriggle under the fallen cedar beam and hurry to where Kora lies pinned under a giant chunk of brain coral. Her entire torso is trapped, and her eyes bug wide. "Help me, Doctor Gristie."

The chunk of coral is huge. Her feet stick out one end and her head the other. With all our might, we lift then roll the rough, spiky coral chunk away, as she howls in panicked pain. "Charlotte, Mom ..."

Kora's torso has been smashed flat. Blood pools around her in a wide circle.

"She's not going to make it," Bombyx says.

Corydalis says, "The LiFT is still there, on the far side of where the Blossoming Baths were."

I say, "We can send her to—"

"Chang," Corydalis finishes.

There is a second explosion then, far too close. Light and dust from nowhere and everywhere fill the hall.

"We saw Chang die, remember?" I say. None of us can really fathom a world without him.

A third thunderous crack, high above.

"I have an idea," Bombyx says. "But she has to live long enough for us to get her in the LïFT."

I gather Kora up in my arms, gently as I can. She whimpers in pain and fear.

Somehow, we work our way around the steaming hole that was the Blossoming Baths. The column that holds the LïFT is remarkably intact, give or take some cracked glass here, a burn scar there.

Bombyx presses the button.

It opens.

I lay Kora's broken body on the elevator floor. She shivers in pain. "Papa Wai ..."

Bombyx picks up a piece of brain coral and smashes the control panel open. Behind it lies a wall of flesh. "There's a batterkite on the roof of this tower," she says. "The one Isabelle arrived in. Can you coax it—?"

I stare at her. "I've never—"

"Isn't it your great gift? The cutting and repairing of flesh?" She produces a scalpel from an inside pocket and hands it to me.

Deep in the folds of my brain, the wormy scale that the great inventor gave me wriggles an affirmation of Bombyx's plan. I guess she's not as thick as I once thought.

I know what to do. "Isabelle be praised," I say, forgetting for a moment the terrible thing Isabelle has done. I begin to cut. Careful, so careful, as though the guts of this panel were the living flesh of my own beloved Peristrophe Halliana, I cut. I pull at muscle and vein. I nudge nerves. I detach and reattach. The wormy scale teaches my fingers something they didn't know before. At last, I pull my bloody hands out from the meat of the LïFT. "Here goes nothing!"

Bombyx replaces the metal panel and presses the top button. I kneel and stroke the dying girl's hair. "It's going to be okay," I tell her. "In just a few minutes, you will see."

I duck out just before the doors slide shut. Follow my sisters to the back stairs and run up up up the cervical spine of the archive to its brainy top. Out of breath, we arrive.

Who should greet us but Myra Mao herself, grinning face wide as a shark's. "Woooooweeeeeeee! We did it! We took that dirty bastard Chang down, and those twisted HöSTers with him!"

"Where have you been?"

"Exercising my mechanical skills, of course. Did you see the rocket go up? That was my doing! And the explosion? No one ever needs to be tempted by that dead man Marcus Traskin or sneaky Elzbieta Kruk or doddering Chang again. Or that silly K2 Ko. Am I good or what? Me, Tania, Isabelle, and the launch button at Cosmopolitan Earth, that is. Good thing these hands are handy." She holds them up so we can all marvel.

I'm incredulous. "That was you?"

"Who else, Dr Gristie?"

"I can't imagine."

She looks at me expectantly.

"Well, you can't come with us. You tried to send me and Kora to Eng. You made me dream I had to cut out Peristrophe Halliana's heart."

"Not my business what you dream down there. I sent you down so you could be with her. Safe from Chang and safe from Elzbieta. I thought it was what you wanted."

"You threw us into Isabelle's arms so she could use us to make a captive Grist sisterhood," I say.

"Do you know how to fly a batterkite?"

I don't. "How can I trust you?"

"I'm not going to fly it. I'm going to Cosmopolitan Earth."
She pulls a twig out of her head. "Here, take this. It's better with
a halo, but you do like needles." She jams it into my skull before
I can protest.

"Ow!"

"You're welcome. Just wanted to make sure you sorry Gristies
get where you need to go. That truck better still be there."

In the foyer to the high priestess's private quarters, the dial
above the LiFT door swings left then right, then left again. It moves
so erratically we're afraid it might break. At last, the door opens.
A giant fish lies there, silver and slippery, covered in long tendrilly
scales, with a pink right fin. I gather it up, clutch its dead flesh to
my chest.

Bombyx runs into Elzbieta's lab. The moist, quivering brain
she used to manage the archive takes up the bulk of the space. We
squeeze past its spongy grey folds. At the back of the room is a small
docking bay. A wet batterkite presents its closed but oozing mouth.

I chant:

Our Mother who art artful
Our Mother of light

The mouth opens. The batterkite accepts us.

I release the wet fish that was the body of Kora Ko to the floor.

"Do you know the latitude and longitude of New Grist Village?"
Bombyx asks.

I search the worm in my head. I set the coordinates and grasp
the batterkite's wet lever. The kite lifts from the crumbling ruin
of the New Origins Archive. From its mucus-covered window, I
think I see a ghastly yet elegant figure lying dead in the exposed

ruin of Chang Hall. Turkey vultures circle, closing in on their meal. Farther below, near the main entrance, a tiny figure climbs into the wheelbarrow that brought us here.

The sun is going down. It sends rays of light through water vapour, smoke, dust, and radiation from the death of Chang. It makes a cloud ocean of fabulous purple, mauve, silver, and gold. The batterkite dives into this dirty but miraculous beauty, free to glide us home.

PART V

CASCADIA YEAR: 269 TAO (TIME AFTER OIL)

UNITED MIDDLE KINGDOM CYCLE 83, YEAR 18 (METAL SNAKE YEAR)

GREGORIAN YEAR: 2301

THE STARFISH TREE 43

NODE: INSECTS AWAKEN
DAY: 1

IT'S BEEN A HUNDRED AND FIFTY-SIX YEARS SINCE I WAS THE GIRL
you are asking about. The world has changed so much. I'll do my best to remember, and to explain to you how it was in those days, but you have to understand—nothing is the same. When I was a girl, the possibility of doublers, starfish, and grooms did not even touch my consciousness. All I knew were boys and girls, men and women. Groom Elder Kirilow Groundsel was young at that time, tending her Peristrophe Halliana, while her mother double, Glorybind Groundsel, watched over them both. When she wakes up from her nap, you can ask her about it.

A cool, pleasant breeze blows through the alpine valley, and the ancient starfish tree shudders and sways.

What I know of the time before I got mostly from the man I thought was my uncle before he left us. But he was embarrassed to tell it, so I don't really know what 'lying together' entails, though if you ask me, it sounds painful. You should be grateful you don't have to do it to make a daughter double. You and me—we are alike. We fruit! I know how painful it will be for you, because Corydalis Ambigua birthed a whole litter of you right at the base of my trunk.

Don't snigger, Flos Syzygii. You were one of that litter, born beneath these very leaves. When you pluck your first replacement heart or liver from my branches, don't you dare scoff. You must remember my pain, as I remember yours.

Flos Syzygii flushes bright red, and the Kora Tree turns a set of freshly sprouted eyes on her.

Hm. So slow to learn. The tree has no mouth. It vibrates language.

In the old days, after lying with a man, a woman would grow, as you do, like a giant sister egg, for the same forty terrible weeks that you will all one day endure. And all for what? Not a litter of daughter doubles but only one.

"Only one daughter double?" gasp the young Grist sisters.

"Groom Elder Bombyx says sometimes there were two, or even three," says precocious Plumula Nelumbinis.

Yes, rumbles the Kora Tree. *I've heard of that. But all the girls at my dancing school were born in litters of one.*

"Tell more!" cries Flos Syzygii, rapt now.

When they were with child, the women were treated with gentleness and care by everyone around them, at least until the men got really sick, and then there were murders sometimes. Gruesome, angry ones that got more depraved as the men became fewer and fewer. You don't want to know those stories. And I won't tell them. You still get the tiger flu that consumed the men, you know. Everyone was susceptible, though women had better immunity. If your immunity was compromised, like Peristrophe Halliana's, you could die. That is why you must drink Miracle Milk when Groom Elder Kirilow brews it for you. I know it tastes bad, but it's better to drink it than to die of the flu.

Fanned out beneath the Kora Tree like synchronized swimmers

from the time before, the young daughter doubles stare up through her leaves to the bright sky.

"No doublers?" says Solani Lyrati. "No grooms and no starfish trees? Did they at least have the old kind of starfish?"

Well, says the Kora Tree, *they did, but they didn't know it. I myself was one of the old kind of starfish, but I didn't know. Can you imagine? Not knowing your own nature? But it was a time of information blackout. Everything they knew in the time before was stuck on Chang and Eng, and only the elites had access. Even now, our wisest Grist scholars don't know everything they knew."*

Plumula Nelumbinis claps her hands. She's heard this story before. "And you came and planted yourself at New Grist Village to save us all!"

I wasn't quite as generous as that, says the Kora Tree. *Not at first, anyway. I nearly died. I had to be uploaded to a batterkite and become its consciousness. And then we discovered that the tentacles of the kite doctored carefully and left to lie long enough atop fertile soil could become roots. Bombyx Mori and Kirilow Groundsel worked for many years to make me what I am and to seed the entire Starfish Orchard that nurtures the great Grist Garden.*

The little doublers turn to admire the Starfish Orchard that surrounds them in a leafy, comforting dance of light and shadow.

"Are there gardens beyond Grist Garden?" asks Plumula Nelumbinis.

There was once a garden called Saltwater City, says the Kora Tree. *It was a very dirty garden. And another called Cosmopolitan Earth. And more too, I think, but my memory is not what it was. Ask Groom Kirilow when she comes.*

A fresh litter of younger sister doubles comes up the hillside then, to gather around the base of the Kora Tree.

"What did we miss?" asks little Iphigenia Bulb.

"Everything," says Flos Syzygii.

Never mind, says the patient Kora Tree. *I'll start again from the beginning.*

At the very top of her branches a little tendril lights up momentarily, calling out to no one. She wills it to dim.

DEEPER WITHIN THE ORCHARD, IN A CAVE IN THE SIDE OF THE MOUNTAIN, the ancient groom elder Kirilow Groundsel rises from her bed and climbs into her rocking chair. She picks up the pipe that once belonged to her mother double, Glorybind Groundsel, stuffs it with her own special blend of cannabis, sage, and forget-me-do, lights it, and takes a deep, satisfying draw. She looks up to the mantle at all the organic and inorganic oddities she's collected over the years. Contemplates a wrinkled, blackened bit of matter that the weathered and creaking Bombyx Mori gave her the day before yesterday.

"Found it in your old medicine cabinet and thought you'd like it back," Bombyx had said.

It looks like a dried mushroom, until Kirilow brings it close. The five fingers are still clearly distinct. "I wonder what that flu-sick Salty would think if she could see us now?"

Kirilow sits back in her chair, and smokes and rocks. Her eyelids droop. Just before she tumbles into sleep, a wistful thought rises up. *Maybe today is the day I'll set out for the ruin of the New Origins Archive. Maybe the blue door is still there. Behind it and down the stairs, maybe I'll find my beloved Peristrophe Halliana, alive and well in the Dark Baths.* Her eyelids drop down as the old pipe smoulders, then goes out in her hand.

Far beyond the earth, in the deepest reaches of space, the old communications satellite Eng lurches along her still-deepening orbit, a long ellipsis that will take her a thousand years to complete.

ACKNOWLEDGMENTS

THIS BOOK HAD ITS START IN A WRITING GROUP THAT CONVENED OVER email in the mid-2000s. I'm so grateful to the whole group: Pamela Mordecai, Martin Mordecai, David Findlay, Jennifer Stevenson, Nalo Hopkinson, and Hiromi Goto. It was also supported by a generous residency in the English Department at Simon Fraser University. I'm grateful to Roy Miki, Sophie McCall, Steven Collis, Jeff Derksen, and especially David Chariandy, who gave up his office so that I would have a place to write. Further work was done through the generous support of a guest professorship at the University of Augsburg. Many thanks to Katja Sarkowsky, Rainer-Olaf Schultze, and Claudia Glöckner for their generous care during that time. I am also most appreciative of a writer-in-residence position I had at the University of Guelph. Thanks especially to Jade Ferguson, Helen Hoy, Thomas King, Smaro Kamboureli, Mark Fortier, Alan Filewood, and Michael Boterman. The wonderful Sophie Mayer published my short story "The Starfish Groom" in a special "Utopia" issue of the queer British literary journal *Chroma*, which was this novel's inception.

I had lots of generous feedback as well from fellow writers, editors, and friends who read various drafts. Thank you from the bottom of my heart for the time and thought you gave *The Tiger Flu*: Ellen Pond, Rita Wong, Ian Williams, Yukiko Toda, Meredith Quartermain, Patrick Crean, and Robert Majzels, who also came up with the title.

I am especially grateful to Hiromi Goto, dear friend and editrix extraordinaire. Where have you been all my life? Thank you for your brilliant feedback and suggestions. This book would not be what it is without you.

Special gratitude also to the wonderful Warren Cariou whose editorial support offered so many helpful insights in the realm of contemporary narrative ethics and beyond. I especially appreciated our conversation about oolichans and caplin.

Thanks hugely too to the whip-smart Shirarose Wilensky at Arsenal Pulp Press for the copy edit that kept on giving. If there are any flaws in the book now, I have no one to blame but myself.

Many thanks to Oliver McPartlin for the beautiful design, and to Cynara Geissler for publicity already done and publicity to come. Thank you to Robert Ballantyne for his work behind the scenes. I know how much thought and care goes into what you do.

So much appreciation to Brian Lam for taking this book on with the incomparable professionalism, grace, and aplomb with which he always engages. Thank you for continuing to believe in me.

Thanks also to many students and colleagues at both the University of British Columbia and the University of Calgary who supported this work in small and large ways through conversation, commiseration, and other forms of moral support. Thank you to my writing community broadly—the many friends, colleagues, readers, and interlocutors whom I've met on various travels inner and outer. It's not possible to name everyone, but your impact is felt nonetheless.

Finally, loving thanks to my family Tyrone Lai, Yuen-Ting Lai, and Wendy Lai, and to my endlessly and generously supportive partner, Edward Parker, who puts up with the mania, panic, and mess on a daily basis, fixes everything, and who read not one draft but three. You're okay, I guess.